To

The *JESUS* Film Project,

and all those involved in
this crucial ministry.

Portraits

Balcony

Blind Faith

Endangered

Entangled

Gentle Touch

Heaven's Song

Impasse

Masquerade

Montclair

Stillpoint

Walker's Point

LINDA CHAIKIN is the award-winning author of numerous bestselling books, including *Empire Builders*, winner of the Angel Award for excellence in fiction. With over 300,000 books in combined sales, her epic stories and endearing characters have captured a loyal readership. She and her husband, Steve, make their home in California, where she writes full time.

One

Mount Kilimanjaro stood alone, endowed by its Creator with a perpetual crown of snowy white, while below stretched the Serengeti Plain, bearded with sun-bleached grasses and dotted with dried thornbush. Flat-topped acacia trees bit their way up through the earth's brittle crust, giving speckled shade to a small herd of zebra. The animals stood motionless except for the nervous flick of their tails.

Nearby, at a meager water hole, a pride of lions ambled single file against the horizon of the bright East African sky, the dry wind stirring the amber dust beneath their paws. Two thin cubs, panting from the heat, waited expectantly in the brush. In the distance, lying in the shade of a rock, the male of the pride looked on with golden eyes, his mane ruffling in the wind.

Sable Dunsmoor walked out of the small mission shamba begun by her mother into the still African morning. She stood musing, not about the lions that eyed the nervous zebra, but about the missing money in her personal account.

How very odd. . . . What could have gone wrong?

After a two-year absence from East Africa, Sable felt the heat demanding its toll, and she stood fanning herself with her wide-brimmed hat, her pale blouse sticking like damp gauze to her skin. Her silky hair, the warm color of honey, was braided, then looped into coils at the back of her neck. Her heavy khaki slacks were bloused into her tall safari boots, designed to protect from a host of crawling critters: large safari ants, biting insects, and even worse—several varieties of snakes.

Here in Namanga, Kenya, some two hundred miles inland from the coastal city of Mombasa, she stood alone in a Maasai tribal township on the Tanzanian border. Her rented jeep was parked across the narrow dusty track under an acacia. The breeze died. Not a whisper stirred as her gaze absently drifted past open-air stalls where the leather and bead Maasai jewelry was on sale to the wildlife-viewing tourists on safari. She noticed the Maasai women with empty baskets, followed by barefoot children, walking long distances to trade here at the dusty vegetable market. The women and their long walk reminded her of the need for water wells and of the money that should have been in her account to pay for the construction.

Sable's thoughts turned to Dr. Vince Adler, a man she highly respected and whom she had thought would be here to meet her. The professor of anthropology was on leave from a private research lab in Toronto and was now working on the wildlife reserve managed by the Dunsmoor family. Dr. Adler was a hero in Sable's mind, since his research centered on a cause she found dear: what to do about the effects of continued tribal wars, drought, and famine on the game animals of East Africa. He was especially interested, as was she, in working with her father in preserving the last herd of giant-tusked elephants at Marsabit reserve in the NFD region—the Northern Frontier District of Kenya, an area bordering wartorn Somalia.*

She frowned suddenly. She shouldn't think of Vince as "Doctor" anymore, since an engagement between them was possible in the not-too-distant future, perhaps within a few months after they both arrived to work at her father's elephant camp near Samburu. Thoughts of an engagement must wait, however, since there was a more urgent problem to deal with: what had happened to the twenty thousand dollars to fund her Christian project here among the Maasai?

Sable's throat was dry from more than the heat and dust. She

---

*The NFD borders Somalia, as well as Ethiopia. Samburu, Isioli, and Marsabit are game reserves *within* the NFD region.

swished her hat, scattering the flies. What would she tell her sister? Kate was working temporarily at a medical camp not far from here and was expecting her to begin the well-drilling project before the two of them left with Dr. Adler for the NFD. Their paternal grandmother, Zenobia Dunsmoor, waited some twenty-five miles away at the family-run game-viewing lodge named Kenyatta.

For the past year Sable and Kate had planned their well project in memory of their mother, Julia, who had worked with the Maasai as a medical missionary for ten years before her marriage to their father, Skyler Dunsmoor. Having to watch their mother slowly die of cancer in the hospital in Toronto had been a trial of faith for both sisters. As a loving memorial to a cause Julia cared deeply about, they had worked and saved to fund the drilling of two desperately needed wells. And now . . . the money wasn't there.

There must be a simple explanation, Sable told herself, walking toward the tree where the jeep was parked. Before leaving Toronto, she'd been assured the money had already been transferred to the Medical Mission headquarters here in Namanga, and that the funds would be available to pay the Nairobi construction team when she arrived. She slipped her sunglasses on, musing. Could Kate have already taken it and put it to use? If so, why hadn't she told her?

Deep in thought, Sable hadn't noticed the truck bearing down upon her, driving too fast for the narrow roadway. She heard the engine rev and looked up. Before she could step back, the driver leaned on the horn with a long, ear-splitting blast that pierced the stillness, followed by the ugly sound of heavy tires ripping up the dirt as he stomped on the squeaking brakes. The vehicle bounced and swayed precariously. A brawny truck driver with sun-bleached hair dusting his heavy shoulders under a sweat-stained T-shirt leaned his head out and shouted impatiently as though she were to blame for his reckless driving.

The truck rumbled past, and Sable, embarrassed at being yelled at, stood with eyes closed while holding her breath, embraced by a cloud of dust.

That truck again! She had first seen it when driving in from Mombasa. It had hogged the roadway, following closely behind her jeep for several miles before rumbling past, nearly causing her to swerve off to the side. She shaded her eyes and looked after it, recalling the words written on the truck's side: *Smith and Browning Zoo Animals.*

The association, loosely headquartered at the shipping port of Tanga in northern Tanzania, had an odious reputation among game conservationists. Her father had written her in Toronto that it was associated with an international hunters' group working out of the Far East to supply the lucrative black-market trade in elephant ivory, rhino horns, and leopard skins. Her father seemed to think that few animals were actually captured alive to be sold for zoos or circuses, as their cover suggested.

Sable wasn't sure which angered her most—the destruction of wildlife by the poachers, who had no concern for the elimination of unique creations of God, or the unfortunate fate of the animals that were sold to third-rate zoos and circuses.

That foul crew ought to be arrested, she thought, staring after the big dusty truck as it drove out of town. It was against the law to hunt, kill, or trap in the game reserve without a license from the Kenyan game warden. And animals protected by the endangered species law were not to be hunted at all.

Sable suspected that the zoo hunters were camped out of sight across the Kenyan border inside northern Tanzania to avoid contact with the game wardens in both countries. The two governments were working with wildlife conservation groups to stop the poaching and safeguard their living treasures from international avarice, since world tourism to view the great animals on the reserves was bringing in millions of dollars annually.

Yet the poachers abounded, tracking the herds or individual elephants and rhinos with aircraft, Land Rovers, and machine guns. The animals were helpless in the face of such sophisticated hunting techniques, and the poachers were rarely caught. They were like guerrilla fighters who would attack suddenly and melt away before the authorities could arrive. And even more tragic, some wardens and African tribal members cooperated with the international poachers for bribes. White hunters who had retired from legal safari businesses were also sometimes culprits.

Seated at the wheel of the jeep, Sable started the motor. There was no sense in waiting any longer for Dr. Adler. He must have been detained, and if she were to make it to Kenyatta Lodge by sundown, she needed to leave now. Anxious to see her family again, she pushed aside her concerns for Smith and Browning Zoo Animals and her missing money and drove from the border town of Namanga in the direction of the Dunsmoor game-viewing lodge.

⌒〰〰〜⌒

As the day wore on, the bright East African sky was adrift with enormous pink and cream-colored clouds passing over the sun. So incandescent were the billows that Sable imagined fire smoldering within, even as memories of Kenya burned in her soul and were warm with longing. Yet such memories were painful, too. She blinked back the unbidden tears and straightened her sunglasses, refusing to allow those memories to rampage through her heart. Returning to Africa must not stir to life again the forbidden embers of her past love for Kash Hallet.

The jeep bumped along over the ruts below the fast-racing clouds. As midafternoon neared, Sable noticed one of the ancient baobab, the oddly shaped tree that drew so much curiosity from the tourists. The tree appeared to be growing upside down with its tangle of meandering rootlike branches reaching skyward. This particular old baobab stood majestically on the plain with a flock of darkly silhouetted game birds perched on its branches, reminding her of partridges in a pear tree.

However, it wasn't the birds or the tree that seized her attention. She slowed the jeep to a crawl, and the dust settled silently. The ominous shadow of a single cloud raced across the suntanned plain, momentarily blotting out the amber grass. A short distance from the baobab tree, some bald-headed vultures were squabbling on the ground, displaying their full wingspan, a sure sign that something was dead or dying.

A pack of brown hyenas emerged from the prickly brush and sidestepped nervously at the sight of her jeep. They trotted a safe distance away, cackling as Sable drove toward the suspicious gray-colored mound resting on its side in the dried yellow savanna grass.

No, her heart throbbed, *not an elephant.* Poachers! How had they separated this one from the rest of the matriarchal herd? Was it a bull? Male elephants were solitary except during times of mating.

Leaving the engine running in case she needed to escape quickly, she caught up her loaded rifle from the backseat and ventured cautiously from the jeep.

Slowly she approached the elephant, keeping a safe distance until she could manage a clearer view. She was right—poachers—but her heart was reluctant to admit the next discovery. To come across an elephant like this was traumatic enough, but this particular cow was one she thought she recognized.

Her fingers tightened on the rifle stock. *No, not Moffet! It couldn't be.*

Sable glanced about the dried brush but saw nothing—no calf. Then it couldn't be Moffet, she reasoned. If it were, her baby would be here, too. And, anyway, what would Moffet be doing here so far from her own family unit? She would not have left their protection unless something was wrong—very wrong.

Sable drew near, then stopped; a cry of dismay escaped her lips. She'd recognize that elephant anywhere by its left ear. Five years ago she had helped treat the damaged ear that Kash said had been gored by a rhino in a squabble at a water hole.

She and Kash had first brought the young elephant to the Nairobi orphan zoo years ago after Sable had found the mother dead, another victim of poachers. But before the young elephant became too tame to survive again in the wild, Sable and Kash had released her in the Amboseli Game Reserve, hoping that a herd in this protected area would still accept her.

She swallowed as she stared at Moffet, recognizing the red tag Kash had marked the elephant with before setting her free. She remembered the relief she'd felt when she learned that

Moffet had indeed been accepted by an old matriarch into a small herd. Later, Moffet had given birth to a calf that Sable had named Patches.

Sable approached silently. The sight was far worse than expected because the elephant with its pitiful half-ear also brought back memories of her love relationship with Kash, which had ended as painfully as Moffet's life had.

"Oh, Moffet. . . ." Her throat ached; the words choked off. The poachers had brutally killed her for her two medium-sized tusks. Ivory! Something man didn't need for his own survival, but only to feed his greed.

Her hand clenched when she saw that Moffet was not yet dead, although there was nothing she could do to save her. She could only put her out of her misery.

"Moffet," she whispered.

It was uncertain whether or not the elephant understood her name or recognized the voice that spoke it. The only sounds that filled Sable's ears were the quarreling snarls of the vultures and the high-pitched laugh of the hyenas.

Sable wept, unashamed, hoping the animal could somehow sense her sorrow, could sense that some humans were her friends. There was a bond between the redeemed children of God and His creatures. She cared because Jesus was the Designer. He had produced that which was "good" until sin had come to ravage and destroy! She knew she cried for more than this elephant alone. To Sable, Moffet represented all the elephants of Africa. They were unappreciated for their majestic beauty and seen only as something to slaughter for a simple ivory tusk that would be carved into a needless decoration to adorn some wealthy home.

More than Moffet was dying. For Sable, Kash, too, had died—his honor, character, and a love that was once as strong and tender with passion as a warm African night were also gone. The young man whom she had loved had compromised his character and his love of Africa—for money. The young man who had worked with her father to protect and nourish the game animals had turned into a ruthless poacher himself. He had prostituted his knowledge of the land to exploit what he had once protected.

Insects droned noisily, carelessly, unmoved by the death scene as they landed on Sable's sweating throat. She was too emotionally spent to even brush them away. *Is this what I've returned to Africa for? Savagery? Misery? Death?*

The answer came to her heart with a drumlike cadence of the certainty of the calling of God upon her life. Yes, she had returned in His name to walk amid death and offer the message of Life, to hold forth the true Light where Satan's thick darkness still reigned. She had returned to speak of hope where there was despair, to offer Christ's eternal gift of reconciliation to all who would hear. She had come to show the *JESUS* film to the Maasai and the nomadic tribes in the NFD, to bring Scripture portions in their own languages and medicine for Kate to use in her work as a nurse. Yes . . . she had come home to stay. No amount of suffering would turn her back.

Moffet made a noisy breathing sound, and Sable stirred from her thoughts. She gripped the rifle and approached the suffering animal. She remembered suddenly—the calf . . . where was Patches?

Sable looked about again, her gaze pausing on the ground a short distance away where the soil was marked up with tire tracks, boot prints, and the ugly telltale sign of a scuffle. The poachers had worked to trap an animal and load it onto the trailer truck. Patches. And the poachers?

Smith and Browning! She thought of the truck that had nearly run her down at Namanga and the rawboned driver who yelled at her. He and his hunters were the ones who destroyed Moffet for her tusks, leaving the elephant to die a painful death, and took Patches to sell to a zoo. Sable was certain of it.

She neared the truck and trailer tracks, aware that the herd might be in the area. The marks were clear—and so was the direction the hunters had gone with their stolen treasure. As she had first suspected, the hunters had escaped across the plain for the Tanzanian border, not too many miles away. They would be camped near the Usa River for the night and eventually head for the port of Tanga to load their animals aboard ship.

Sable shuddered at the death rattle coming from Moffet and turned sadly to look upon the elephant. She started toward her when a far different sound came from the boulders, bringing a leap of fear to her throat—the low snorting of a lioness who must have smelled the blood as she was on the prowl for food for her cubs. Sable knew that there were "rebels" in this area—loners among the lions, both males and females, that had been rejected by the pride and were forced to hunt and survive on their own until they matched up with another lone lion to start a pride of their own.

There would be trouble, for the pride that already ruled this territory would fight to protect its food supply from invaders.

Sable hesitated, casting one last glance toward Moffet. Was there time to put her out of her misery?

Risking a face-to-face encounter with the lion, Sable edged near to where the elephant lay. Kash had taught her to be a crack shot, and she raised the rifle, holding it steady as she aimed directly to where the bullet would enter the brain.

"I'm sorry, Moffet. I'll find Patches somehow. Your calf will be all right."

Moffet's eye, with its long eyelashes, blinked toward the sun. The elephant's life would return to its Maker. Sable squeezed the trigger. She fired twice, to be absolutely certain.

At the sound of gunfire the lion quickly bounded away. Sable strode to the jeep and tossed the rifle in the backseat. Her eyes narrowed. This was one time when that truck driver would not get by with stealing a baby elephant for a circus. She was going to get Patches back—one way or another.

Determined, Sable drove the jeep toward the river camp of the zoo hunters. They weren't going to get away with killing Moffet for her ivory. And she wasn't about to let Patches be sold to uncaring hands. She'd get the baby back if it meant confronting the entire operation alone!

Sable swerved into the dusty camp where tents, trucks, and a trailer were parked ahead beneath a stand of acacia trees. She cut off the motor and got out, slamming the jeep door. Her eyes swept the safari hunters lounging about, and she noticed three Europeans and two Africans near the beat-up trailer. A large tent was set up near the river, where an African cook was preparing food. The aroma of coffee drifted to her on the hot breeze.

Ignoring the men, she grabbed her revolver from the glove compartment and shoved it in her holster. With head high, she walked briskly toward the far end of camp, where she spotted some cages covered with tarps. She could only imagine what terrified and angry animals hovered behind those coverings. Several Africans who looked to her to be from the Chugga tribe loitered about. Seeing her stride across the camp, they hid their surprise and stood with blank faces, eyes averted.

One of the three Europeans standing outside the trailer said something to the other two and walked toward her. "Hey! Wait a minute, sweetheart."

Sable turned with studied dignity. She had accompanied her father many times on his rounds as a warden, and she would not be easily intimidated. She casually rested her hand on her holster and stared evenly at the rawboned man with sunburned cheeks. Yes, this was the clumsy dude who had nearly run her down at Namanga. Evidently he was too thickheaded to even recognize her.

His ice-blue eyes wasted no time inching their way up from her ankles to her face. He stopped, raising his battered coffee tin to his lips, where a smile revealed his thoughts. "Name's Pete Browning. If you're lost, Nairobi's that-a-way." He used his thumb to gesture off into the wide African distance.

Sable showed no response to his intended humor and spoke in a chill tone. "I'm not lost, Mr. Browning. I was born and raised here. Furthermore, I know poachers when I run into them."

His smile melted away. He took out a stick of gum and removed the wrapper, tossing the paper to the ground. "You're mighty quick with accusations. Proving 'em is somethin' else." He bit the stick of gum between his teeth and chomped. "You come with a search warrant, little girl?"

She raised her chin and gazed past the man. "I don't need

one. Are you the owner of this ragtag bunch of poachers?"

He chewed thoughtfully. "Poachers?" he asked dumbly. "Why, we're legal reps from the Indonesian Circus Ring. We've the sweetest, legalist little license to hunt you'll ever see." With his thumb, he gestured over his shoulder. "Right in the boss's trailer—all framed an' hangin' on the wall for all game wardens to gaze upon. Comes from the good president of Tanzania himself."

"You were hunting in Kenya, in the Amboseli Reserve. And I suspect your license is a forgery."

He studied her, growing a little more cautious. "Who are you anyway? What d'ya want?"

"I want to see your license revoked and your stolen animals returned to the Amboseli Reserve. I'd like to see you penalized for poaching ivory tusks—but what I want right now is a certain baby elephant. Either you or your rank hunters stole her this afternoon about six miles from here in Kenya. The mother was shot by poachers."

She had his full attention. He lifted his tin mug and drank, watching her, munching his gum. After a good moment he gestured his head toward the trailer. "You'll need to talk to the boss. Any deals will be made with him. But he's not available right now."

She stood her ground. So deals were to be made, were they? Then she may at least save Patches. She had thought this man was the boss, but evidently there was someone else. If this was Browning, then the man inside the trailer should be Smith.

"Suppose you go get the boss, then."

"He's sick. Suffers with headaches. Sees stars and zigzags, I think."

She smiled. "My heart bleeds with sympathy. Perhaps you can bring him . . . this." She opened her bag and pulled out a small tin of aspirin, dropping it in his brawny hand.

He looked at it. "An' who do I tell him is here? 'Miz' Game Warden?"

Sable restrained her temper. "No, the *daughter* of the game warden."

His munching stopped.

"Tell him I want that calf."

He shrugged his heavy shoulders under the torn T-shirt. "Sure, I'll tell him. He won't know what you're talkin' 'bout, though." He chewed his gum. "We don't have elephants."

She was losing patience. "Just call him, Mr. Browning. In the meantime, I'll have a look around while he wakes from his 'stars and zigzags.' "

She turned and walked away, aware that every eye followed her with suspicious concern. Sable kept her hand on her holster, head high as she walked toward the cages, where several Africans had come to stand guard.

She gestured to the covered cages and spoke in fluent Swahili: "What does the European have in there? What has he stolen from the Maasai? Are you from the Chugga tribe here in Tanzania? Do you approve of this evil of poaching? When the poachers kill off all your land's treasures given by the living God, what will you do then? Can you make them anew from the dust of the earth?"

She didn't think the European men who stood some feet away keeping a watchful eye on her could understand the language, although they may have picked up a few words. The African workers shifted their stance, shook their heads as if they couldn't understand her either, and gestured back toward the trailer.

"Someone killed an elephant in the Amboseli Reserve. They were poachers," she said. "They killed for two medium-sized tusks—think of it! Can you point out the hunters who did this? Or did *you* obey them for wages?"

Again they pretended they didn't understand and said nothing.

A masculine voice, unintimidated, did answer—coming from behind her and speaking Swahili as fluently as she. The "boss" was managing his headache and ordering the two Chugga tribesmen to leave him and the woman to speak together alone.

The sound of that voice caused Sable's back to go rigid.

She'd know that voice anywhere. How could she forget it even after two years of trying? Kash Hallet. So he was now the "boss" of this outfit? Then everything Vince Adler had warned her about him was true. That warm and leisurely voice had once told her how enamored he was with her "charms" as they stood beneath the bright African moonlight shining on the snows of Mount Kilimanjaro.

Uncertain as to the depth of emotional impact that awaited their first meeting in two years, Sable's concerns for the baby elephant momentarily vanished. It was now her heart that was endangered.

Two

Confronting Kash was the last thing Sable had expected upon her return to East Africa. She had determined never to see him again, or even talk to him. Now unnerved, she was reluctant to turn and face the man she had demanded to see, afraid of what her heart would still find.

Well, she didn't love him anymore, she told herself. Besides, the kind of "love" she once had for Kash had been infatuation; mere physical attraction, even if it had been as deep and warm with longing as any exotic African night! But all that foolish heart-pounding drama was over.

She'd been younger then, and yes, as much as she disliked to admit it, she'd been emotionally unsteady. But during the last two years, she had done much growing up. Her mother's long bout with cancer and subsequent death had been used of God to teach her so much more of the deeper meaning of love, of commitment between two caring people, of enduring values that lasted beyond the sparkle of youthful passion. And now she had the love of Dr. Vince Adler, a man who embodied the very spirit of humanitarian sacrifice and concern for the suffering. Her attraction to Vince went beyond the physical to include a cause that she, too, could feel strongly about.

Her relationship with Kash had been different. His good looks had overshadowed everything else. She'd been blind to his spiritual shallowness, his self-love, and his greed for money at any cost, which had now led him to the lucrative business of poaching.

Yes, Kash had once possessed her heart, but that was before she really knew what he was like. The past was over. The love-flame was cold and dead, just the way she intended to keep it . . . buried.

With her mind thus fixed, Sable turned calmly, indifferently, her armor all in place, her heart emotionally prepared to resist the man who'd chosen to walk away from her without a backward glance.

Kash Hallet stood there a few feet away. Her eyes flicked over his brooding good looks, which were little diminished by the fact that he was suffering from pain and attempted to hide it with dark sunglasses. His denim shirt, left unbuttoned, must have been quickly thrown on over his well-worn Levi's. The dark hair, the savage yet restrained strength that he presented in leather boots and the wide Maasai-made leather belt, might have been used in an advertisement for the rugged outdoors. He had not changed in two years—if anything, he seemed more adventurous than ever—but she had changed. Though her heart hammered, she was able to tell herself she didn't want his love the way she had so desperately wanted it before.

"So Kash Hallet has returned to Kenya," came her accusing tone.

"I never went far. You're the one who fled—to Canada with Dr. Adler."

Her eyes were distant, and she ignored the insinuation that she had run from him. "Dr. Adler is here, too. He's involved sacrificially with his fellowman and the wildlife that is so much in need of protection from your kind. That you've returned probably explains the recent increase in poaching."

His jaw flexed, but his voice remained too calm. "It does? That you rush to think so disappoints me. Are your charitable indictments part of your missionary work?"

Sable flushed, reminded of who she was in Christ and how her accusations of him were far from being under the Spirit's control. So Kash knew why she had returned.

"I found Moffet shot and left to suffer, her tusks torn out," she said, frustrated that her voice quavered. From the corner of her eye she saw the brawny blond man named Pete Browning come closer to hear their conversation. She glanced at him, then back at Kash, whose bronzed expression revealed nothing of his thoughts.

Sable swallowed back her disappointment, for though she wouldn't admit it, her subconscious had desperately hoped he would deny it. He stood there, apparently unyielding. She glanced again toward his partner, then turned away. "I don't think I need to waste any time asking more questions. It's obvious who did it."

She swept past, keeping a wide berth so he couldn't catch hold of her arm, and hurried toward her jeep. Unable to ignore the flaring pain coming to life in her heart, she blamed it on the trauma of having found Moffet.

Accusing Kash of this crime, when at one time he had cared as much for wildlife as she, was to the point and cruel, but at the moment she didn't care. He had trampled on her heart and left her to bleed emotionally while he ran off to make his fortune. The desire for vengeance, which she thought she had surrendered to Christ, was growing again like piercing thorns inside her soul. She wanted Kash to feel some of her suffering.

He came after her, as Sable had expected, and she ran to her jeep to avoid him.

"Typical, running away again," he said calmly.

His response surprised her. She considered Kash the type to avoid emotional confrontations. She had always wanted to discuss their differences and understand each other, but he had always avoided those discussions, as though she were backing him into a corner. As a man he could handle conflicts of all sorts, yet when it came to dealing with intimacy of mind and heart, he had always withdrawn, unable or unwilling to tell her how he "felt." Instead, he had insisted she didn't play by the rules. Rules! What rules? Why did he always want to hide behind "rules" that were fair when she wanted to talk about emotions and feelings?

Kash would never explain. And now—he dared to accuse *her*

of having been the one to run away from him!

His taunting continued. "I thought you were wiser than to believe in a man like Adler—or should I call him Saint Vince? Build your brave new world on his integrity, and you'll hit bottom when he falls."

Sable stopped and whirled to face him, her eyes moist with a frustration she couldn't control. Instead of denying the crime of poaching, he brought up Dr. Adler.

Kash stopped, too, deliberately keeping distance between them as though he knew that this time she was the one who wanted it there. She suspected that he watched her intensely beneath those sunglasses, and that if she stayed now, she couldn't win . . . she'd lose again. *I don't love him.* Her eyes smarted, but she placed her hands on her hips and tried to appear aloof.

The heat and dust fed the flare-up of tension, and for a moment the tug-of-war continued, each seeming to wait for the other to give in first.

To free the moment from its certain doom, Sable called, "Never mind about Dr. Adler. He's an innocent bystander. You killed Moffet. How could you? You, who once saved her from poachers. What did it feel like to shoot an animal that trusted you?"

His expression showed none of the guilt she might have expected to see as she remembered back to better days when he'd been attentive and caring, before ruthlessness had placed a steel casing about his heart. She wouldn't remember those times, she told herself; they would drag her down to defeat.

Aware that she was neither reasonable, nor likely to be under the present circumstances, she ran to her jeep and slid behind the wheel, quickly slamming the door and switching on the ignition. She backed out in a half circle, stepped on the accelerator, and sped away, leaving a shower of dust behind.

A moment later when the dust settled, she cast a last glance through her rearview mirror and saw him standing with one hand on his hip. She visualized the frustration that must be smoldering within, and she winced to herself. No matter. He deserved every bit of it.

But as she drove on, she sighed and leaned back into the seat, aware of the guilt that was surfacing. The warning that she was behaving wrongly had been there all along, but only now when the emotional clamor began to subside did she pay closer attention. Each beat of her heart ached. Suppose he hadn't killed Moffet? Was it possible the entire hunting group had been innocent? She didn't have to like the rawboned Mr. Browning to admit that they might not have been the poachers.

That was hardly possible. She had followed the tracks into their camp. And except for Kash, they'd all behaved as though they had something to hide. And Kash could be a master at concealing his feelings.

"He should have been an actor," she said harshly. "He'd win an Oscar for best performance."

Oh, Lord, she prayed, discouraged with her failures. The groan within spoke to Him of what she could not express in words.

She wouldn't analyze her feelings now. She couldn't accept them anyway.

As she drove, she blinked hard and tried to release herself to experience nothing more than the wild African terrain. She headed across the plain toward the seasonal Lake Amboseli, a route that would offer a shortcut home. At this time of the year the lake would be dry. Now, more than ever, she wanted to arrive home to Gran's embrace and be ushered into her old, familiar room. If she went by the lake route she could be at the lodge as the evening shadows were falling and avoid traveling alone at night, which could be dangerous.

"I won't think of Kash," she told herself. "By tomorrow he'll break camp and move on toward the coast."

It would be good to see Vince. His dedication to his scientific endeavors made her feel calm and sane.

Three

The seasonal road across Lake Amboseli was deceptive.

The dry season was the best time to see large herds of game animals congregating at the few watering holes, and the area of the Amboseli Game Reserve called Old Tukai contained one of the most remarkable concentrations of animals to be seen in all Africa: not only rhinos but elephants, buffalo, lions, cheetahs, giraffes, baboons, monkeys, and herds of plains game were common. To the novice tourist, anxious to set off for a photographer's paradise view of Mount Kilimanjaro and the exquisite game animals roaming the vast yellow grasses of the plain, the lake road would appear safe to travel upon, but appearances were not what they always seemed, especially in Africa.

"But I'm no tourist," Sable muttered to herself. "I should know better than to get stuck in the mud like this."

At the height of the dry season the lake became a vast, shimmering plain of white dust, but today it was wet, cracked mud, mud so sticky that the wheels of her jeep were hopelessly mired. She'd been careless, thinking of Kash, and she'd paid for her mistake.

Sable sat behind the wheel, staring across the great expanse of cracked clay, troubled by more than her predicament. Gran should have warned her that he was back in Kenya. She used a handkerchief to pat her pale throat and with a sigh of resignation opened the jeep door and stepped down. She winced as the sluggish mud squished beneath her safari boots. "Yuck—" She ran her sweating palms along her pants and settled her hat while she looked about. Despite her frustration, she knew the mud served a vital purpose for the hippos and elephants that loved to wallow in it. The mud sealed their hides from vicious biting and stinging insects and the blistering sun. The Creator's design was perfect for what He intended to accomplish. The same mud that left her jeep stuck and her spirits downcast was, for the animals, a healthy deterrent against insects.

She stared at the jeep tires sunk deep in the mud. She'd never get out now. She pushed her hat back and glanced about, wondering what to do next. It was miles to the lodge. What she needed now was a tame elephant to pull her out. She thought of Moffet, new grief settling in. Unlike Indian elephants, African elephants did not make good pets. But Moffet had been unusual. She'd been tame enough to be harnessed with a rope. She reminded herself of what wildlife conservationists knew so well, that taming animals in the wild put them at risk. It left them vulnerable and too trusting of humans, who, in many cases, could not be trusted with their God-given responsibility to rule the environment as a treasure.

Danger, however, was impartial; humans, too, were at risk from the animals, and allowing herself to get stuck in the wilds with evening approaching had been unwise, especially in Old Tukai in the southeastern corner of the Amboseli Game Reserve. For a tourist, a guide was essential to make it through the swamp and woodland with its intricate network of tracks. Sable was far from being a greenhorn tourist, since she'd been born and raised in Kenya as the great-granddaughter of Hiram Dunsmoor, who had settled in what was once called British East Africa. Her knowledge of Amboseli was nearly as keen as that of the Maasai tribe, which worked with the Kajaido District Council to administer the reserve.

She slipped her sunglasses on and, shading her eyes with her hand, stared across the great expanse of Africa. Would Gran begin to wonder and send someone to look for her? Gran knew she had planned to meet Dr. Adler at Namanga, but it was getting late now, and Gran would surely wonder why they hadn't arrived yet. Sable had no idea what had happened to Vince, and perhaps her grandmother would assume they had both driven on to see Kate and observe the work at the Maasai medical camp. Kate had assumed the directorship for the family-owned medical relief organization begun by their mother, which was now temporarily set up some miles west of Old Tukai but would soon be moved north toward Samburu.

Bringing in the supplies, however, would prove difficult, since there was a threat of a renewed outbreak of tribal warfare in that area. The desperate need of thousands only strengthened Sable's resolve to accomplish the task, in Christ's name, to those He loved. For His sake she chose to love them.

She recalled the story of a medical missionary nurse working with the disfigured leprosy victims. As she cleansed and handled the loathsome flesh, an onlooker was horrified and exclaimed, "I wouldn't do that for any amount of money!"

"Neither would I," said the missionary. "But I'll do it without cost for Jesus who loves them."

Unlike her sister, who was a nurse, Sable was actively involved in Bible distribution and evangelism, showing the *JESUS* film in the native language of the tribes. Her supplies were still in Mombasa. Food, Bibles, and bicycles were to go to the Kenyan missionaries working out of Nairobi with the Maasai. Yet getting into the restricted area depended on whether a hunter-guide could be hired. From what Gran had told her on the telephone, there wasn't a guide or safari hunter willing to risk the region for the low wages they could pay for his services.

There was another reason she must get through. Marsabit, in the Northern Frontier District, was the final habitat of the giant-tusked elephants—what remained of them. The poaching had become a nightmare for those who hoped to save them. Now there were the Maasai—another of His handiwork, a far more precious work who needed not only help, but the Light to shine upon their hearts.

She turned to look behind her. It was a long way back to Namanga and not much closer to the foul camp of Smith and Browning Zoo Animals. If she chose to walk back, which she wouldn't do to avoid another meeting with Kash, anything could happen to her on foot. She opened the jeep door and removed her revolver from the glove compartment, placing it in her Maasai-made leather belt about her waist, a precious gift from a Maasai evangelist. He was one of the fine young men to whom she would have the joy of giving a bicycle so he could visit his people and present the Scriptures.

She closed her eyes and prayed silently over her dilemma, confessing her sin in getting angry with Kash and Mr. Browning, but before she had even ended her prayer she heard the sound of an engine and turned hopefully. *A Land Rover!* Perhaps Gran had sent Mckibber, Kash's uncle, to locate her.

She watched hopefully as it came into view, tearing down the track. Sable shouted and waved her hat, but of course the driver couldn't possibly hear her. Swiftly she climbed into the jeep and leaned on the horn with a loud and plaintive call of distress.

The vehicle slowed, then the driver, surmising what had happened to her jeep, backed up and turned onto the smaller track that was seasonally in use beside the lake.

"Thank you, Lord." Sable grabbed her bag from the seat beside her and, smiling, started to get out, glancing in the rearview mirror. As the driver walked around the front of his vehicle, her breath caught and her eyes narrowed. Kash!

She sat there looking in the mirror, debating whether she wished to get out or not—as if she had a choice in the matter. And Kash waited patiently for her decision as though he had all the time in the world, leaning against the side of the Land Rover, arms folded.

Sable got out of the jeep and stood there, bag in hand, not quite knowing what she actually expected him to do about her dilemma, or whether she even wanted to be obligated to him. After their emotional confrontation back at the trailer camp, his smile was the last thing she had expected. So he wanted to make a truce. She didn't know why, but it brought great relief. She hadn't wanted their first meeting after two years to be so emotionally intense. Their last confrontation had been seared on her mind as they separated in the throes of misunderstanding and frustration.

"Now, this is a sight to remember," he called. "The independent Sable Dunsmoor, daughter of the internationally known wildlife conservationist Skyler Dunsmoor, naive enough in the ways of Africa to get herself stuck in the mud! And after I lectured you at least ten times when we were growing up to never drive a jeep into a riverbed."

She winced, her feminine pride needled by his amusement, and something else . . . the sound of his voice when in a pleasant mood stirred too many deep and hurtful memories. Nevertheless, she managed a rueful smile. "And I suppose you're just going to stand there enjoying my failure?"

His smile remained. "Why not? There's no use both of us getting muddy."

"As you wish," Sable said with a casualness she didn't feel. "I don't need any help anyway."

"Aptly spoken by the brave *Miz* Dunsmoor."

"If you say 'Miz' one more time—"

"I'll cheer you on as you inch your way across."

"But I do need a lift to Gran's place."

"I wouldn't think of leaving you for the hippos." He reached onto his seat and removed a camera.

"What are you doing!"

"I can't resist. I want to catch you playing in the mud. The last time, as I recall, you were a little girl making mud pies for me and Seth."

She flushed, remembering. Seth was his older brother by five years. She started across the gluelike mud, and he deliberately held the camera on her as he lounged against the Land Rover.

"Did anyone ever tell you what a mean-spirited hyena you are?" she called.

"Yes, lots of times. I remember when you used to call me something nicer. . . ."

Sable's boot wouldn't lift from the sucking mud, and she lost her balance and fell backward, holding in her cry of humiliation.

"Ah—perfect," he said and snapped the shutter, not once but several times, and she heard him laugh, then toss the camera onto the seat. He smiled. "This is for blackmail."

It was bad enough that he'd come back, crashing the emotional barrier she had placed around her life, but now she had to be embarrassed as well.

"Ah, the bitter dregs of life. You've had more than your share of tragedy recently, haven't you?"

Yes, and you're part of it, she could have said, but that sort of remark would never play well with Kash, and she would be displaying a crybaby attitude. She had already blown their first meeting by raging at him as both judge and jury.

"Shall I take pity and rescue you?" came the mild invitation. "If I don't, you might be there until the new rains."

"Come near, and I'll see you dragged down to the wallow!"

"Ah! Sweet vengeance. But I can't resist such a fun challenge."

"I mean it."

"I'm sure you do. That's the fun part."

"I thought you had a migraine!"

"Maybe a good mud bath would ease my pain and frustration. What do you think?"

"Stay away!"

He shrugged. "Far be it from me to play gallant knight when the damsel in distress bluntly refuses. Then go ahead. Struggle on your own. You always did insist on it."

She always did insist. Was that true?

He leaned back again against the Land Rover. "I should've brought more film. What do you think our magnificent Dr. Adler would pay for these?"

"Anything for money?" came the quiet but meaningful question.

He sobered. "Now, I thought you knew me better than that. No, not *anything* . . . and I didn't shoot Moffet."

She found her heart desperately wishing to believe him, perhaps too desperately, because there was still something inside her that wanted to believe that the Kash Hallet she had previously known still existed. The wistful sound of his voice brought her a pang as he said thoughtfully to himself, "I loved that elephant . . . Moffet and her silly half-gone ear. . . ."

Sable blinked hard. There was no mistaking the tone of those words. Kash did remember the better days of their youth, the wildlife projects they had worked closely together on, the long safari journeys with her father and Mckibber, the campfires, the Kenya moon, the—

No, she thought, forcing herself to stop the merry-go-round of memories.

He snatched up the camera again. "Vince will appreciate such rare vintage photos of his fiancee."

His voice held nothing. So he knew about the upcoming engagement. Was that the reason he had attacked Vince's character back at the trailer camp? He had never liked him. Then again, why should Kash care who she became engaged to?

He didn't—he was just trying to avoid thinking of the elephant, she told herself. Sable snatched up her muddied bag. She figured he was concentrating on the camera in order to forget. She knew him well in some ways, yet overall he remained a stranger.

She pulled her suitcase from the back of the jeep, and this time more carefully, Sable made her way toward the road. When she reached the Land Rover, he said smoothly, "You'll get mud on my seat."

That did it! Throwing her suitcase on the ground, she turned swiftly, words bubbling to her lips, but they died there. He'd removed his sunglasses, and she was unprepared for the onslaught of confusing feelings that flooded her soul as his cobalt blue eyes held hers, all casualness melting away.

He reached his hand and gently stroked the looped braid at the back of her neck. This gentle move took her off guard, for it was the last expression of his emotion that she would have expected.

"Sable—"

She turned away, vulnerable, shaking her head, her fingers gripping her handbag. She closed her eyes. "Oh, Kash, why did you come back?'' she asked weakly. ''Why didn't you stay away!''

A breath escaped him, as though resigned to her rejection, and he leaned back against the vehicle, again looking up toward the sky. The absolute silence of the reserve held them both prisoner. Somewhere a bird screeched, and there followed a distant trumpeting of an elephant.

''Unlike Vince, I was born and raised here, remember?''

''Yes, I remember,'' she half accused. ''I also remember how you chose to walk away—from everything.''

''Not everything.'' He reached over and took her hand, prying it open and disclosing the stain of rich mud drying on her palms. ''Unlike Vince, who doesn't really care about Kenya, you and I are both attached to this earth. We were born and raised here, and we belong to this land.'' He smiled. ''But we British have the prickly end of things this time. Our families have a history of two hundred years in this piece of East Africa, and for once we know what it's like to be the rejected race, the unwanted outsiders. We fell in love with a country that isn't ours, and we can't have it! It's rather maddening, isn't it? We're not the lords of the earth now, but strangers and pilgrims. We can't own land here.''

His words hurt, for he was right. And she did understand. Sable thought of the Dunsmoor ranch that had ceased to exist in the days of her grandparents and of the Hallet land now owned and operated by members of the Kikuyu tribe working for the government.

He rubbed his thumb over her palm where the mud was caked and dried, and while she was aware of his touch, it wasn't at all clear that he was aware of her. Rather, Kash seemed to be contemplating the soil, for he touched it almost longingly.

''Maybe we're both destined to love what we can't own,'' she said quietly, but she had more on her heart than Kenya, and while his dark head was bent, her eyes misted, following the handsome and chiseled line of his jaw. Suddenly she remembered what she had programmed herself to forget—his warm lips on hers, the strength of his embrace. She remembered with a vividness that left her weak.

"Too many Hallets have been killed here to forget," he said. "Like Abel, their blood calls from the ground. My grandparents by the Mau Mau, an uncle in the war, and . . ."

But Kash didn't go on. He looked at her, all the fire gone from his eyes now. In its place a calm determination settled in his gaze as he grew reflective. He released her hand and by so doing seemed to also release any claim to her emotions, leaving her unexpectedly disconnected.

"I came back for several reasons. This is where I belong, and I'm staying this time. One way or another."

Sable stared at her hand, aware that with his touch withdrawn it felt as empty and aching as her heart.

Yes, she thought with an unemotional resignation that matched his, *Kash belongs to Africa, not to anyone or anything else*. Like the great Serengeti Plain and the animals that roamed it—free, but always in danger of drought, hunger, savage death, fire, wind, and storm.

Sable turned her head and looked toward Mount Kilimanjaro as the golden sun crowned it with a mysterious, untamable glory.

A silent interlude passed before he opened the door.

"Never mind the mud," he said with a smile in his voice.

She slid onto the leather seat, weary now, worn by the onslaught that had played on her soul.

Kash tossed her suitcase into the back. "I'll send someone to fetch the jeep." Walking around to the driver's side, he got in and started the motor.

She noticed that he frowned, his lashes narrowing, and she remembered that he wasn't well and that his head must be causing a good deal of pain.

"Did the aspirin help?" she asked meekly, feeling guilty when she recalled her motive in giving them to Mr. Browning.

He cocked his head and looked at her.

Of course the aspirin hadn't been strong enough to ease the pain. She looked away. "I'm sorry. Want me to drive?"

"And get my Land Rover in the same mess you got the jeep?"

She turned to protest and saw a smile as he started to drive.

In a brief time they had left Lake Amboseli behind and were on the track in the direction of the gaming lodge.

"You're wrong about Vince," she said, no accusation in her voice. She was growing more curious about the reason for his remarks.

"You're the expert where he's concerned."

There was more to those casual words beneath the surface. "I know him better than you, but where Dr. Adler's concerned no one is an expert."

"Granted, he's a deep thinker. Too profound for us poor commoners."

She refused to take the casual bait.

He looked at her. "Are you sure his noble passions aren't prompted by some New Age philosophy?"

She looked at him, shocked. "New Age? He's a Christian. Vince will also help my father at the elephant camp in Samburu. I wish you wouldn't attack him. I'm going to marry him," she said boldly, for self-preservation.

He looked at her, and a ghost of a smile was on his lips. "Are you?"

It unnerved her, and she turned abruptly to stare ahead.

"I'm curious about this sudden warmhearted devotion to Dr. Adler."

"It isn't sudden," she said with confidence.

"Two years ago you were in love with me. Now you're going to marry him. I call that sudden."

"Your conceit is unbearable. You think all you need do is show up again after all this time, and that will change my opinion of Vince. It isn't quite as reckless as you want to make it sound. Two years is a long time to not hear from someone who simply walked out of my life."

"I didn't 'walk out' of your life. I was waiting for you to grow up a little. And your opinion of him will change fast enough when you know him better. If not, you'll make the biggest mistake of your life."

"And, of course, you know all about Vince's character."

"I know enough about him," he insisted quietly. "Vince isn't what he pretends."

She stared ahead. "You never liked him," she accused.

He shot her a narrowing glance. "He's old enough to be your father."

"He's thirty-eight," she corrected airily, "not old at all."

He remained silent, adjusting his sunglasses.

"You needn't concern yourself about my making a mistake," she went on. "I'm old enough to make my own."

"Some mistakes are forever."

"Yes . . ." She settled back uneasily. "I know how I'm going to invest the rest of my life, and I won't be wasting it chasing empty dreams or letting anyone decide to be the manager of my destiny. I've come back, like you, because I belong here. I've come to work with Vince and my father at Samburu."

From the corner of her eye she saw his head turn and felt his gaze studying her, so she folded her arms and stared straight ahead as though confident of tomorrow. She had been—until an hour ago.

"Did you say Dr. Adler wants to work with your father researching the elephants at Samburu?"

She wondered at the intensity of his question and looked at him. "Yes. Why?"

He looked back to the road, thoughtfully.

"Why do you ask?" she repeated when he remained silent.

"What if I told you Vince is working with Toronto colleagues at Lake Rudolf? Would you reconsider going to Samburu?"

Vince working at Rudolf? "What would he be doing there?"

"Maybe he's supporting an evolutionary cause."

"You mean looking for fossils? Impossible . . ." she began, then paused. "Anyway, my reason for going to Samburu is to help my father do research and to show the *JESUS* film. It's a personal goal, but I expect to work it into my schedule." She folded her arms. "Nothing can convince me to change my mind. As you said back at the lake—we know this land, the animals, the tribes. We love it, and we belong to it, like the Maasai."

He smiled. She looked away, assuming his smile was over amused pleasure in her dedication to the land, which they shared too deeply. She hastened, "Even if Vince wasn't born here, he cares about the animals."

"Trying to convince me or yourself? He doesn't understand Kenya—he never did. He was an evolutionary fanatic searching for fossils with a Dr. Willard at Rudolf, and he's added some New Age religious philosophy."

"That's absurd, Kash! He's never even mentioned Lake Rudolf. He's a conservationist to the core, and I told you, he's a Christian."

"Is he? He claims to be, but he's using the term very loosely. And as for the animals, Skyler would die to protect the elephants, but Vince—" He stopped, as though he had said too much.

She realized that Kash sounded anything but the callous young native gone bad—and the leader of an elusive poaching outfit. She studied the side of his face curiously. There was no mistaking the fervency in his voice about protecting the elephants, and it contradicted everything he outwardly represented. "I don't understand you," she began quietly.

Kash stepped on the accelerator. "Vince hired Dr. Katherine Walsh to work with him at Rudolf."

A woman? Who was Katherine Walsh?

A hundred questions rushed to her mind, but she avoided them all, for Kash couldn't be right. He was mistaken . . . or was he trying to plant doubts about Vince in her heart? Whatever the reason for his wanting to do so remained hidden, but she would eventually find out.

"How do you know all this?" she asked. "When were you in Samburu? When did you see my father or even know about what's happening there or at Rudolf?"

"I can't explain now, but Vince is here."

"I know that. He called me in Toronto two weeks ago."

"Did he know then that you were going to try to show the *JESUS* film to the Maasai?"

"No," she admitted reluctantly.

"Vince will ask you to go with him to Samburu, to bring him to meet your father, but I'm asking you not to go."

Surprised and wondering at his motives, she mulled his words over in her mind without an immediate reply.

"I don't see why you should care," she said after a minute.

"I care. That's all I can say right now."

"But Vince doesn't need *me* to bring him to my father," she protested.

"No, but he'll need you to 'contact' your father. Skyler has disappeared into the wilderness, and it's his wish that no one, including Vince, find him until he's prepared to show himself."

All this was new to Sable, and she didn't know what to make of it. Why would her father disappear into the wilderness and not wish to be found?

"None of this makes sense to me. Even if it's true, what makes you think I can help Vince find my father?"

"For the same reason Vince thinks so. You're his daughter."

"So is Kate."

"But you're the one interested in elephants, like Skyler."

"You know an awful lot for having just arrived back in Kenya. So why shouldn't Vince be brought to my father's camp?"

"What if I told you he has plans to hunt ivory?"

His suggestion left her speechless. She stared at him in astonishment. Of all people, he had the audacity to accuse Vince of poaching!

"There isn't a man more dedicated to wildlife," she insisted.

"Maybe . . . but I doubt it. Even if he has an interest, it's not the same as ours."

She had no argument for that. There was a certain affinity between the great-grandchildren of the Kenya colonizers that outsiders didn't understand. Vince was from Toronto, and even though he had studied Africa for years and knew more of its ancient history than even she did, it was impersonal knowledge.

The history she shared with Kash bled and throbbed with pathos and heartbeat.

But what of Kash's poaching? How could he claim to still have an interest in the animals that he was now killing and capturing for money?

Kash had lapsed into what she took for a moody silence, but it may have only been his way of contemplation. Whatever it was, she found it most attractive and looked away again, annoyed with herself for still feeling drawn to him.

She glanced in the backseat and noticed the hunting rifle, maps, baggage, and the camera he had teasingly taken her picture with when she had slipped in the mud. What was he up to? What was he doing in this area of Amboseli now? What did it have to do with Smith and Browning Zoo Animals?

The Kenyatta Game Viewing Lodge was twenty miles away now. They had left the Old Tukai region of Amboseli, with its swamps and acacia woodlands and soon entered the reserve's plains, which consisted of hot, dry thornbush country. As Kash drove along they could see the Maasai herdsmen with their thin, horned cattle. The cattle reminded Sable of the drought and famine that were never far removed from Africa. Here on the Amboseli plains the nomadic Maasai moved from place to place for grazing land, burning the fields behind them to promote the growth of new young grass. Only in the Old Tukai area were the Maasai forbidden to bring their cattle, in order to preserve the area for the wild animals.

They passed the mustard-colored acacia trees, saw a long-legged ostrich scooting through the plains dust, an impala leaping gracefully, a little dik-dik, and a herd of zebras.

Kash slowed and she wondered why, glancing at him. "Elephants," he explained.

Sable didn't see them, but they had knocked down trees everywhere so that the branches made a wild tangle of deadwood, like white bones.

Kash swerved suddenly, and Sable clutched the seat as the Land Rover dove and bucked into thick thornbush. For a moment she didn't know what had happened.

"Elephants," he repeated grimly, "and they're not happy."

She looked toward a clump of dry, yellow trees not more than fifty feet away, her heart thumping with both fear and excitement. There were five of them, stately and enormous, and then she saw it—the carcass of another beast.

"Oh no," she whispered and began to open the door to get out when Kash's warm hand grasped her arm.

"Don't move—" he warned in a quiet voice. She waited tensely, wise enough to know there was something else she hadn't seen. Off to the right a bull elephant came through the trees, his trunk lifting.

"He's going to charge!" she gasped.

"No, he's halfhearted. See his trunk?"

The elephant's trunk was extended to smell the air rather than rolled under to protect it in a charge. It sidestepped threateningly and flapped its ears, then walked away into the trees followed by the small herd, and to Sable's joy a baby elephant slipped in between two huge elephants and moved off toward the river.

When they'd gone and the dust had settled, Kash opened the door and got out. Sable followed.

"Poachers," he said flatly.

"I can't bear it again today—what is it, Kash?"

"A rhino."

She turned away, emotion choking her throat.

"It must have happened around the time Moffet was killed." The restrained anger in his voice alerted her. She turned and looked at him, knowing now that he couldn't have done it. She'd been wrong. A swell of pride flared up in her heart and something else—a warning that she could care again too deeply.

"Are . . . are you sure?" she asked to cover her feelings.

"Same tire tracks. I noticed them this morning where Moffet was."

"You noticed. . . ?" she began, surprised. "Then you already knew when I came to the trailer camp?"

"Uh-huh."

"But I don't understand. You're the boss of the zoo hunters."

"Yes, but I can't explain now."

"It's despicable," she said, her voice shaking. "It's the poachers who are the beasts! To kill a beautiful animal like this for nothing except a rhino horn."

Kash stooped in the dust to examine the footprints, all but destroyed now by the trek of game and the other elephants. "Money," he said simply.

Something in his voice troubled her, and she searched his face.

Several brown hyenas emerged nervously from the dusk. Above, buzzards circled and landed in a tree, stark and colorless against the lavender sky billowing with silver clouds.

Sable stood looking at the rhino and thought of Moffet. "Moffet trusted everyone. It was so unfair, so cruel. . . ."

He looked over at her, frowning, and stood. He walked up and, in a moment of silent understanding, put an arm around her shoulders, drawing her toward him. It seemed so right to be there with him, to accept his comfort as she had in the past. But receiving it now only brought the realization of how dreadfully she had missed it these two years. She pulled away as though an electric current had run between them. Had he felt the same?

"Come on, let's get out of here," he said in a husky voice and, taking her arm, led her back to the Land Rover.

Four

Amboseli was one of Kenya's largest and most scenic wildlife reserves, with the entire plain dominated by the shining snow-covered cone of Kilimanjaro in northern Tanzania rising to an astonishing height from the burning Serengeti. One of its two peaks, Kibo, was the highest point in Africa, over nineteen thousand feet above sea level, and sixteen thousand feet above the flat, hot plain of the reserve. To sit beside a fire outside the safari tents on a clear night, with the moon shining on the great ice cap high above, and hear lions roaring not so very far away was for Sable a cherished memory of having worked with her father, Kash, and Seth in earlier years.

The Land Rover emerged from the mountain's great shadow past several tall Maasai warriors, each carrying a serviceable spear. Their ocher-smeared bodies were reddish gold, and their elaborately plaited hair and the clean-cut lines of their somber aquiline features were, to Sable, reminiscent of the finely featured Ethiopians. Evidently recognizing the Land Rover and its male driver, they saluted back gravely, always courteous but distant, as was their way.

She glanced curiously at Kash and saw his handsome profile, shadowed by his hat, as equally noncommittal. "You've been gone for two years. I'm surprised they'd know you."

His deliberate silence intensified her curiosity. Was there any reason to think that he hadn't been gone? The possibility that he'd been in the area all this time without letting anyone know was rather intriguing. Why might he have wished to conceal it from her?

Undaunted, she persisted. "How is it they recognized you, that they knew you?"

"I've been working with the Kajaido Council," he admitted.

The Kajaido Council worked with the local Maasai to manage the Amboseli Game Reserve, and Sable was taken off guard. "For how long?"

"About a year now."

"How come Gran doesn't know you're working with the Maasai?"

"She does. Maybe she didn't think it was important enough to tell you."

Everything Kash did was deemed important to Zenobia. Her grandmother had always thought well of him and his brother, Seth. During Sable's stay in Toronto, her grandmother's letters and telephone calls had kept her informed about what the family was doing and what was happening at the lodge, but if Kash had been back for a year now working on the reserve, why hadn't she mentioned him? It was unusual. Sable had been under the impression that Kash had been in South Africa this whole time, working as a hunter-guide for a large international safari business.

Then if Kash had been home these past months working with the Kajaido Council and the Maasai, had her grandmother kept him informed of Sable's intentions about Vince and the work at Samburu? No wonder he knew the reasons for her return. But the mystery surrounding her father remained, as did Kash's association with Smith and Browning. One thing seemed clear: she would get few answers to these questions from Kash now.

"Then you actually returned to Kenya before I did," she said.

"Yes, I've been back about a year now."

"I wasn't aware you decided to come back. . . ."

"No, when I returned you'd left for Toronto with Vince."

She glanced at him uneasily. His casual tone suggested that she'd planned that excursion with Vince, when it had actually been the other way around, but it didn't seem wise to discuss Vince when Kash was so negative about him. The purpose of her visit to Canada had been anything but a holiday. She wondered if he knew about her mother.

"Did Gran explain about my mother?"

He turned his head, thoughtful. "Yes, she told me."

Was that all he was willing to say? If Gran had explained about bringing Sable's ill mother to Toronto, then he should understand why she wasn't home at Kenyatta when he changed his mind and came back. She had gone with Vince because he had arranged for a specialist to treat her mother. Vince had been her encourager when she thought Kash had walked away, not that she would have deliberately sought his emotional support. She'd actually tried to avoid leaning on him.

What was the verse in Psalms? "It is better to trust in the Lord than to put confidence in man."

The Lord Jesus would not fail when even a husband could not provide all the emotional strength a wife might need. Her mother had told her as much in Toronto when Sable had mistakenly blurted out, "Why isn't Father here with us?" Tears sprang to Sable's eyes as her mother's wasted body came to mind, and she could hear her saying weakly, "Husbands are only human. I'm not resentful that Skyler isn't here. Don't you be. Something's gone wrong . . . something in the reserve . . . I sense his prayers. . . ."

Her mother had often told her and Kate, "Find your deepest emotional support from your relationship with the Lord. Who knows us better than He? We are His daughters."

Her mother could say that, thought Sable, because for years she had labored alone as a missionary nurse with the Maasai and knew by trial and experience the faithful intentions of the Lord Jesus. Her mother had known what it was like to pass the so-called flower of youth and still be single with no prospects in view, fearing aloneness, yet knowing God could supply her heart's desire as easily as a rose can bloom from a bush with thorns. Therefore, she was unafraid, confident in her aloneness.

Julia Dunsmoor could wrestle through prayer, stand for the Lord amid Satanic opposition in getting out the gospel in a hard place, and at the same time have no one close enough to share her deepest emotional needs. Sable's mother had learned through trial and error how to cry out to her heavenly Father and cultivate that close union with Him. And according to the truthfulness of His promises, she had found Him sufficient for everything. Only after this long trek alone had the Lord brought Skyler into her life, resulting in marriage and children. Yes, her mother had been special.

I want to know Christ like that, but am I willing to make the investment? To stand the dry times as well as when rivers of living water flow through my soul?

"God isn't in a hurry," her mother had told her. "He will take all the time He needs to form you, shape you, chisel you into following the pathway to Christlikeness. And He knows the very things to bring into your life—or take away—to help you find that place of rest and blessing."

Sable became aware of Kash—he had slowed and was watching her with restrained interest.

"When I came back to Kenyatta looking for you, Zenobia told me about Julia's illness, and I wrote you in Toronto."

She turned her head, masking her utter surprise. He had written to her?

He looked back to the road and pressed on the accelerator, and the needle began to climb. "I asked if you'd like me to come and be with you."

Her heart gave an odd little jerk.

"You didn't answer."

Sable wanted to tell him that she hadn't received any letter, and yet it seemed wiser to not allow her emotions the undisciplined reaction of spilling all over him, desperately grabbing the first "feeler" of renewed interest he'd shown in two years.

"I suppose Vince was all the help you needed," he suggested.

The almost gentle nudge brought her a moment of deep satisfaction. It was reminiscent of the way Kash sometimes tried to gauge her interest. In the past she had always rushed to throw "passion-wood" on the sparks, perhaps smothering them before they were ready.

She glanced uneasily toward the speedometer, somehow thinking it might match his mood, and breathed, "Your presence would also have been . . . appreciated."

Silence.

"Then why didn't you bother to contact me?" he asked casually.

Why hadn't she received his letter? Had she been so concerned with her mother that it had somehow slipped through the cracks? There had been mail, lots of it, from all sides of the family and friends, and church associates as well. Perhaps it had simply gotten buried in the pile.

She mustn't rush to judgment and think the worst—and what could the worst mean? That someone—Vince, for he was the only one there—had deliberately kept Kash's letter from her?

Vince was not deceptive or melodramatic. And one of her weaknesses was that mail sometimes stacked up for days on end and littered the coffee table, waiting to be opened at a more "convenient season." Yet even if Kash had written, could one letter from him compensate for having left for South Africa without a good-bye? And if he'd been disturbed because she hadn't answered, then why hadn't he pursued the issue? He could have asked her grandmother or Kate why she hadn't written him from Toronto. He knew she had gone with Vince. Had Kash been overly concerned that a romance might begin, he could have flown there to make his own presence felt. Kash's arrival would have been all she needed to rush to his arms. Instead, from what he said, he'd been here in the Amboseli region for the past year.

Sable decided to walk around the unpleasant moment. Kash surely had other women interested in him; it would do him good to realize she could now rebuff his renewed romantic interest. Perhaps his motive was only to hurt Vince, since he disliked him so much.

Kash's mood suddenly matched her own indifference, and the speedometer slowly ebbed. "My coming wasn't necessary. We both know how capable Vince is in a crisis."

She cast him a glance, and his smile was disarming.

"He's even donned the red cross of Christian relief," he said.

"Why is it I'm inclined to think you mean the very opposite whenever you speak well of him?"

"How could you ever get that impression?" he said with a wry smile.

"I would think you'd be pleased I've arrived with supplies for the Maasai."

"Your sincerity goes without question."

"Thank you, sir."

"Don't be so prickly. Vince is something else. Tell him if he's really interested in the Maasai, he can build a well to bring them water."

Mention of the well brought to mind the missing money, and she moved uneasily. She wouldn't tell Kash, knowing what he'd say. "So what are you doing working with the Maasai?"

"Teaching ranching techniques. A major problem faced by the Maasai is overstocking their land with cattle. In the old days this didn't matter so much. If the animals multiplied it was simple enough to invade a new area to provide the grazing. Now, with limits on their expansion, their numbers of cattle are becoming too great for the land to support. They graze so heavily the grassland is destroyed, leaving dust. When the rains come the soil is washed away."

"So the Kajaido Council is trying to encourage enclosed ranches?"

"You can see a few of them along the road between the Athi River and Kajaido."

"I didn't know you were involved with the Maasai. It's a fine work you're doing, Kash."

"To get back to good Dr. Adler—I suspect his sudden charitable interests have more to do with the access it gives him into areas off limits to hunters. Plenty of opportunity for poaching without getting caught, wouldn't you say?"

She turned on him. "What! With your suspicious presence at Smith and Browning, you dare suggest he's involved in this hideous butchery?"

"How swiftly you don angel's wings to fly to his defense. Just be sure your humanistic little do-gooder isn't using your cause—and your money—to support the evolutionary bone-diggers out at Lake Rudolf."

"Evolutionary—humanistic—what are you saying?"

"He's a colleague of Dr. Willard."

"He is not! And even if he knows them, so what? He doesn't support their cause."

Kash looked back to the road, seemingly undisturbed by her response. "Before this is over I'm going to prove he's involved in poaching. If I were you, I wouldn't be too anxious to marry him."

Sable was too overwrought to discuss the matter sensibly. First he insinuated that she might jump into an engagement because Kash didn't move fast enough to suit her fancy! And now suggesting Vince was a despicable poacher! And—a hypocrite as well.

"You haven't a very good impression of my character, have you?"

"Your character shines."

She was slightly mollified. "Yet . . . yet you say Vince has ulterior motives, and you think *I* go around contemplating marriage without knowing what the man is really like?"

"Vince was clever enough to make use of your emotions at a time when you were vulnerable."

Sable gave a brief laugh and behaved offended, even though she had questioned her own motives more than once. "Absurd." She snatched her hat and fanned her warm face. "You're only perturbed because you can no longer easily manipulate little Sable Dunsmoor—"

"Manipulate! Now I've heard everything."

"Yes—a puppet on strings, that's how you want to keep me, just waiting breathlessly in the 'parlor' for Kash Hallet to decide to favor me with a call. As if I ever would again!" She jammed her hat on and folded her arms. "I'm no longer a teenager in love—and I'm no longer interested in—"

The Land Rover bumped to an unexpected stop at the side of the dusty road. Kash turned abruptly to face her, his arm on the back of the seat.

Sable glanced about uneasily. "Elephants again?"

He removed his sunglasses. "No," came his challenging tone.

She looked at him for an explanation and found his eyes burning like warm blue fire. His lashes narrowed, and she swallowed a nervous lump forming in her throat.

"Don't look at me like that."

"How do you want me to look at you?"

She leaned away. "Stop it—whatever you're doing. . . ."

He reached for her with both hands.

"Kash, no—"

"Yes. Commitment is one thing you've long accused me of avoiding. I did . . . but for your sake, not mine. What could come of it? I had nothing to offer you. I was the overseer's son. I also stayed away from you because I thought you were too good for me."

He smiled, and the back of her neck prickled as she moved toward the door, fighting for the survival of her heart.

"You're still too good for me, too sweet and noble. But I've decided, Sable, that I want the best, regardless. And I'm going to take you away from Vince."

Sable's breath stopped. "Oh—you are, are you!" she challenged.

He bent to kiss her, and mesmerized by his gaze, she barely managed to duck, knocking off his hat as he leaned his head toward hers.

"No," she said weakly, "we mustn't do this. It's . . . it's wrong."

"Why is it wrong? After all, it's about time, isn't it?"

"I'm . . . almost engaged. You know that."

"And I hope to prevent it." Kash lifted her hand. "I don't see any ring. So you're not breaking any vow to Vince. I knew you before he did; I intended to have you before he came along. Nothing has changed."

"Everything has changed."

"For the better. We're both older. And I've got money now."

The thought of money sobered her like a splash of cold water. "I don't know how you made your money, but I don't want it. It's no substitute for commitment, and spiritual character can't be bought."

"And you think Vince has both?"

"I'd rather live in a tent on the reserve than with a man who's sold out everything he held decent and godly for money!"

His eyes smoldered. "You think I've done that!"

"Yes—"

"You insult me but trust *him*, a phony. All right, have it your way."

And he pulled her toward him. Her head fell back against his arm, and he kissed her thoroughly.

Sable's heart pounded in her ears. Too weak to struggle, nor certain she wanted to, even when the sound of a motor roared and a horn blasted angrily.

Kash released her, and Sable jerked away, frightened and feeling guilty as two jeeps came to a dusty halt. Rushing footsteps neared the side of the Land Rover where Kash sat. Sable, dazed, was looking up at Vince. His usually remote dark eyes kindled like heated coals. His straight black hair glinted in the sun as he threw open the door to the driver's side and, grabbing the front of Kash's shirt with both hands, hauled him from behind the wheel—or was Kash getting out deliberately?

Sable couldn't make a sound, but her hands clenched as she heard the swift smash of doubled fists.

Both were sizable outdoor men, but she feared more for Vince. Sable came to herself as if awaking from a drugged sleep. "Stop it! Stop it!" She clambered over the seat to crawl out the open door and looked about desperately for someone to come between them.

Mckibber was standing by his jeep, arms folded across his wide chest, watching.

"Mckibber! Stop them!"

"I'll get meself busted tryin'." He opened his mouth and pointed to a missing eyetooth. "Lost it three years ago comin' 'tween Kash and Seth. Won't be losin' my front tooth over Dr. Adler. He best take care of hisself."

Sable heard a thud and whirled to see Vince sprawled across the back of Kash's Land Rover, bloodied and dazed. She winced, sickened and angry over the ridiculous display between two grown men.

Kash was picking up his hat from the dusty road and flicking it clean.

She strode up to him, her eyes rebuking, but he looked defensive. He plucked the handkerchief she wore at her belt and blotted the blood from the corner of his lip.

"You're not leaving with him. Get in the Land Rover, please."

Their eyes held steadily. She must refuse; if she didn't, it would appear she'd made a decision to choose between the two of them.

"I'll leave with whomever I choose. It so happens I wouldn't have either of you!"

His slow smile brought an ache to her heart. "Well, that's a start. Vince and I are on equal footing now."

"You're so sure of yourself . . . of me," she whispered, frustrated with his behavior.

His gaze grew sober. "No. Sure of Vince. In the end he'll blunder. Stay away from him, Sable. I don't want to see you hurt. I'm going to see him come to trial for the death of Seth."

The death of Seth Hallet!

He turned and walked away, leaving her to stare after him, stunned. His words resounded in her mind. The death of his brother . . . Seth was dead? How, and when? Why hadn't she been told this earlier?

Kash got in his Land Rover and started the motor. Mckibber walked up, leaned in, and said something. Kash nodded, then drove away.

A small trail of dust lingered.

Sable stood in the road, astounded by the impact of his words. Seth . . . killed.

A shiver ran through her. He blamed Vince.

Five

There was no time to consider the dreadful implications of what all this might mean. Vince had pulled himself to his feet and was walking unsteadily toward the open door of his jeep. In dismay she ran toward him.

"Wait, Vince, please." She took hold of his arm. "I can explain."

"I'm sure you can," he retorted, "but at the moment I'm not in the mood for excuses."

Excuses. Rebuked, her hand fell away. His sharp gaze provoked embarrassed feelings, as though she were an immature girl who was to blame for two men brawling over her.

Had he been anyone except Dr. Adler, she could have borne her embarrassment with more dignity. Despite all Kash said about him, Vince was a studious man, sophisticated in a Sherlock Holmes sort of way, with a keen face, eyes that were dark and pensive, jet black hair with a touch of early gray at the temples, and expressive hands featuring long, slender fingers.

He'd been around thirty-five when she first met him at a wildlife conservation class he was teaching at the university in Nairobi. He had been hired on for a quarter in order to fill in for Dr. Willard, who had taken a leave of absence to dig fossils at Olduvai Gorge. At first, Sable had been skeptical. Some of the things Vince said resembled New Age teaching, but when she questioned him more closely, he had denied it and told her he'd been raised in a Protestant Bible church in Canada.

During that summer, she and Dr. Adler had developed a casual friendship that developed into his growing interest in her father's work at Samburu and Marsabit documenting the habits of the elephants in the region. One thing had led to another, and when her mother was diagnosed with cancer, Vince had been supportive, recommending a medical center in Toronto.

Her father had made the decision to have her mother flown to Toronto to the research clinic on the outskirts of the city in the Canadian countryside. There was little to lose, he had said, since the clinic expected no payment; there was only the cost of the plane fare. They were doing this for the greater cause of trying to find more effective treatments for cancer. Since Julia Dunsmoor had given so many of her years of faithful service to the well-being of Africa, her people, and her wildlife, making a case study of her unusual condition was small payment.

And so Sable had flown with her mother and Vince to Canada, where in the intervening six-month period she had become convinced of the genuineness of his cause to help humanity. And he was, as he said, a staunch Christian. He'd become an inspiration to her. She marveled at his knowledge of natural science and revered his commitment to wildlife conservation.

Before she realized where her emotions were bringing her during that long ordeal, Sable had come to depend on Vince, who had been there to handle a myriad of details when her father could not. Sable, besides losing her mother, had just gone through the painful realization the year before going to Canada that Kash's intentions toward her were deliberately uncertain. He had left to take a job in South Africa, where he had also planned to contact his parents' families, without a hint of willingness to commit himself to furthering their relationship. After he had gone it wasn't long before her mother's diagnosis was rendered, and there followed the discouraging events in Canada and the rainy morning at her mother's funeral. And Vince had been there.

Now, standing beside the road, rebuffed by his angry rejection, she lapsed into silence. He reached into the back of the jeep for the water canteen, and she walked up to where he leaned splashing water on his bruised face. "I want to explain," she began again, desperately. "Please don't brush me aside as though my words can't be trusted. I respect you too much to offer foolish denials and excuses."

His humid dark eyes silenced her. "Even a doctor should be allowed weakness of temperament in expressing indignation at finding my future fiancee wholeheartedly cooperating in the torrid embrace of an old flame."

She flushed with embarrassed resentment. *Wholeheartedly cooperating—?*

"I wasn't aware, Dr. Adler, that my future had already been settled in my absence and without my knowledge. An engagement is a matter as yet to be discussed, which means—"

"So now it's *Doctor* Adler—which means, if I read your manner correctly, that you've changed your mind about us. All because of the arrival of a reckless, headstrong safari hunter who doesn't mind shooting endangered species for ivory!"

"That wasn't what I was going to say. And I'm making no excuses for Kash Hallet. I had no idea he was back."

"Unfortunately, you'll need to get used to the idea, since we both may need to deal with him in the future."

"What do you mean?" she asked warily.

He appeared too overwrought to explain and said through tight lips, "You say you didn't want this to happen?"

"No—"

"Do you honestly expect me to accept that?" he demanded.

"Accept my honesty in being fair with you? Yes! Unless you think I'm so giddy and immature that I can't be trusted. In which case I've neither the reputation nor the honor to be any man's wife!"

"We both agree Kash Hallet is not just any handsome young adventurer. You were in love with him once. And you must admit this scene doesn't speak well of either of you."

Stung, Sable paled under his rebuke.

Dr. Adler grabbed the jeep door and swayed on his feet as he lowered his tall, lanky frame behind the wheel.

Concern for his condition on the long ride to the gaming

lodge urged her to set aside her own injured feelings. "Please, Vince, you mustn't drive off like this alone."

"I am quite all right. It is you who needs to pull yourself together." Looking past her stricken face, he motioned to Mckibber. "See that Sable is brought to Miss Zenobia."

"What of you?" she asked worriedly, feeling guilty. "Where are you going? The sun will set soon."

"I want to be alone." He revved the motor. "I've had rather a shock of sorts today. Anyway, I've business out at the Maasai camp. I'll speak with you at the lodge on Tuesday."

Vince had a way of provoking feelings of guilt, and she hastened, "I'd like to come with you."

"I'd prefer that you didn't." Without a farewell he drove away, leaving her standing at the side of the dusty track staring after him.

Mckibber Hallet, Kash's South African uncle, walked slowly up to stand beside her, his worn leather safari boots kicking up dust. He hadn't changed all that much in the two years she'd been gone. He still looked to Sable like the American country singer Willie Nelson. He wore a battered zebra-skin hat—a hat he made sure everyone knew had come from a zebra carcass already killed by a lioness and abandoned to decay—and beneath the hat his face was as hard and drought-stricken as the African earth he called "Mother-home." Although born in Cape Town, he had left there after the death of Kash's parents and come to East Africa looking for his two small nephews. He had stayed, becoming friendly with Sable's father and especially Grandmother Zenobia, who ended up depending on him.

His sun-emboldened skin color caused his eyes, as blue as the vast sky, to glimmer even more brightly as they gazed out from his wizened face, his thinning gray hair drawn back and tied. Despite his age—he had fought with UN forces in the Korean War—hard work had helped to retain his muscled torso; a figure that suggested an old cowboy all the way down to the revolver shoved in his handmade leather belt and his rugged boots.

His bright blue eyes followed her troubled gaze, watching

as Dr. Adler's jeep faded into the speckled shadows of the flat-topped thorn trees of the plain.

"Oh, Mckib," she breathed, discouraged. "I've made a terrible mess of things. Maybe Kash was right; maybe I shouldn't have come back."

"Don't go blaming yerself." His odd brogue retained his South African roots mixed with British African, unique to the now displaced families of the early settlers.

"If you be wanting my opinion," he went on, "Dr. Adler's to be faulted. Was unwise to stampede Kash like that, grabbin' him by the shirt. If Kash hadn't protected hisself, Adler woulda tried to crack his front teeth."

Sable winced. Even if she agreed, she wouldn't come out and admit it. "They both behaved like schoolboys."

"More like a young lion, is Kash."

She wouldn't argue that. "You always defend him, Mckib, and you shouldn't. Not when he's bordering on the line between trouble and recklessness."

"Be not all Kash's fault. He's come home smartened up and with good plans."

She glanced at him, wondering, and Mckibber rubbed his fingers across his lips, still staring thoughtfully after Dr. Adler's jeep.

"Odd behavior for a professor. Calls himself *Doctor* of Anthropology. First time I ever seen him not lookin' like Sherlock Holmes puffin' his peace pipe."

Mckib's bias toward Kash didn't surprise Sable. He doted on his nephew. Kash had always been his favorite when growing up, even though the most difficult of the two boys to handle.

Mckibber had been a famous safari hunter and had taught the two boys priceless secrets. When they were teenagers, Kash and Seth had joined Mckibber in starting up their own hunting and photographic safari business out of Nairobi. The Hallet name had meant something special in the safari world, gaining business from all across Europe and the Far East. Then something had happened.

Sable never quite knew what it had all been about. Her

mother had become ill at that time, and her thoughts were consumed. But she remembered the Nairobi newspapers had spoken of an accident of a wealthy business tycoon on a vacation to bring home a trophy to impress rich friends. The man was killed on the safari. Somehow the Hallet name was blackened, and their license had been revoked. Their guides were faulted for the man's death, but Seth had insisted he was innocent. Seth had then moved to Tanzania and worked for another safari service while Mckibber had come back to work for Zenobia. But Kash—

Kash had simply disappeared with no explanation. Then a brief time later she had learned he had gone to South Africa to work and look for his extended family.

Sable supposed that with Seth now dead, Mckibber would be even more inclined to hold tightly to Kash. She wanted to ask him about Seth, about why Kash had blamed Vince for his death, but the moment didn't seem right.

"Kash shouldn't have come back," she said quietly. "He let us all down."

Mckibber shrugged his casual disagreement. "Depends on how one looks at it. He thinks he had good cause for leaving. And a better cause to come back . . . I'm thinking he did, too."

She looked at him, and Mckibber's eyes softened. "Even though, if he'd been more a gentleman and less of a brewing storm, he'd have explained how things was between him and you before he took off like that." He looked at her. "When you told him he didn't have enough money to marry you, well, you sure needled his pride."

"I never told him that," she insisted, but flushed, remembering back to a scene she'd had with Kash before he left. He may have misunderstood her. . . . "A brewing storm" his uncle had called him. Well, Kash was still one, she thought.

Sable dismissed the disturbing memory of his lips on hers and steeled herself against dangerous further involvement. While Mckibber's defense of Kash was reasonable considering he was his uncle, she was reluctant to excuse him, even if Vince had provoked the physical outburst. The safer route where she was concerned was to sympathize with Vince, even if his response had surprised her.

She was bewildered by the almost spoiled and pouting behavior of Dr. Adler, since it was foreign to everything she remembered about him in Nairobi and Toronto. He'd always been the restrained, intelligent, pipe-smoking doctor of lanky good looks, willing to sacrifice for the wildlife causes she and her father embraced. And more recently he'd taken an active role in international protection of tribal lands from careless oil and mineral development.

"It doesn't matter now what happened two years ago between me and Kash. The past is over. I've my own cause for being home, and Kash has nothing to do with it."

Mckibber looked at her with quiet eyes that suggested he understood. "Knowing Kash, he had something to prove, maybe to hisself. You've a right to be mad at him—but don't forget it was Vince who bellied up his fists first. I've been around him enough to know he isn't as saintly as he likes to put on."

"So Kash told me."

"And he was out of place talking down to you like that. You're worth both of 'em, if you ask me."

She smiled wearily. "You always have a way of cheering me up. I've missed you and Father so much!" She put her arms around him, and as he patted her head awkwardly, she allowed herself to release her uncertainty for the first time.

"I don't know what to do," she sighed. "Kash—he's so mean and unfair! This is his fault."

"You're right there. I wonder if he knows just what a can of worms he opened up. He's been determined to detour you from going to Samburu since he knew what you were coming back to do."

"He can't stop me, Mckib. I've got to go. It's a cause I believe in."

"I think you got a real problem on your hands this time, since Kash knows he made a mistake two years ago."

"Oh no, he doesn't—he's against Vince, is all. And I don't know what to do."

"You'll find the way, little one. You're just like your mother was. She knew where to turn for answers when the way was clouded with confusion. There was a time when she almost didn't marry yer father. Just don't let either one of them fellas intimidate you. You do what God tells you. If Kash has his way he'll swoop you away to his own dreams. And Dr. Adler . . . well, he's more subtle. Maybe that means even more trouble in the future. Things are odd-like round here since Skyler left and Dr. Adler's come."

Odd? she wondered. She raised her head tiredly and looked into the age-wise eyes, smiling wanly. "The trouble with you, Mckib, is you're prejudiced in favor of your nephew."

"No secret there. Come on, what we both need is a good cup of Kenya coffee. Zenobia's probably standin' on the porch waitin' for us. Wait till she hears 'bout what happened between Vince and Kash!" He shook his head. "She can't make up her mind about those two—and right now it looks like neither has the advantage."

Sable looked at him in surprise as they got into the jeep. "I'm astounded anyone could rival Kash for Zenobia's favor." She closed the door, and he started the engine and pulled away.

His smile was gone. *Does it have anything to do with the death of Seth?* she wondered, and for the first time her concerns brought a chill of fear. Kash had blamed Vince, which made no sense.

There was so much to ask Mckibber, but she felt she could endure no more for one afternoon. Downcast in mood and physically drained, she anticipated a cool, fragrant bath once she arrived at the lodge and a cup of Zenobia's fresh, strong coffee, grown by local African planters.

Mckibber, too, was musing over thoughts that must have troubled him. "Have you got the supplies for Samburu unloaded all right?"

She had left them in the crates at the Dunsmoor warehouse on the wharf at Mombasa. "I'm expecting them in another day or so. As soon as Father arrives, they'll be ready for us to truck to Samburu."

He looked at her. "Hate to be the one to tell you, but Zenobia wants you to know before you arrive. He's not coming. A message from Isiolo says he's gone off in elephant country again on research. No one's seen him."

So Kash had been right. What was her father up to?

"What about a guide to bring us to Samburu? My father mentioned having hired someone out of Tanzania."

Mckibber bypassed the reference to her father. "I'm trying to locate one now. With fighting 'bout to start up near the border with Somalia, finding a guide worth his salt is hard to come by. An' I'm too old," he said flatly. "I'd ne'er make it."

Sable smiled. "I'd trust you anywhere. I suppose Vince, too, is trying to find someone?"

He looked at her, then back to the road. "He is, but after that debacle when he was in Tanzania, there isn't many who'd hire on under him. Too much risk involved."

"When was Vince in Tanzania? What debacle?"

He shrugged, as though he'd said too much, and changed the subject. "I woulda met you in Mombasa myself, 'cept a mite of trouble cropped up at the lodge. Took longer than we thought to take care of it, and I'm not sure it's cleared up yet. Zenobia's upset."

"Not a safari accident? Gran told me about a group of New York photographers who stayed out after sunset and encountered a lion." She chuckled. "They landed wonderful photos, she said."

Mckibber was not smiling. "No, nothing so fine as that. Vince's find yesterday made her near sick. And next week's the big international conference she's hosting for the conservationists, so between everything that's happened recently she's pretty depressed."

The mention of trouble overshadowed any excitement over the long-awaited wildlife conference, her first in three years. "What did Vince find?" Sable asked uneasily, watching him.

"More poaching, this time 'round the sanctuary. It's not just a tragedy for the animals, but Zenobia—you know how she loves 'em. It's an embarrassment, since she's left in charge now that Skyler's away."

More poaching! The thought made her stomach knot. "I thought you and Vince were helping Gran."

"We are, but you know your grandmother. She holds everything dear, like it's her failure if something goes wrong. She's sensitive 'bout her age now, and Vince don't help. Oh, he's supportive enough, but he's always encouraging her to retire and leave the business to him."

Mckibber's frown convinced Sable of what he was thinking about Vince, that he wasn't the most qualified to perform as a game warden in her father's absence.

"With doctors of renown comin' to talk on how they can protect the animals, having poaching going on under her nose is galling."

"What was it this time?" she asked quietly, not sure she wanted to know.

"The white rhino."

"Oh no. . . ."

"Yep. Vince found it. There isn't another in Amboseli. Maybe a few near Lake Manyara in Tanzania. It's got Zenobia all upset. She felt responsible for that particular rhino. She was here when they trucked it in two years ago."

Sable told him about Moffet and the black rhino that Kash had found.

"Skyler better get back soon" was all he said. "I do my best, as does Zenobia. And Kash's been holding more than his own since he came a few months ago. But something's going on round here that's bigger than the best of us. Maybe this conference can figure out what to do about the poachers. Just wish I could get my hands on them hunters when they're at it! Trouble is, the slimy rats gets away—they shoot them machine guns at us while we're fighting back with revolvers."

His steely eyes hardened with affirmation. "Nothing taken but the horn on the white one. Zenobia said she should have kept it in her sight even if it meant trailing it day and night. The animal was left to rot! She had a baby, too. Vince hopes something can be done to save it.''

Sable sank dejectedly into the worn seat. Poaching would soon force many of the great created in East Africa into extinction. "I wish we could catch them," she murmured.

"There's a bounty on the poachers now—your grandmother's raised it, but . . ." He paused and glanced at her. "Vince is upset about it.''

She looked at him, surprised. "Vince is upset?"

"Says she's pret' near hocking the Dunsmoor shipping line at Mombasa to raise money. That's your inheritance, he says."

She picked up the tension in his voice whenever he mentioned Vince Adler. Like Kash, Mckibber had never gotten along with him, and now that her father had left Vince in charge of the lodge, she sensed the strain between the men had grown more pronounced. Mckibber didn't believe Vince was sensitive enough to know what was really going on with the animals.

He'd be interested to hear that Kash agreed with him. Perhaps he already knew what Kash thought, since the two had been close while Kash and Seth grew up on the private game sanctuary. She wanted to ask him about the death of Seth and why Kash blamed Vince, but she doubted if Mckibber could give an answer without overly defending Kash. She'd wait to ask Zenobia.

" 'Course," he said, "even if Zenobia did hock the shipping, it's no one's business but yours and hers, seeing as how it's being left to you."

Sable didn't take the bait and ignored his watchful eye. She glanced about casually. "Did Vince learn anything about the death of the white rhino?"

"No. And Zenobia wasn't happy. She insisted he try to find out if the Maasai saw any illegal hunters about in the last few days, but I'm guessing he won't learn anything."

She looked at the side of his hard brown face. "You mean the Maasai won't talk to him?"

"They'd talk. That's not what I'm meaning."

She hesitated to probe any further, fearing he meant to cast further shadow on Vince. Enough suspicion had been aired for one day. What Sable wanted was clear, unbiased answers.

⟨∭⟩

The sun was getting ready to set, and the sky reflected a handful of rose pink clouds. There'd been little rain during the past month, and the track that led to the gaming lodge was thick with well-traveled dust. As the jeep brought them through the gate, Sable sat staring ahead at the familiar sights of the now government-owned game sanctuary of a thousand acres. There were enormous sun-drenched plains where herds of zebra, gazelle, and wildebeest roamed at will under the blue cloud shadows that drifted by as idly as sailing ships on a summer sea. It was wonderful to be home again. As for Kash, she would avoid him, and she would yet prove to Dr. Vince Adler that she could perform her duties as professionally as anyone, including her sister, Kate. The past with Kash was over. She would not think of it.

Sable looked about with satisfaction, and Mckibber, too, had lapsed into the same silence that suggested he was drinking it in. Long before Sable had been born, the land was settled by the Dunsmoor family from Melbourne. They had developed the land into a successful sheep ranch. Then, with the Mau Mau uprising in the 1950s—or the "Emergency," as England had called it—East Africa had gained independence and Kenya had been born a nation in 1963. Its first president, Jomo Kenyatta, had then begun what he called the "Kenyanization" of the land, which simply meant that all nontribal Kenyans who would not become citizens must give up their plantations, shops, and businesses to non-white Africans. Her grandparents had willingly given up their British citizenship to become citizens of the new Kenya, but in the end it didn't matter; they had been forced to give up the ranch.

"I earned what I have honestly enough," her grandfather had complained. "The Dunsmoors have been here for over a hundred years. This land lay waste until the colonizers turned it into what it is today. If it belonged to anyone it belonged to the Maasai, and they didn't resist us when we came. Now the Kikuyu," he had said of Jomo Kenyatta's tribe, "have taken it away from the Maasai and the Europeans."

Somehow her grandfather had arranged between the British and Kenyan governments to turn the sheep ranch into a game sanctuary, working to reestablish native wildlife, with the Dunsmoors remaining to manage the new reserve and tourist lodge for the government. The president's close advisers had agreed under the condition that the ranch name be changed from "Dunsmoor" to "Kenyatta."

Her grandfather had reluctantly agreed, for it was said that Jomo Kenyatta had been the leader of the Mau Mau rebels, although he denied it and the British could never prove it.

In the end, there'd been no choice for her grandfather. The Dunsmoor ranch, first begun in the 1880s producing some of the finest Merino wool in East Africa, had become a game sanctuary renamed "Kenyatta." The sheep had been sent to market, with the selling price going to the government, supposedly to help the Kikuyu tribe. Her grandfather had managed to survive financially, since foreign investment was permitted in businesses, especially in Nairobi and Mombasa, and he'd been able to invest in a shipping business in Mombasa. Giving up the ranch had been a grief to her grandfather and Zenobia, but they had managed to live a good life together in Kenya for a decade more, and he'd even been buried on the land beside his parents.

According to Zenobia, her son, Skyler, had adjusted readily to the new calling of wildlife preservation, and Sable had been happily born and raised contentedly at the old Dunsmoor family house. The house had changed, of course. There were new additions of hotel-like guest rooms, a dining room, an enormous game-viewing veranda near the water hole, where safari enthusiasts could sit in comfort while sipping tea or cool refreshments and watch the animals come in the evening to drink. Kenyatta was now one of the best-loved game-viewing lodges and a photographers' paradise.

Although government owned, the lodge was maintained

largely through private funding from international conservation groups. Sable grew up meeting many well-known conservationists who came to the lodge from all over the world to meet with her father and hold conferences among themselves on new ways to preserve Old Africa from being destroyed by the new. And Skyler Dunsmoor was considered by respected international conservationists to be one of the foremost experts on elephant preservation in this part of East Africa.

But if she felt that she belonged here with the tribes, Kash's roots in East Africa went back even further. Like the Dunsmoors, the Hallets had owned a ranch in the same area, but his grandparents had both been killed in the Mau Mau uprising. They had lost their land, and there was no hope of ever getting it back. The Hallet name had been all but forgotten except as safari hunters and guides. In the end, with the changing times and the political winds that blew in the 1960s, there'd been no alternative.

Like herself, Kash and his older brother, Seth, had been born on Kenyatta, but instead of the old house, they'd been born in the overseer's bungalow. His mother, Mara, had been brought to the Dunsmoor plantation after the Mau Mau had killed her parents. She'd been fifteen then, and a witness to her parents' brutal death. Sable's grandfather had found her hiding in the nearby jungle, half-crazed with fear and emotionally damaged. It had taken months to get Mara back on her feet and in her right mind. The Dunsmoors had raised her until at eighteen she married one of her own cousins, Thomas Hallet from South Africa. They had lived on Kenyatta for seven years as overseers until the two of them went home to South Africa to arrange a new home in Cape Town. Tragedy had struck; the plane went down, and they both died in the crash. Seth, the firstborn, who was seven, and Kash, two years old, had been left at Kenyatta.

Both Seth and Kash had grown up working with Mckibber and Sable's father, and in their late teens they had begun a safari business with Mckibber out of Nairobi. And then something happened to change things for them. What it was, she didn't know, for her own tragedy with her mother had struck then, and the long emotional struggle facing separation and death had followed. Her older sister, Kate, a strong Christian, had been prepared to face their mother's death; her mother had as well, but not Sable. Sable had been tossed to and fro in her Christian dedication, so in love with Kash and Kenyan wildlife that the Lord and the Bible had taken a lower priority in her life.

The winds of adversity had blown harshly, and there had been a time when she thought they could engulf her untested faith. Yet God, in His love and faithfulness, had molded and shaped her into pursuing a new passion—one that embraced His cause. He had also been gracious enough to allow that cause to include the things Sable, too, cared deeply about: Kenya, its tribes, and its majestic wildlife.

⟨⟨⟨⟩⟩⟩

The vehicle turned off the rough road onto a track that crossed a stretch of barren, rock-strewn ground bordered on one side by trees and a glint of water. The jeep bounced in and out of deep dust ruts and over boulders and roots and tufts of parched yellow grasses. Leaving the hard sunlight, it ran under the leafy shade of a giant tree to emerge onto a large sweep of yard. A rambling ranch-style double-story house with wide verandas looked out on the watering hole, showing lavender blue in the twilight and graced with some visiting pink flamingos.

A half dozen dogs of assorted shapes and sizes rushed out to greet the jeep, barking and snarling vociferously, followed by two Kikuyu houseboys in blue jeans and white shirts. The more dignified Maasai refused Western ways and rarely permitted themselves to become servants of others, including Europeans. The two boys removed her suitcase and bag from the back of the jeep and called, "*Karibu Kenyatta!*"

"Thank you, it's good to be home again."

A door at the far end of the veranda opened, and a tall, robust figure walked toward Sable and stood waiting at the top of the shallow porch steps—Zenobia Dunsmoor of the Kenyatta Reserve.

Six

Grandmother Zenobia wore blue dungarees, an embroidered denim shirt, and safari boots. Her long silver hair was braided and pinned to the top of her head, and as was her custom, she carried her big multicolored straw hat, although the glare of the sun's rays was already ebbing. To Sable, Gran was neither old nor rattled, but almost royal in her African way, indomitable, warm, and tough. Sable longed for the recovery of their relationship even more now that her mother was with the Lord, her body resting in the cemetery in Toronto.

"Gran!"

Though unsentimental about many things, when it came to family, Zenobia was highly demonstrative, and she clasped her arms about Sable as though she were a butterfly soon to flutter away. Her voice echoed with a strong suggestion of surprise as well as relief.

"It's so good to see you home, dear. And I'm sorry to not have been able to meet you in Mombasa, but there's this nasty business of the poaching. Even Mckib got sidetracked. Thank goodness you got my message and were able to make it to Namanga by yourself. How well you look! Come along inside the lodge."

Zenobia stopped and looked about, evidently surprised. "Where's Vince?"

Sable hoped Gran wouldn't learn of the fight between him and Kash. It would be dreadfully embarrassing. "He found it necessary to go on to the relief camp to meet with Kate," she explained casually, hoping she didn't sound disturbed by the change in plans.

"A fine thing," grumbled Zenobia. "One would think he's going to marry Kate instead of you."

Sable laughed. "She wouldn't have him."

"You're right there. She's still grieving over Jim. I'm glad I was never the woebegone sort of romantic. It keeps one from ulcers. Come along."

Sable smiled.

"I'll have Jomo brew a fresh pot of Kenyan coffee."

"I was counting on that. Oh, it's great to be home!" She followed Zenobia across the porch.

"Rather odd—about Vince, I mean, unless he's bringing Kate home tonight, but she sent a message telling you to meet her at the Maasai camp. There was something about a well that she was all excited about."

Sable masked an inner flinch. It would be dreadful to disappoint Kate. With all the events of the day, Sable had almost forgotten about the missing money for the wells, but she didn't want to let on. Gran knew nothing about the wells yet, for it was meant to be a surprise for her. Gran had always looked favorably on the Maasai tribe, and Sable knew she would be pleased with such a memorial to her daughter-in-law.

"I told him not to travel at night with these poachers about," said Zenobia, frowning.

Mckibber called up from the jeep to the porch, "Dr. Adler won't be coming to supper tonight, Zenobia. There's a meeting about getting those supplies up to Samburu. He can't hire a guide."

"Just as well. You'll all get ambushed by thugs touting machine guns." It was clear that her grandmother was uneasy about their planned trip to the dangerous Northern Frontier District, so close to the hostilities in Somalia.

Zenobia turned from Mckibber and spoke again to Sable. "Come, dear, you will want to see your old room. I'm sorry, but the house will soon be filled with the conference guests. I hope you won't mind. It will be more like a hotel stay than a home-coming to a grandmother's house smelling of gingerbread and tea."

Sable laughed and slipped an arm about her grandmother's thick waist. "I like my unconventional granny and her house just the way they are. When will the conservationists be arriving?"

She sighed. "On Thursday . . . but your father won't be coming. Did Mckib tell you?"

"Yes. I suppose Kate's as disappointed as I am."

"Kate's like you. She won't quit. Insists on opening the medical clinic in the north. I'll lose both of you to tramping off on your own. You know I don't want either of you to go up there with Skyler."

"Now, Gran, you also know that's the reason I've returned home. Besides, we won't need to be heroic and on our own. We have Vince. And maybe even Father will surprise everyone and show up unexpectedly, fresh from the African wilderness." Her expression darkened. "I'm sure he has much to say to the con-servationists about the decline of the elephants in Marsabit."

"Yes, well . . . if Skyler does show up, Vince will be the hap-piest fellow at Kenyatta. He's desperate to see him."

Sable remembered what Kash had told her. "What about? The elephants?"

"He didn't say. I suppose so. He won't talk to anyone but you, dear. One would think he's found an old map to Solomon's mines."

"Sounds dangerous," she smiled. "I prefer to gather data on the elephants and show the *JESUS* film."

"Let's hope Vince has the same cause on his heart."

Sable stopped and gave her grandmother a searching look. "What do you mean? Why wouldn't he?"

Gran laughed shortly. "Pay an old woman no mind. Come along—don't tell anyone, but I've a secret letter from your fa-ther. It's addressed to you alone, so I've not mentioned it even to Kate."

"When did it arrive?" she asked excitedly.

"A week ago. And I've behaved myself—I refused to steam it open."

"It wouldn't matter if you had. Where is it? Do you have it on you?"

"No. I'll go to my office for it now. You can read it after you wash the dust from your face and take your things up to your room." Zenobia turned to go, then paused as though she were very tired and said, "I hope you'll stay, Sable."

She knew what her grandmother meant. Sable smiled and remained cautious about her plans. "Of course I'm staying, Gran! It's wonderful to be back in Kenya."

"You know what I mean. I wasn't thinking of Samburu, but here at the lodge."

"And I do want to stay, but you know Father's expecting me and Kate. Her nursing skills are needed with the tribes, and Father has all his research journals to be put in order for publication." She added carefully, "When he returns here, I'll be with him. I want to take up Mother's position of helping both of you manage the reserve."

Gran was silent for a moment or two, then her fingers tightened about Sable's arm and she looked into her granddaughter's face with clear eyes full of anxiety. "You must choose for yourself, Sable, as must Kate. However, there are some things I must tell you—things that will affect your future."

"I'm not afraid of the future, Gran, if that's what you think. I've given everything to the Lord. Even if I don't understand all that's happened to me, I believe that He has a purpose meant for my good and His glory. He's guiding my steps now. I feel as if the Lord has called me here, and because He has, I don't intend to let anything or anyone persuade me to run away back to Toronto."

The emotion and strain remained in Zenobia's tanned and age-lined face, but her eyes softened with pride. "I always did appreciate your strong will. You and Kate both. Whatever men you two marry will be greatly blessed."

Sable smiled wryly and remained silent.

"Now that you're close to the Lord, I'm certain you'll consider matters carefully," Zenobia went on. Then she frowned. "I had thought Vince would be here, and Kate, too, but we'll go on without them. Perhaps it's better this way. You'll have time to think and decide on things on your own. Vince can be very persuasive."

They walked across the wide hardwood floor of the dining commons toward Zenobia's cluttered office, a room Sable had visited a thousand times while growing up.

"I wanted you to come, but not because of the needs at Samburu," said Gran again, looking at her, a troubled glint in her eyes. "The Lord knows we have more than enough needs right here. And there's the shipping business at Mombasa."

"Yes, Mckib mentioned it. Are you sure you want to sell it?"

"Goodness, it's not a matter of what I want, but what I must do. The financial difficulties are beyond us unless Vince can bring in new investors." She frowned again. "I hope I made the right decision about that. He's been running it for me the last year. Did he mention it to you when you were in Toronto?"

"No, I suppose it slipped his mind. I'm surprised. What does Father think of the idea?"

Gran sighed. "Skyler, unfortunately, hasn't been back here in months. He's so taken up with the elephants out there in the bush that I don't think he even cares about the family business anymore."

Sable could hardly believe it of him. "He's always been interested in the shipping. If he's taken up with elephants, Gran, it must be very important. He'll explain everything."

Gran didn't reply, and her silence made Sable uncomfortable.

"It was Kate's idea to have Vince run the shipping," Zenobia went on. "She knew I needed help and thought he would be reliable until Skyler returns. I admit Vince is trying, but Kash isn't pleased, and that troubles me. He wants to buy the company."

The news came as a total surprise. "Kash? I'm surprised he's able to do such a thing."

Zenobia appeared disturbed. "He's offering a good price,

but Vince is against it. He doesn't trust his business connections.'' She frowned. "That's the same argument Kash uses against Vince.''

Sable watched her. "When did you see Kash?''

"He came to see me a few days ago. He didn't want you here, least of all up there in Samburu with Vince around. He claims Vince isn't what he pretends. That he has some agenda of his own.''

"It's absurd, all of it,'' said Sable, growing more uneasy by the minute. "I can't believe Vince is deceptive. But I do wonder how Kash came into enough money to want to buy the Dunsmoor shipping business.''

"He says his work in South Africa was quite lucrative.''

Sable wasn't sure it was as simple as that. If that were true, then why was he now working as boss for a third-rate zoo hunter's company out of Tanga?

"He was only there a year,'' Sable said. "How could he have made so much in such a short time?''

Zenobia looked away. "Well, there is more . . . but we'll talk of it later, after you've had a chance to wash up.''

Sable decided Zenobia must know about Kash's illegal activities. But why then would she even consider letting him buy the shipping business?

"Of course, Mckib vows that Kash knows what he's doing,'' said Zenobia.

Sable laughed her doubts. "Mckibber is his uncle. What can we expect him to say?''

"You're right . . . but somehow Kash never seemed the sort of boy to be involved in poaching or anything else ugly and illegal.''

"He's not a boy anymore,'' said Sable tiredly. "And it so happens I ran into him today.''

Zenobia gave her a quick searching glance. "So,'' she mused, "that accounts for things. I was wondering why Vince went off in such a huff again.''

Vince's angry behavior earlier that day had surprised Sable, but because her grandmother thought it somewhat typical, it alerted her. "Why did you think so? Vince has always behaved with such restraint."

Zenobia shrugged. "You forget, Vince has been a member of the family here for the last six months. I've gotten to know him well enough. He's temperamental, but a good sort nonetheless."

Sable told her about her adventure in meeting Kash, about Moffet, and the camp of Smith and Browning.

"Browning said Kash was in charge," said Sable, troubled. "What does Mckibber say about that?"

"That Kash can be trusted, and he knows what he's doing."

"I have serious doubts about that. Seems to me his activities these past couple of years have been questionable at best. Vince has persuaded me that whatever money he has now has been acquired illegally. If I were you, I would never allow him to buy the company. If nothing else, it will add to the tension between him and Vince, but it could also be disastrous for our family. I think we'd better listen to Vince this time."

Her grandmother was thoughtful. "That may not be so easy."

Sable wondered what she meant. She also thought of what Kash told her about the risk of going to Samburu with Dr. Adler. It seemed he had more on his mind than mere safety of travel or the danger that could come from renewed fighting among opposing tribes in the area. What was it that Kash knew that he wasn't telling her? And just what did he really want—the shipping business in Mombasa?

"I've talked your ear off, and you haven't even gotten out of those dusty clothes yet. I have more to tell you, but first you go up to your room, dear, and wash up while I get the letter from Skyler. Then we can relax and have our coffee."

As Zenobia bustled off to her office, Sable wondered what the letter from her father had to say and why he had chosen to write her in secret.

Sable descended the wide staircase a few minutes later, feeling somewhat refreshed after washing her face and hands and putting on clean shorts and a T-shirt. A lingering bath would have to wait until later. Right now she was anxious to hear what else Zenobia had to tell her and to see the letter from her father. She stood looking about, drinking in the sights and sounds of "home." The lodge was, despite a reprieve from tourists, a busy place, where the service people were cleaning the dozen guest rooms in preparation for the conference. The dining commons was the main gathering place each evening for the highlight of their stay: grand and stylish dinners, a la 1940s style, with portraits of Gregory Peck and Ava Gardner on the log walls commemorating their parts in *The Snows of Kilimanjaro*—the movie of Hemingway's story. All the wood furniture had cushions done in simulated zebra fur, and there were majestic enlarged photos of lions, elephants, leopards, and rhinos. The highly polished floor smelled of new wax. The encircling viewing veranda that looked down on the watering hole had private tables and chairs, with binoculars available. A wide flight of stairs went up to the rooms, with private baths and terraces, and room service was carried by white-jacketed waiters who had mastered their elaborate British tone better than the English natives.

The gift export shop opened off from the dining commons, and Sable made her way through the open doorway to look about. Zenobia had still not returned with the letter, and Sable wondered what was keeping her.

She glanced at the familiar barrels of Kenyan coffee beans, delicately carved wooden boxes of spices from Zanzibar, and other tourist attractions—safari boots, jackets, stacks of postcards, rolls of candy mints, and Wrigley's chewing gum. Zenobia's beautiful watercolor paintings graced the walls, depicting majestic scenes of the wild African terrain, Mount Kilimanjaro, and Maasai warriors carrying their spears.

The mounds of goods were all familiar to Sable. Zenobia, a third-generation Kenyan, had long participated in the trade from Dunsmoor shipping. In the old days the family had shipped ivory and hides, but that was long before the slaughter of wildlife had brought many species to the brink of extinction.

Zenobia owned a much larger shop in Mombasa, where she went with Kate twice a year to buy from the dhows—little trading boats that came in a flotilla with goods from Zanzibar. She then exported goods on the Dunsmoor shipping line to cities in Europe and the Far East.

Sable peered through the dusty glass-topped counter and scanned the Maasai jewelry made of leather, polished stones, and beads. There were animals, too, carved from polished wood and stone, bright tribal scarves, and fetishes. Behind the counter were displayed the more expensive pieces, including items priced up to a thousand dollars: brass-decorated chests and carvings. . . .

She stopped, her gaze stumbling across a large elephant carving that appeared to be of genuine ivory.

She went behind the counter and carefully lifted it from its display. It couldn't be . . . Gran would never carry real ivory or animal skins. Yet closer inspection convinced her she was wrong. It was ivory, and some skins of giraffe and zebra were also genuine.

Zenobia finally emerged from her office and called to the tall African who came from the kitchen, "Jomo, we'll take that coffee in the dining commons."

"I'm in here, Gran," called Sable, her voice strained.

"Oh, all right, dear. Jomo, bring the coffee to the shop. Odd," she continued as she entered with a frown. "I knew I placed the letter in my desk. I must have mislaid it yesterday when I was moving things about looking for a bill that needs paying. I've been looking for it all this time. Shall I pour?" She proceeded to fill the two enamel mugs that Jomo had laid out on the small table by the window. "Don't worry. I'll remember what I did with it. I couldn't have tossed it in the trash."

Sable turned, holding the ivory elephant. "Gran, how can you sell this?"

Zenobia straightened from the table. "What?" She shook her head and squinted at the elephant as though she'd never seen it before. Then she sighed, and her eyes swerved apologetically to Sable.

"Oh yes. That *thing*. Dreadful, isn't it?"

"You know it is."

"Just makes me sick."

"Gran—what's it doing here?"

Zenobia went to switch on the overhead lighting, and the cluttered room came to dusty life, showing up pillows in acrylic fur and stuffed animals. The stale musty odor of the clutter filled Sable with distress.

"It isn't mine," said Zenobia crossly. "It's a horrid reminder of the trouble I'm having with the shipping. I wish Skyler would come home. I'm getting too old to handle all this. . . . Neither are the skins mine," she added with a defensive wave of her hand. "I thought you knew me better."

"I do. So I'm wondering how it could possibly be here."

Zenobia heaved a sigh and sank into a chair at the small table. "Come drink your coffee before it gets cold."

Sable felt guilty over the cross tone she had used with her grandmother and came around the counter, still holding the ivory elephant. "I'm sorry. It was depressing to see it here. What if the conservationists arrived early and saw these? Think how embarrassed we'd feel."

"Yes, especially after the white rhino . . . poor Bones," she murmured of the beast. "He was special, you know—the only white one in these parts. I promised the conservationists I'd protect him, and now . . ."

"Gran, surely these weren't brought up from *our* warehouse in Mombasa?"

"Yes, they were, and as I said, they don't belong to us. Furthermore, I don't know how they got there in the crates."

Sable walked up to the table and stood looking down at her. "Who found them?"

Zenobia lifted her blue mug. "Kash."

Sable's heart stopped, then she felt sick.

"They're from the Ivory House in Mombasa," Zenobia admitted dully. "You remember it, don't you?"

"The auction house?" Sable asked, surprised. "It's closed down now. Kash couldn't have acquired them from there," she said, mild accusation in her voice.

"One can still find ivory for the right price."

Sable knew that, of course. She thought back to the colonial section of Mombasa. In Treasury Square there were several public buildings, and by the railroad near the old post office there was the old Game Department Ivory Room established in 1912 as a storage and display room for elephant tusks, rhino horns—superstitiously in demand in East Asia as an aphrodisiac—hippo teeth used for carvings, and other trophies recovered from poachers or collected from animals that "died naturally" or were shot as part of control programs. There were twice-yearly auctions. Sable had read that in one such auction, more than seven hundred thousand dollars worth of ivory and trophies were sold, including thousands of pieces of ivory, rhino horns, and hippo teeth.

"Private dealing in ivory is prohibited indefinitely," she protested. "If Kash got them in Mombasa, he did so on the black market."

"You're right. However, Kash didn't buy them at the auction." Zenobia paled. "He found them in the Dunsmoor warehouse."

Sable lapsed into silence. The family warehouse . . . what were black-market items doing there? Did this mean there were more such illegal objects?

"Kash brought these here?" she repeated numbly.

"I'm sure they were old items," Zenobia hastened. "They were goods once confiscated from the poachers and their merchants."

"All the more reason not to make use of them. Money is still being made by slaughtering the animals. Who can say with confidence that some dealers wearing the mask of Kenyan law aren't deliberately working with the poachers in the black market? The white rhino for instance . . . and Moffet's tusks. For the prices these will bring, the temptation for the law to look the other way is too great."

Zenobia winced. "Get them out of my sight. But I promised Kash, you see. He knows someone coming to the conference who wishes to buy them . . . who has great interest in such things."

Sable set the elephant back in its place. "It's an affront to leave them in the open with the international conservationists arriving next week. Does he actually think there are black-market operators among them? Or does he think Vince arranged to have them in the warehouse to load on the Dunsmoor ships?"

Kash wasn't telling the truth. He couldn't be. The family didn't ship illegal items on the black market. What's more, Zenobia knew it as well, so why was she covering for him with lame excuses? It appeared that her grandmother simply refused to believe Kash was capable of wrongdoing, even in the face of mounting evidence against him.

And yet . . . Kash was no fool. If he meant to keep his work in poaching a secret, why bring such items here to flaunt under the nose of the Dunsmoor family, who were all avowed conservationists?

Sable turned to face her grandmother, who looked pale and drawn now, as though the subject matter had made her ill. Sable's anger began to smolder.

"He has a lot of nerve bringing this here to sell. And whatever makes him think he has any right at all to place these items in the shop? And what was he doing snooping about the Dunsmoor warehouse in Mombasa? Who let him in?"

"I did," admitted Zenobia. "He came asking for the key, and I gave it to him."

Sable watched her, bewildered. "But why?"

"Dear, you'd better sit down, too. This will take a while, unless you want to wait and have dinner first?"

It was obvious her grandmother hoped she would agree to delay this talk, but Zenobia's reluctance to reveal what was on her mind only made Sable more intent to know the truth. She sat down opposite her grandmother. "Dinner can wait. I want to know now."

"It begins unpleasantly enough with the death of Seth Hallet."

Sable swallowed, her hands clenching in her lap. "Yes, Kash told me this afternoon. I was so shocked, I could hardly believe it was true. How did he die? And when?"

"It was a dreadful tragedy. No one seems to have any notion how it could have happened. Seth was an expert when it came to knowing animals—just like Kash and Mckibber. He was killed by a charging rhino on a photographic safari in Tanzania. Most unusual, you'll agree."

Sable's throat went dry. "Kash blames Vince. It doesn't make any sense. Vince never went to Tanzania—"

She stopped, remembering. Mckibber *had* said something about "that debacle when he was in Tanzania."

"Do you know why Kash would think Vince was somehow involved?" Sable asked.

Zenobia picked up a fan and cooled her pale face. "Kash hasn't said. He wouldn't, of course, unless he had certain proof. But he was quite certain you shouldn't have come home yet. And he's just as determined you shouldn't work with your father at Samburu."

"So he told me, but he wasn't willing to explain why he felt so strongly about it. I'm going to be working with my father and Kate, too, not just Vince. But Kash's opinions will have no sway over my decisions, Gran. I've a calling, and I intend to see it through to the end. I'm going with Kate and Vince to be with my father." She stood. "As for Kash, when he walked away two years ago without an explanation, he forfeited any right of involvement in my future."

Zenobia watched her, distracted. "Kash would disagree. He feels he had a legitimate reason for going away when he did, and it was you who failed to answer his letter."

"I didn't receive his letter," she said quietly.

"Did you tell him?"

"No," Sable admitted.

"Why not, for goodness' sake?"

"Because . . . he'd just accuse Vince of destroying it. Besides that, I'm not certain I want to reopen a door long since closed and bolted."

"Bolted from the inside, Sable?"

"I was sure *he* bolted it first! It's too late now. I'm going on with my plans."

"You know what your mother would say: 'You've no right to plod stubbornly on when the Lord's making it clear you're coming to a new crossroad.' Better slow down and do a lot of praying and Scripture searching. It's when we think we have all the answers that we're in the greatest danger of making a wrong choice."

"Oh, Gran, please, not now. I just got home, I just met Kash for the first time in over two years, and he dared—" She stopped, reliving the emotion that rushed into her heart.

"And he dared what?"

To kiss me, Sable could have confessed, but she looked away and stared out the window. "Don't worry about my rushing to become engaged to Vince," she said tiredly. "We had our first disagreement only hours ago. Neither of us are in a candlelight mood."

"Candles, bah. Love is born in the nitty-gritty. You need to marry a man who cares about many of the same things you do."

"Well that certainly rules out Kash. He's a total stranger to me now, even more so than Vince. I don't understand either one of them . . . and I don't care to discuss my engagement just now. I'm terribly sorry about Seth's death . . . you know how much I liked him. I can understand Kash's pain over his brother. They were so close, so much alike. But accusing Vince of somehow being responsible is absurd."

"I'm worried about all this just the same. When has Kash ever done anything absurd? He's always been mentally solid and as calm as a windless night."

Sable had no answer, for down deep in her heart she knew this to be true. The truth was she knew Kash well—she knew what to expect of him emotionally—and when he refused to share his thoughts, his heart, there wasn't anything she could do to force it. It was Vince who had surprised her today. She'd never seen him so angry, so threatened, and even cutting in his remarks. He had shown a side of himself she hadn't known existed. She tensed, thinking how close she had been to an engagement. Was she really sure he was the man the Lord had for her?

Gran was right. It would be unwise to accept an engagement ring now. She must see Vince in all sorts of situations before she really could say she knew him. Kash, however, she had seen at his best, his worst, and all places in between. And always her thoughts wanted to return to that well-traversed path to where their hearts had beat as one.

"Kash called on me a week ago about the shipping," Zenobia explained. "It was at that time he asked me to stop you from coming to work with Vince. I told him there was little I could do about it, that you were coming as much for Skyler as Vince."

Sable watched her grandmother with alert interest. "So he came here just to discuss shipping?"

Zenobia hesitated for a moment. "He discussed several things. Seth was one, you and Vince another."

"And the shipping? Did it have to do with the ivory and skins he found and brought here?"

"No, he didn't know about them the first time he came. But he did ask for the keys. It was the company's financial problems that brought him here."

"How did he know about them?"

"Mckibber must have mentioned something. He knew that Vince was trying to save the company from ruin by finding other investors to buy in, some wealthy entrepreneurs from Indonesia and Taiwan. Kash warned against it. As I told you, he wants to buy the company . . . including your shares."

Sable's gaze held her grandmother's. "Mine? Why?"

"This is the heart of what I wanted to talk to you about." Zenobia sighed and set her mug down. "Perhaps I should have told you before you left Toronto, but I thought it best to tell you in person."

Sable tensed at the concern in her voice.

"When your grandfather and I had to give up the land, he bought into the Mombasa shipping line and eventually was able to buy out the other British businessmen from Hong Kong. I've recently discovered that the finances he used were not entirely his own."

Something was wrong. Sable could feel it in the pounding of her heart. And it had to do with Kash. . . .

"Not 'entirely'? You mean, Grandfather didn't use the money he earned from selling his sheep to the government?"

"Yes, but it wasn't nearly enough. I didn't know it then, but a large amount of it came from the Hallets."

The Hallets? "How—when they had so little? Wasn't that what we were always told?"

"It's what I always thought," Zenobia said quietly, fingering her cup.

Sable leaned forward in the chair, watching her grandmother's strained face in the light. "We were told that was the reason the family took in Mara," she said of Kash's mother, "that she'd been left without anything, both her parents killed in the Emergency."

"All that's true," Zenobia agreed. "But in South Africa when he visited his relatives, Kash discovered his mother's father had filed a claim in the Australian gold rush and made good before he settled in Kenya."

Sable mused for a moment, uncertain how the news affected her. "How do we know it's true?"

"There's no question about it. Mr. Hendricks, our lawyer in Mombasa, did some investigating after Kash's inquiry and produced a document signed by Jack," she said of her late husband, Sable's grandfather. "In the document, Jack told of how he'd gone back to what was left of the Hallet estate in Kenya and retrieved a good deal of money in Australian gold pieces. Evidently he knew about it all along but never told me. The Hallets had a vault, and it was left untouched by the Mau Mau." Zenobia looked away, obviously ashamed of her husband. "Your grandfather invested that gold in Dunsmoor shipping, buying it out. I never knew."

Sable gripped her coffee mug. "Are you saying," she said in a low dry whisper, "that Mara Hallet, as a young girl, never knew about the gold her parents had put away?"

"Evidently not." Zenobia looked old and pained. "And to think she lived here for several years before her marriage to her cousin Thomas Hallet, thinking she was receiving Christian kindness from me and Jack."

"Then—when Mara and Thomas died in the plane crash, they didn't know. There was no will for Kash and Seth?"

Zenobia shook her head, looking intently at her fingernails on her wrinkled hands. "They never knew. Nor Mckibber. He still doesn't know, unless Kash has told him recently."

Sable didn't think so, since Mckibber would have mentioned it when he discussed the shipping with her earlier.

"So Kash came to you about it?"

"Yes, when he learned what Vince wanted to do about foreign investors. Now that Seth is dead, Kash inherits all that belongs to the Hallets."

All those years he and Seth had grown up working with her father as the sons of an overseer of Kenyatta. As Sable digested all this, Zenobia said quietly, "So it appears the Dunsmoor shipping line belongs equally to the three of us—you, Kash, and myself. And since I'm leaving my portion to you . . . well, you see, don't you? You and Kash must work this out."

Sable swallowed. There must be many thousands of dollars owed to Kash from the years Dunsmoor shipping was prosperous. How would she ever pay him back?

"Kate has no part in it," said Zenobia. "I'm leaving her the shop in Mombasa. So you see why Kash must be involved in any decision you and Vince will make about other investors."

"Then Vince doesn't know?"

"That Kash is an owner?" Zenobia fanned herself. "No, not yet. When Kash was here last week he asked me not to say anything yet."

Sable wondered why.

"I told him I wouldn't. That I'd talk to you first. Kash is

dead set against these Far Eastern businessmen, though he didn't say why."

Sable thought she knew, and the galelike winds beginning to blow against her were indeed troubling. She recalled what Kash had said about international poachers with Far Eastern connections. She glanced in the direction of the carved ivory elephant—mysteriously found in a crate in the Dunsmoor shipping warehouse. She thought she knew now why Kash had brought it here.

He must think Vince is involved, she thought. The idea set her on edge. And if Kash did think this badly of Dr. Adler, naturally he could convince himself that he also had something to do with the death of Seth. But what gave Kash the notion he would be involved? His reputation for animal conservation and interest in the tribes was impeccable.

"So Kash wants to buy me out, does he?" she murmured.

"I'm certain it's because of your possible engagement to Vince. Kash wouldn't want a partnership with him."

"Because of his dislike for him. There's no other reason for it, Gran. Vince isn't guilty."

"I'm not so sure Kash's ambitions are as simple as that. There's also the matter about you. The two of you were in love once."

Sable shook her head. "He never was. He never wanted to commit. He was a friend, is all."

"A friend," said Zenobia with mild disbelief.

"On his part that's all it was. On my part—well, I made a dreadful mistake chasing after him. I'm ashamed to think of it now. I was deceived into believing the liberal talk of how it's proper for a girl to tell a man of her interest before he's taken the initiative. I don't believe that anymore. Anyway, I certainly made him nervous, didn't I?" she said with a laugh at herself.

"Oh, I don't know. Kash isn't the nervous sort. And from what I remember, he was doing a good deal of chasing after you."

"Yes, but looking back . . . I think he became a bit cautious." She stood, embarrassed when she remembered how she rarely prayed and left things with God, but moved in to "make" them happen. "It's over between Kash and me. I want it that way, even if I don't marry Vince. At the moment, I want nothing more than to work with Father in Samburu. I'm going to tell Vince I think it best the engagement be postponed."

Zenobia's eyes were suddenly bright. "Are you? I think that's wise considering the innuendoes afloat. After all, if love is genuine and he's the one the Lord has for you, you needn't worry about it all slipping through your fingers by waiting and testing the waters. No one ever lost by waiting on the Lord, but much has been lost by rushing into romance and marriage."

A thousand swirling thoughts left Sable feeling overwhelmed and confused. *I'll keep them both at arm's length*, she decided. *To make a decision now would be foolish.*

"So what do you think?" Her grandmother's question interrupted her thoughts. "Do you wish to sell your share of the company to Kash?"

Her first response was negative. Even if Hallet gold had been used years ago, the Dunsmoors had built the company. She didn't like to surrender anything that was old and historic, even if there was debt. It was goading to think Kash wanted her out, whether his motive was dislike for Vince or not.

"I'll need to think about it first, Gran. I'm not anxious to give up the past if there's a way to keep it. I may owe so much to Kash that I've nothing to sell. In which case, he could end up getting the company by absorbing the debt."

Zenobia pushed herself up. "Kash isn't the sort of man to do that. He's still interested in you, dear. I could see it in his concerns."

Sable took a last sip of her coffee. "I also want to hear first what Vince has to say about these Far Eastern businessmen Kash is so against."

"A good idea, but you know Kash," she warned. "He's persistent when he decides what he wants, and he has plans."

"He'll need to be patient," said Sable airily. "I won't be rushed into selling just because he doesn't approve of Dr. Adler. What does Father say about all this?"

"I'm sorry to say he doesn't know yet. I haven't had opportunity to talk to him since Mr. Hendricks informed me of the Hallets' share in the company. He wouldn't know any more than I did." She sighed and walked with Sable from the shop.

"If only he would come to the conference next week. Actually, your father is the main reason I wanted you to come home. I'm concerned about him, Sable, and from some of the things Vince tells me, we have good cause to worry. He's been disappearing from the Samburu camp for weeks at a time."

"Father knows the wilderness; there's no reason to worry."

"I can't say I blame Kash for not wanting you to come now. With the possibility of renewed tribal fighting and Seth's mysterious death, it would have been better for you to stay in Toronto until things were cleared up. But I was selfish. I wanted you home—and preferably home to stay with me instead of going off with Kate."

Sable caught up her hand, smiling. "You weren't selfish, Gran. I belong here with the rest of you. If there's trouble, we can't hide from it. I'm not a child anymore."

Zenobia looked more vulnerable than Sable remembered. Gone was her tough shield, the way she had carried her revolver in her belt and drove about alone in her Land Rover. The gray hair was thinning; the sharp blue eyes appeared less alert and even afraid. Sable held her hand tightly.

"I must go to Samburu, but when my work there is done, I'll come back to Kenyatta. Father and I both."

"It isn't just Samburu that disturbs me, but the death of Seth."

Sable, too, was worried, but she wanted to hide it from Zenobia. "Because Kash blames Vince?"

"Yes. . . ."

"Surely he gave some hint as to why he would think so. What possible connection could there be between Vince and Seth Hallet in Tanzania?"

"Kash won't say. He's too polite. He thinks I'm old, and he wants to soften things for me. I'm afraid of serious trouble between them. And now that you've come, I don't see a pleasant end to it. Kash wants to come between you and Vince, and his motive may be more than jealousy over the past."

They had come to the stairs that led to the upper floor.

Zenobia stood searching Sable's face thoughtfully. "You look weary. I'd best let you rest awhile before we have supper. Now that Vince and Kate won't be here, we'll dine alone. You need not get dressed up. Supper will be ready when you are."

Sable watched her grandmother walk across the dining commons to her office; then fingering the carved wooden banister and heading slowly up the stairs, she thought of the ivory carving. Moffet came to mind. She recalled her stay in Mombasa and arranging for the supplies to be delivered by truck to Kenyatta. She remembered seeing the stately Dunsmoor merchant ships in the harbor. She'd watched one such ship leave port with exports for Taiwan. She thought of the ivory elephant. Just who were these investors that Vince hoped to convince to buy into the company?

Sable's old familiar bedroom was large and comfortable, as she had left it years earlier. The windows had been cleaned for her arrival and looked out onto a wide strip of thirsty lawn where a blaze of drought-resistant flowers grew in the nearby garden. The best part was the view of the water hole. As a girl she had sat up in the late hours with Kate watching the big animals come to quench their thirst.

Sable turned to stare thoughtfully at her reflection in the mirror: a remarkably pretty young woman who insisted she no longer loved the renegade Kash Hallet.

"Yes, of course I'm going to stay in Kenya," she murmured to herself. "I belong to the Lord and to Kenya and perhaps to Vince, as well. And as for Kash—it's over, even if he thinks it isn't."

She threw off her sandals as she went into the private bath adjoining her room to enjoy a soothing soak in the tub after her long and emotionally trying day. From Namanga to the lodge! And soon, all the way to Samburu to work with Father. How could Gran even think she would not go? Did it have anything to do with the trouble of finding a willing guide? Well, Vince and Mckibber were bound to find someone. Those supplies must get through.

Seven

When Sable came down to dine alone with her grand-mother, she was surprised to find other guests waiting in the large dining commons—Mckibber, Vince, and Kash.

A rush of conflicting emotions sent her heart pounding. What was Kash doing here, and Vince? He couldn't possibly have driven out to the camp where Kate waited and be back this soon. What had caused him to return? And more important, how would he and Kash get along now? Evidently, they were behaving in a restrained manner—at least Gran's lamps were still all in one piece!

Kash was standing at the open doors to the terrace, looking out at the lavender and green Kenyan sky. The small water hole was below, the one source of water for the wildlife that came each day in the cool of the evening to drink thirstily. When Sable entered, Kash turned around and their gaze met, then fell away by mutual consent.

There followed a few tense moments of silence in the large room with its warm wood tones and casual furnishings. Dr. Vince Adler spoke first, his voice not betraying the intense conflict between the three of them earlier that afternoon on the road from Namanga.

"Sable—welcome home!"

No one else appeared to notice that he'd taken charge, welcoming Sable to her own home as though he were the greeting patriarch. Vince, wearing a white short-sleeved shirt and casual slacks, his lean, tanned body energetic as he walked across the polished wood floor, held out his hands and took hers, smiling at her, but his eyes were serious, imploring her to react as though this were their first meeting of the day.

Zenobia knew better, of course, but Vince didn't realize this. Sable cooperated smoothly, since trouble of any kind was the last thing she wanted, and she said lightly, "Why, hello, Vince. I thought you'd gone out to the Maasai camp."

"Yes, I was going to, but then I thought it best that we go together, so I came back. We'll go first thing in the morning."

She drew her hands free from his and turned to Zenobia. "Hope I've not kept you all from supper, Gran."

"We wouldn't think of going on without you, dear. Anyway, you're not more than a minute late . . . um, you've said hello to Kash, haven't you? Goodness! How long's it been now? Several years at least since we've been together as a family."

"More like a few hours," said Sable breezily, casting a too-friendly smile in Kash's direction yet managing to avoid a locking gaze.

"We've met already today, Zenobia," he said, striding across the floor from the open terrace door.

Zenobia knew this already, but she feigned surprise, glancing from Sable to Vince to Kash. "Well . . . how nice we're all together again."

Kash seemed to ignore Dr. Adler, walking right past him to stand before Zenobia. "Unfortunately I won't be staying. I was just running the truck in this direction and stopped by for a moment."

"Utter nonsense, dear boy, you must stay and have supper with us now you're here. Isn't that right, Sable? There's plenty of food and more than enough chairs at the table—" She turned brightly and called, "Oh, Jomo? Do set another place for Kash!"

Sable, aware of Vince standing close beside her and of the tension passing between the two men, looked at Kash, her expression casual, but as their eyes met, her cheeks warmed. She touched her hair self-consciously, where it was still damp from her bath and drawn back simply from her face. "Yes, of course. Do stay, Kash."

Restrained amusement flickered in his brief smile, as though he knew how his presence made her relationship with Vince awkward, and that she hoped he wouldn't stay.

"Thanks, but I'd best be going."

She made no reply at first. "You're feeling better? The migraine?"

Zenobia looked concerned. "Oh dear, that again?"

"It's nothing. I actually came to borrow Mckib for a few days." He looked at Sable. "And to return your jeep. I hauled it out of the mud."

"Oh. That was thoughtful." She wondered why he wanted Mckib.

He showed a slight, wry smile. "Think nothing of it. I also have the photographs of you—if you're interested."

The photographs of her in the mud! Her eyes implored his as Vince spoke for the first time, his tone curious and blunt. "What photographs?"

Sable turned to him quickly. "It's nothing, Vince. You wouldn't be interested. They're merely photos of . . . Lake Amboseli."

She waited, half expecting Kash to contradict, but he did not, and a quick glance his way confirmed a smile.

"I do wish you'd stay, Kash," said Zenobia, but he'd caught up his hat from a chair and was now the essence of congeniality.

"Another time, Zenobia. If you don't mind, though, I'll borrow Mckib, and we'll be on our way."

"Oh well," she sighed, "if you insist." Coming up beside him and looping her arm through his, they walked from the dining commons toward the front door. "Do bring your uncle back as soon as you can, dear, and I insist you must stay for luncheon next time. I'll have Jomo fix your favorite. The way he always used to when you came as a youngster to see Sable."

"We have a date, then," said Kash, smiling down at her. Sable wondered fleetingly if he was actually thinking of her, not Gran.

Sable was aware of the heartbreaking charm he could exercise when he took the trouble. That he had already won her grandmother's affection long ago was no surprise. Whereas Vince sometimes seemed pretentious, superior, and a bit hard to get close to emotionally, Kash was warm and lovable—at least around Gran. With younger women, however, he remained exasperatingly aloof.

"Why does he need Mckibber?" mused Vince, looking after Zenobia and Kash as they disappeared into the outer entranceway.

"I don't know," Sable said, turning curiously to Mckib as he walked toward them from the dining commons to follow Kash. He, too, appeared to deliberately ignore Vince as he stopped and looked at Sable.

"Kash brought you something you'll be happy to see" was all he said, and he gave a wink before striding after his nephew.

Sable looked after him, wondering, then as the front door opened, she heard a sound that caused her heart to leap. A whimsical smile broke out on her face, and without a word to Vince, she turned and walked quickly to follow.

The others were already outside when she came out the front door and walked across the large rambling front porch to the steps, grasping one of the posts as she looked ahead into the deepening African twilight. Gran came up beside her as Sable noticed the trailer truck parked in the driveway. Kash was giving orders in Swahili to two African zoo workers, and Mckibber was calling several of Gran's workers on Kenyatta to come and help.

Sable's eyes glistened with delight as the baby elephant, the calf of Moffet, was lowered from the bed of the truck to the dusty ground. Patches was safely inside the barred cage, her little trunk uplifted to smell the breeze and her gray ears flapping.

"What's this?" Zenobia asked as Sable smiled toward Kash and started down the steps in his direction.

"Moffet's baby," Sable called over her shoulder and walked across the warm earth toward Kash.

He had finished giving orders to the zoo workers and had

opened the big cab door of the truck to swing himself up behind the wheel.

"Wait, Kash."

He looked down at her, one boot on the truck step, his hand on the wheel. In the twilight he was every inch the handsome and masculine young man she had always wanted, always loved, and her eyes softened as they met his. Sable restrained her emotions, refusing to let them spiral out of control.

"Thank you," she said quietly.

Kash made no audible reply at first, but his eyes said enough to cause a rise in her heart rate. "I wouldn't want anyone else to have Moffet's calf. If it belongs anywhere, it's here on Kenyatta."

Sable watched him climb behind the wheel of the truck, then turning away, she walked to where the Kenyatta workers were carefully handling the cage. They would bring Patches to the "pet area" of the sanctuary, where Zenobia housed a number of injured or orphaned animals: everything from a pink flamingo named Sam to an old lion unable to hunt for himself and rejected by the Kenyatta pride. Now Moffet's orphaned calf would join the compound to be hand-fed until old enough to reintroduce to the wilds.

The truck's engine rumbled to life, and Mckibber climbed up into the passenger side. Sable watched them until the truck disappeared, then slowly turned to walk back to the lodge. She looked up to see Vince walking across the yard toward her.

"An elephant?"

"Yes," she said. "The calf of Moffet—an elephant Kash and I saved years ago. I found her dead today . . . on my drive home from Namanga."

His eyes reflected dark and luminous in the twilight. "I'm sorry you had to be the one to find her," he said sympathetically. "I should have met you and driven you home to avoid all this. I suppose bringing you the calf soothes Hallet's conscience," he said wearily, looking on as the workers maneuvered the cage onto a flatbed to bring it out to animal recovery.

"What happened on the road today—between you and

Kash—I won't permit it to occur again," she said defensively.

"I wasn't speaking of what happened this afternoon but of poaching. Hallet's involved up to his ears, or should I say all the way to the bank?" Vince shoved his hands in his trouser pockets and stood looking at the elephant with a frown on his lean, sun-tanned face. "It's one thing to bring you a calf to win your sympathy. It's quite another matter to be running Smith and Browning."

"You're not suggesting he's involved in Moffet's death?" Sable asked, although only hours ago she'd been the first one to think so. Somehow, now she didn't want to believe it. Kash had denied involvement. Why shouldn't she believe him? But in truth, he hadn't denied poaching. He had only said that he hadn't killed Moffet. And what of the money he had? Had he really earned it legally? Or, as Vince seemed convinced, through black-market dealings in ivory and skins?

The breeze blew his hair across his forehead. "I'm not an investigator, and therefore I have no proof," he said with casual dignity.

"Kash denies poaching."

"He would. I've learned from a good authority that the Tanzanian police are just waiting to nab the team of Smith and Browning on their return to Tanga. We shall soon know how deeply Hallet is involved in this nasty business."

Sable looked at him, masking her worry, knowing he studied her response as he filled his pipe and lit it, the breeze tossing the smoke away from his face. "A pity a good safari guide like Hallet had to become involved. Zenobia tells me he grew up on Kenyatta, working closely with your father in wildlife management."

"Yes . . . he did, and Seth, too. They left to begin their own safari business out of Nairobi. If Kash is involved in poaching, he bluntly denies it."

Vince bit on the end of his pipe and stared into the deepening darkness. "I understand he blames me for the death of his brother. A rather bizarre notion, I would say. I never met Seth."

She turned to face him curiously. "Why would he think so, Vince? As you say, it is odd. And Kash isn't impetuous—he keeps things to himself. If either of the two Hallet men were hot-blooded, it was Seth. He'd feel strongly about things and would sometimes rush in to try to make them right."

"Perhaps," Vince said, removing his pipe from between his teeth, "you should ask him why. You might get a straight answer."

Surprised, she searched his face. He was casual enough. "Are you serious?"

"Why not? I'd like to know, and I'm sure you would, too. Any bright young woman would want to know why an old flame accuses her fiance of arranging his brother's death."

His caustic words were troubling on more accounts than one. "*Arranged* his death? Don't be silly, Vince! He doesn't think that. Why . . . why, he couldn't. Why should he?"

"Yes, why should he? I leave that for you to decide. Better yet, ask him. Quiz, probe him for answers, find out—for my sake, if you will."

"Well yes, of course I could ask, but isn't it making too much of a rather wild suspicion? Maybe it's wiser not to feed the fire."

"My very point, dear. This methodical and unemotional young friend of yours from the past now appears determined enough to go to any extreme to win you back. All's fair in love and war, as they say, but accusing a romantic opponent of *eliminating* one's brother?" His pipe had gone out, and he struck a match to light it again.

Sable watched the tiny flame dance in the darkness and felt a chill flare up into her heart.

"That sort of behavior may demand psychiatric care," Vince said quietly.

Sable's eyes swerved to his. Her throat pinched. Absurd, she wanted to say. Ridiculous . . . but Kash *had* accused Vince, both to her and to Zenobia. He believed it, or he'd never have claimed anything so dreadful.

"I'll ask him," she said quietly. "If I see him again."

"You'll see him again. We both will, and that's what bothers me."

She drew in a breath. "There's no reason for either of us to be in close contact with Kash Hallet. We'll be going to Samburu soon, and he's going with the Smith and Browning hunters back to Tanga. If, as you say, he's involved in poaching, then the authorities will take action."

She wondered why he made no comment on her statement and simply smoked his pipe, one hand in his pocket as he gazed off, drinking in the gathering darkness and the sounds of wildlife stirring on their cautious trek to the water hole to drink.

"We'd better go indoors," she said. "Gran spotted a leopard yesterday. And dinner will be getting cold. Jomo will be upset."

She started to walk back toward the lodge, the windows aglow with golden light, when his voice intercepted her. "Sable, I behaved like a fool this afternoon. My main reason for coming back to see you was to apologize."

She stopped and turned, expectantly, seeing his serious expression. "I'm glad you said that, Vince."

He smiled crookedly, knocked out his pipe, and stepped on the tobacco, grinding it into cold ashes. Placing the pipe in his pocket, he walked up and stood in front of her, both hands taking hold of her shoulders. "I apologize, not because I trust Kash Hallet where you're concerned, but because I was wrong to not trust you. My one defense, I suppose, is what I've learned about him—he's volatile. You know him well enough to know I speak the truth. That's why I brought up his absurd accusation against me. It shows his mental state. He's wild and reckless inside, as much an embodiment of old Africa as the spear-carrying Maasai."

Volatile? If anyone could be accused of volatility, it was Vince. The shock of that discovery today on the road had jolted Sable into wanting to back off from an engagement until she saw him perform in more testing circumstances. Right now, she admitted he was behaving the respectable, intelligent man she'd known in Toronto, but there was more to him than she'd realized.

"I accept your apology," she said quietly. "I should hate for you to think I'm the kind of woman who would say she was seriously considering an engagement to you while still attracted to an old flame who suddenly returns. The truth is, Vince, I haven't made up my mind about anything yet. I know I've learned to respect you. Your friendship and assistance in Toronto was badly needed by me. But—"

"But you're over needing a crutch now?"

"I didn't say that's all you were. That speaks rather pitifully of us both, doesn't it? Love, marriage, friendship, commitment—it must all be there for a relationship to work. And faith in the Lord, too; perhaps above all, faith in shared Christian values."

"I thought we had all that."

"So did I."

His gaze was prying, but she didn't look away. She had to be fair to him, to herself.

"You're saying you no longer think so?"

"I don't know . . . about a lot of things. What happened today has upset me."

"That's to be expected," he commented dryly.

"Not just seeing Kash again—because I prefer to stay away from him, too. I've discovered something about myself, about you, and Kash. And I think it's wise to postpone an engagement until I know what God wants me to do. Right now I want to be with Kate and with my father at Samburu."

"I see," Vince said coolly. "Suddenly everything must be placed on hold until after Samburu."

Sable refused to relent. "Yes. It's wiser this way, for all of us."

"I would not be a gentleman if I argued, would I?"

She remained silent.

"Then, we agree to wait, to see where the road may lead us. And I admit I, too, am quite taken up with the need to get on with what we're here for."

It was this dedication she respected about him, and she smiled. "I knew you'd see it for the best. The supplies will arrive from Mombasa soon, but Mckibber told me we're having trouble hiring a safari guide. I thought it was already arranged."

"It was." He frowned. "Arrangements were made weeks ago with a respected agency working out of Tanzania."

"Tanzania?" she repeated curiously, thinking of Seth. "I would have thought Nairobi."

He shrugged indifferently. "I didn't make the original plans. Skyler did."

This was the first she'd heard of her father's involvement.

"They promised us their best guide and he was paid in full, but he backed out at the final moment. Blamed the danger of the bush country and rebel fighting. The government isn't anxious to have travelers in the area now. The drought's also caused a hardship."

"All the more reason to get in there. I don't see how the guide can change his mind if he was already paid!"

"He's returned the money. Don't worry. We'll get there, even if we go alone with Mckibber."

"Mckibber says he's too old for the rigors."

"No matter. I'll find someone. We've got to reach your father and learn about the elephants."

Sable studied his troubled face, thinking that the postponement of their engagement had gone surprisingly well. Both of them had spoken as calmly as two people deciding on buying a new stove. She reminded herself it was this solidity that had first attracted her to him. Yet, after seeing Kash again, she wasn't as certain.

"Gran mentioned your need to see my father. Can you tell me what it's about?"

Vince shook his head thoughtfully. "It must wait until I see him. I hope you'll understand my decision and not feel I'm thinking less of you for keeping it to myself."

She wondered that he couldn't share, or wouldn't, but smiled. "I won't pry. Maybe I'm just too tired now to be overly curious."

"What I can tell you is there's more than one reason why we must get through to locate him."

"The threat of cholera? Yes, Kate would know of that."

"I'm not speaking only of the needs of the refugees from

the war in Somalia, but of Skyler. We're concerned about him."

She believed Vince was sincere from the tense expression on his face. "Concerned . . . but why? And what do you mean when you say 'we'?"

"Dr. Katherine Walsh. She's been working closely with him until recently. When he disappeared into the bush again, she was obliged to return to her uncle's work at Lake Rudolf."

Sable remembered what Kash had told her about Katherine Walsh. "It was you who hired her, wasn't it?"

He looked at her, unblinking. "Yes, she's always been a close colleague. She's dependable and well educated. You'll like Katherine."

Katherine. "Why is she concerned about my father?"

"It's not just Dr. Walsh, but others at the camp, myself included. Sable, you won't like to hear this, but your father's been behaving strangely since your mother's death. Perhaps he didn't take the necessary time to grieve. He's been going off alone into the wilderness for weeks at a time, claiming he can 'talk' to the elephants. He's growing into a recluse. The last time Dr. Walsh saw him she hardly recognized him. His hair had grown, he had a beard, and he had little to say to anyone at the camp. The last word I've received from Samburu was that he'd been gone for three weeks and no one could find him. He has a way with the elephants when the rest of us can't get close. However, no one's heard from him recently. I've been calling to the Samburu lodge frequently to see if there's any news. I'm expecting a call back within a few days, before the wildlife conference."

The news did little to settle her growing anxiety about getting there with the supplies. Could something have happened to him? Could the rebels have captured him, or even killed him?

"I'm sorry to worry you," he said quietly. "I haven't mentioned this yet to Kate. I think it best if you didn't either until I hear again from Dr. Walsh. Kate has already lost Jim. The possibility of something happening to your father will adversely affect her work. I don't want to sound cold," Vince went on, "but you know how much we'll need her medical skills. Katherine Walsh's expertise is in natural science, as is mine. We can treat

the ill, but Kate is the medical expert. And, of course, we desperately need you."

Sable wondered. "Yes, of course. . . . When will you hear
again from Dr. Walsh? You say she's now at Rudolf?"

"Yes, Dr. Willard's her uncle. Now, Sable, let's not jump to
assuming the worst conclusions about Skyler. It's more likely
he's out in the wilderness tracking a particular elephant—one
named Ahmed*. The beast has the biggest tusks we've yet discovered—almost two hundred pounds apiece. Skyler claims he
can communicate with the bull."

Sable was disturbed by his suggestions. Her father was a sen-
sible man. While he cared about the elephants in the Marsabit
region, he was no kook who believed he could communicate
with Ahmed. Something was wrong, but she hesitated to let
Vince know of her doubts.

"Yes, I'm sure that's what it is. . . ." she said. "He's depressed over my mother's death. They were very close. Did Gran
mention the letter from my father arriving? Unfortunately, Gran
misplaced it, so I haven't seen it yet—but perhaps it holds the
information we need."

His black eyes sparkled in the moonlight. "Did she say when
she received it?"

"No, but I gathered from the way she spoke that it arrived
just before I did."

"That's hardly possible. I heard from Dr. Walsh two weeks
ago, and she hadn't heard from Skyler in a month. Unless . . ."

She looked at him cautiously. "Unless what?"

"Unless he'll fool us all by showing up at the wildlife conference after all. A surprise may be in keeping with his new
quirks."

Sable tensed. "Vince, I wish you wouldn't speak about my
father that way. He's not unbalanced!"

He rushed to soothe her. "Sable, I'm terribly sorry. How

*The historical elephant Ahmed was given Presidential protection by Jomo Kenyatta
when hunters vowed to take its tusks. Ahmed lived a full life and is preserved in the
Nairobi Museum.

thoughtless of me. Please understand I didn't intend anything personal."

She drew in a breath. "Yes, you're right. I suppose everything has been a little too much to deal with all in one day. What I want is a guide with dependable men to bring in our supplies— and now, a hot meal and a good night's rest. I'm exhausted."

"Yes, dear, you have a right to be. Come along." He smiled, looking relaxed for the first time. "I'll make sure your plate is heaped high. And Zenobia can see that you sleep like a log. Tomorrow I'll bring you out to the camp to see Kate. She's anxious to give you a tour of the medical work before we all move on to Samburu. I know how much interest you both have in the Maasai tribe."

Vince walked her toward the porch as the bright Kenya moon shone golden above the acacia trees. "As for a guide, there's a chance of finding a good team in Nairobi. I'll be going there before the conference to see what can be done on short notice."

Thinking about seeing her sister and visiting the Maasai brought to mind the missing funds for the wells. Sable considered bringing the matter up now, but there'd already been more than enough to discuss for one night. It could wait. She would speak to Kate first.

Could she believe the concerns that Vince raised about her father's mental well-being? Even Zenobia had voiced her worry. Why hadn't Kash? He seemed to think her father was of sound mind and body. What reason would Kash have to think differently than the others?

Next time she saw Kash, she would ask him.

Eight

*T*he next morning when Sable came down dressed for her drive with Vince to visit Kate at the camp, Zenobia met her at the dining table, where scrambled eggs and beef waited.

"Vince isn't here, but he's left you a note."

"Gone? Where?"

"He had to leave for Nairobi while it was yet dark. A call came late after you went to bed last night."

"Nothing serious, I hope."

Zenobia sighed as she buttered her toast. "The conferees are arriving a day ahead of schedule. And Vince will be the speaker, since Skyler isn't going to be here. And, oh yes—I've spent hours looking for Skyler's letter and can't find it anywhere!" She passed the coffee urn to Sable. "I'm so mad at myself," she scolded. "It's a tragedy, dear. I *really* am getting old and senile! But I won't give up. I'll keep looking. And oh! Before I forget— Kash called, too, from Kajaido. He asked me to give you a message. Kate's asking for you to come today."

Sable was surprised. "When did he see Kate?"

Zenobia shrugged, adding sugar to her coffee. "He's been seeing a lot of your sister."

Sable looked across the table at her. "Oh?"

"Anyway, Kash made it clear I was to tell you to drive out there this morning. He'll meet you at the camp."

Sable took a sip of her strong black coffee.

"By the way, he said not to take the rented jeep—there's

something wrong with it. And he wouldn't want to fish you both out of the mud again, whatever that means. He said to take my Land Rover. And to think I won't have it to drive. I intended to take the dogs and go out to see Patches this afternoon. I want to make sure the boys do a good job feeding her. She's likely to prove difficult at first.''

"You can still see Patches. We'll stop on the way. Why not come with me to visit Kate? By now she'll be dying to see you and gorge on some of your chocolate chip cookies.''

"You take the cookies for me, dear, and the Land Rover. I'm going to tear my office upside down to find that letter while you're gone. I know it's there somewhere. I'll have Jomo run out this afternoon in one of the other cars to see Patches. Can you find the Amboseli camp? It's a good twenty miles from here.''

"I'll find it. I've a load of Bibles, too, I brought from Mombasa. I wish I could have brought the bicycles. The truck bringing the supplies should arrive soon, maybe today. I wonder if any of the professors will be going with Vince and us to Samburu?''

"The itinerary doesn't include that. There'll be the lectures, the slides, then visits to the reserves and a trip out to Kajaido to see firsthand how the Maasai cattle ranchers are doing with the stationary ranching experiment. A few of them seem to be doing well, but I find it highly unlikely the majority of them will ever break with their nomadic lifestyle.''

"Some of the conservationists may change their minds about visiting Samburu when they learn Father isn't there,'' Sable mused. "They'll wonder what it is that he has found more important than the work there.''

"If Vince and Mckibber don't come up with a guide, I don't see how the supplies can be brought in,'' said Zenobia, looking worried. "On the news this morning mention was made of another UN peacekeeper shot at Mogadishu. Authorities are advising everyone to stay out of the NFD area. As for your father coming to the conference, I don't think he will. Not as long as he's worried about that elephant herd.''

"The last giant-tusked elephant herd in the NFD,'' said Sable. "They've got to be protected from poachers!''

"Kash can tell you about them. He came from there recently—" Zenobia stopped. "So that's it! Skyler's letter—it was Kash who brought it."

"Kash?" Sable was so surprised she stood to her feet.

"I wonder. . . ." mused Zenobia, her brow wrinkling.

"Kash brought the letter?" repeated Sable, bewildered. "Why hasn't he mentioned it to me?"

"Yes, I wonder. Perhaps he just told me about it but forgot to give it to me. We were busy talking that day, and Vince arrived . . . and maybe I simply *thought* I placed it inside my desk. Anyway, dear, do ask him when you see him today. He'll have to remember."

<hr />

Of Kenya's parks and reserves, Amboseli was one of the largest, containing over a thousand square miles. Sable recalled how Kash told her he was working with the Maasai as an adviser. *How can he possibly be involved in poaching?* she thought, frowning as she drove Zenobia's big Land Rover toward the camp. Seeing Kash again after all this time was causing her to question whether or not she had been right in believing Vince that Kash had turned to illegal activities to make money. The evidence seemed to be there, but her heart kept telling her otherwise.

However, it was no secret that even game wardens were sometimes the enemy—like a policeman gone bad.

Sable shut it all from her mind to bask in the dramatic scenery everywhere dominated by the majestic Kilimanjaro. As she drove through the hot, dusty thornbush country, she glimpsed the plains animals in herds: the rare and beautiful fringe-eared oryx with its black-and-white face and long straight horns. She slowed the Land Rover as she came across the shy and graceful long-necked gerenuk. As they browsed from thornbushes they stood up on their hind legs, munching and watching her. These were some of the animals the Lord had designed to survive the dry season—able to go without water for long periods.

This area of the Amboseli Reserve was also used by the Maasai for their cattle, unlike the southeastern area near Old Tukai, where she'd gotten stuck in the mud flats of Lake Amboseli. Because Old Tukai was a national park, the cattle were not allowed to graze there. During the dry season it contained one of the most remarkable concentrations of game animals in all of Africa: rhinos, elephants, lions, cheetahs, giraffes, baboons, monkeys, and plains animals of all types.

Sable slowed as the camp came into view. Temporary canvas buildings were set up with various pieces of equipment, and the medical tent, the largest, was partially shaded by acacias. A few goats and chickens were penned farther away, and water barrels were stacked beneath a tree, reminding her of how precious water was in the area—and how desperately the Maasai women with children needed a well nearby.

Sable honked a greeting as she drove slowly into the compound, trying to keep the dust down. At the sound of the horn, her older sister came out of the medical tent and, seeing who it was, let out a cry, waving excitedly, the crimson red cross sewn boldly onto the front of her sweat-stained khaki shirt.

Sable was quickly out from behind the wheel as Kate came running to meet her. "It's about time you came home and got to work again," she taunted, laughing as they embraced, holding back joyful tears. This was their first meeting since the death of their mother.

Unlike many sisters, she and Kate had never competed for acceptance and personal identity. Their relationship had grown as simply and as strongly as Gran's sturdy bright zinnias behind the lodge. Both Kate and Sable were satisfied with their God-given callings in life and were able to appreciate their differences without feeling threatened. Kate was strong, rarely discouraged, and could joke about her disappointments and the flaws in her appearance. She didn't see her work as a spiritual sacrifice to further the kingdom, but an honor bestowed upon her by the Lord.

"I'd rather be here amid the heat, dust, and flies than anywhere else in the world. At night I can see Mount Kilimanjaro, hear the lions and elephants, and still keep secret company with the King of Kings."

That was Kate Dunsmoor. For years Sable had lived under her spiritual shadow, but rather than being jealous of her peace, she'd been wooed by it to search for her own intimacy with the Lord Jesus.

Although sisters, they were dark and light. Kate was a brunette, and her long straight hair was unassumingly drawn back from a pretty face with high cheekbones sprinkled with sun freckles. Her eyes were blue, and she was an inch taller than Sable. She wore jeans well because of her height and straight legs, and she had recently bemoaned her twenty-eighth birthday.

"I'll never marry," she had written to Sable in Toronto and had drawn a smiley face next to a frowney with two teardrops.

Sable had smiled at her cartoon, but there was sadness in her smile. As Gran had said at the lodge yesterday when she arrived, Kate still secretly grieved over the loss of Jim Murray, the missionary whom she had expected to marry since the two of them attended church together and sang in the school choir. Five years ago he'd contracted cholera in one of the relief camps where he was working with the team as a male nurse, and those in authority had sent him home to Nairobi for treatment.

Kate had expected Jim to come back. While she carried on her work she waited for letters to begin arriving in answer to her own, which she wrote every night. Several months elapsed with no response. She had driven to the lodge to call Jim's mother and "casually" inquire how he was doing.

"His mom seemed embarrassed to hear from me," Kate had written to Sable. *"Later, I found out why."*

After recovering his health, Jim had announced his decision to give up medical missions and enter the "non-missionary world" as he had called it. He began working in an auto repair shop and eventually married the owner's daughter.

Years later Kate confessed to Sable that she still grieved the loss of her teenage sweetheart, insisting, *"I will never love anyone else."*

She looked older now, Sable thought as she drew away from their embrace. Kate was not one to smear her face with creams and ointments, and the hot African sun had given her more than a tan. Tiny premature age lines at the corners of her eyes showed how tired she was. Her face, however, shone with an inner contentment that made her truly lovely.

It's just too bad she can't meet more eligible men while doing this work for the Lord, thought Sable in a protective mood.

Who knows? It may turn out that neither Kate nor I will ever marry, she thought, smiling wistfully. *But if this is God's best for us, we won't feel sorry for ourselves. The Lord himself is our portion, our joy, our life.*

"Oh, Kate, it's great to see you again! But look at you," Sable teased. "You're a mess! When was the last time you wore lipstick?"

Kate made a face at her, beckoning her toward the tent. "And who's to see it and think I'm kissable—him?" She pointed.

Sable followed the direction of her gesture and saw a penned, rangy-looking hyena that chose that moment to offer its hysteric laugh.

"He's got a bad leg," said Kate soberly. "I interfered with nature yesterday. He was about to be eaten, and I intervened. Think I'll send him to Gran. What shall I call him? Lover Boy?"

Sable smiled as Kate began to sing loftily, "Somewhere my love, somewhere he waits for me . . . Somewhere my love, somewhere beyond the sea. . . ."

Sable grimaced. "Never mind. Tell me about the work here." They entered the medical tent, where a stately, barefoot Maasai woman wearing a long brown wrap sat immobile on a stool, a small thin baby in her arms.

Kate sobered, becoming professional as she examined the baby's running eyes.

"Skin and eye disease are the result of a lack of water. It could be solved simply enough if they could just get enough water to bathe their children. Imagine, Sable! These women must walk eight miles each way to the nearest water. She leaves early every other day and returns carrying four gallons of water on her back—not enough to wash her children or their clothes or her dishes—only enough for her family to survive."

Sable handed her the medication to clean the baby's eyes and smiled at the Maasai woman, who watched her. To Sable's surprise the woman spoke in clear English. "Doctor Kate tells us you have come with a gift from the Christians to build a well for us. We are very grateful for the love of our fellow Christians. I, too, am a Christian. Many of the children see the talking film of Jesus speaking to us in our tongue. They believe."

Sable glanced at Kate and the child, then back to the dignified Maasai woman, who watched her evenly.

"Yes," said Sable, her voice quiet. "I came to see that two wells are built."

Even Kate turned her head and looked at her expectantly. "When?"

Sable concentrated on the baby. She didn't want to explain what had happened in front of the Maasai woman. She needed to talk to Kate privately. *I'll get the money again somehow*, she told herself. *Please, Lord, make it possible for them to have the wells, given in your Name, so your daughters can have water to keep their babies from disease.*

I'll get those wells built if I have to sell my portion of the shipping to Kash.

Sable smiled. "Very soon," she said brightly. "Before Doctor Kate and the others leave for Samburu, we'll have men come from Nairobi here to build them."

The woman nodded, and although it was not the Maasai way to smile, her eyes did, and even the baby stopped her fussing.

"There," said Kate. "All done. Bring her back in ten days. And apply a little of this ointment every morning and night."

When the woman had left the tent, Kate sank wearily onto a cot at the back of the tent and popped open a can of Coke. "Mckib brought these out a few days ago. Have one, if you don't mind it warm."

"Thanks, no, but Gran sent you cookies. The chocolate's all melted, though."

Kate drew up her long legs, crossing them as she watched Sable soberly. "What about the wells? What went wrong?"

Sable looked over at her, surprised. "How did you know something's wrong?"

"You hesitated when she asked you. And when you spoke you stared at the baby. If you had the money, you'd have been excited."

Sable sighed and sat down. "I sent it through my bank before I flew out of Toronto. When I went through Namanga before seeing Gran at the lodge, I stopped to make sure it was there because I wanted Mckibber to take care of hiring men in Nairobi right away."

Kate drank her Coke without so much as a grimace. "You mean the money didn't reach Namanga?"

"It got there all right, but it was withdrawn four days ago and transferred to Nairobi."

"Well, that's easy. We'll just drive over there and get it. We'll be right there to hire the construction team."

"I called over there while in Namanga. They insisted the money was already used for the work here."

"That doesn't make any sense!"

"No, it doesn't. I . . . um . . . am going to ask Vince about it next time I see him."

Kate's eyes narrowed thoughtfully. "You think Dr. Adler took the money?"

"No, of course not," she hastened, for she wasn't certain yet. The bank had promised to look into it and get in touch within the week. "He may have been under the false impression it was to be used for the Samburu trip."

"Instead of the wells here, you mean?"

"Yes. And if he did, it's my fault, because I should have made it clear that these were private funds belonging to us for Mother's memorial."

Kate considered and lapsed into silence. Sable, too, said nothing more, and after a moment Kate said, "Tomorrow we'll take the Land Rover and tour the area where the wells will go. By the way, if our money was spent, just how do you expect to build them?"

"I will, that's all." Sable stood. "If necessary I'll take out a loan on my shares in Dunsmoor shipping."

"And if you don't marry you'll end up in old age getting your soup at the rescue mission."

"Now whose faith is less than a mustard seed? You can brave all this alone, but now you worry about your sister standing in a soup line."

"Yeah, I suppose you're right."

"Cheer up. Gran is leaving you the export shop in Mombasa. You can retire there to your needlework and sell Maasai jewelry to the tourists. Think of all the tales you can entertain them with about staring down hungry lions in your youth."

"Don't laugh. There was a lion the other night, about eight feet long and sniffing loudly around my tent." Kate changed the subject, growing sober. "You're sure about the wells? If you are, we could start digging before the wet season comes."

"I expect to have the construction papers signed before we leave for Samburu," said Sable, with more hope than certainty.

Kate looked at her curiously. "Did Vince tell you our guide changed his mind about the safari? We've got to find another man, Sable. It's important we join Dad at the camp before matters worsen in the NFD. If actual war breaks out, the authorities may not let us in even if we find a guide."

Sable told her that Vince was in Nairobi trying to locate a safari business willing to sign on for Samburu.

"We've got until after the wildlife conference," said Kate. "After that, we'll need to strike out on our own."

Sable gave a laugh. "Gran will have a nervous breakdown. What about hauling the supplies? We'll need at least two trucks."

"Vince can drive one. You and I can take turns driving the other."

It was like Kate to say this, but Sable knew it wasn't that simple. Their one hope seemed to lie in Vince's success in Nairobi.

"The Lord will provide if He wants us there," said Sable.

"You're absolutely right, so we won't worry about it now," Kate said in her no-nonsense way and, glancing swiftly at her watch, set her empty Coke can down. "There are a few women with children waiting to be seen. They've walked at least three miles to get here. I'll take care of them, then we'll have lunch. Kash is coming."

Sable's expression remained as smooth as glass. "Yes, he told Gran he'd meet me here. I wonder what he wants to talk about."

Kate arched a brow. "You mean there's a long list of subjects to choose from?"

Sable remained silent, remembering the things Vince had said the night before in the yard.

"I'll show you to my tent," Kate said quickly, and Sable was grateful that her sister didn't press the point.

"You are staying a few days with me, aren't you?" Kate went on. "The conference doesn't start until next week. And Vince will swing by here first on his way back from Nairobi."

"Yes, I want to stay. I told Gran I might. She has enough to keep her busy with the arrival of the baby elephant."

Kate shook her head sadly. "It's a shame about Moffet, but as much as we liked her, she's only one of the many animals in the recent rash of poaching. It's despicable."

The bright sunlight struck them as they stepped out of the larger medical tent. Several Maasai women were waiting patiently in the sun, holding babies. Several sick children squatted in the dust, and the persistent flies buzzed.

Kate called to them in Swahili and said something to one of the children, who shyly covered his face with both palms and giggled, then she motioned Sable to follow her.

The dust rose as they walked past the jeep and a bigger tent where the aroma of food and coffee poured out. A fly netting hung in the open arch, and Sable saw the kitchen staff preparing the noon meal. There were an older couple, a stout young man, and an African girl.

"Do you see Kash often?" asked Sable casually.

"Since he's been back, he's come to visit on Sundays, sometimes with Mckib, who brings me Gran's personal supplies for the week and my mail from Nairobi. A few people in our church write me the news; otherwise, I wouldn't get any mail at all from old friends. Most of our group at church belong to the young married Sunday school class and have toddlers. We've drifted apart." Kate's blue eyes fixed on her, squinting in the sunlight, for she seldom bothered to wear her hat. "Why do you ask? About Kash, I mean?"

Sable laughed lightly and cast her a glance. "Oh, nothing. I just thought . . . well, never mind."

Kate studied her. "Don't tell me you're jealous?"

"What right do I have? It's certainly none of my business what he does, or you for that matter. I was curious is all, because Gran said he was seeing you a lot lately."

"You can set aside any concerns. We're friends, nothing more. He's been coming more often since Seth died and asking questions about Dr. Adler." Kate glanced at her. "I think Kash was angry when he learned you were coming home to work with Vince."

"Has he asked about me much?"

Kate hesitated. "You know him better than I. What do you think?"

"I don't know if I know him as well or not," Sable said quietly, looking off in the direction of Mount Kilimanjaro.

"That's an odd statement. You've dated him off and on since your seventeenth birthday. I always thought the two of you would go off together one day and get married in Nairobi."

Sable glanced at the ground, watching the dust rise. "I'd never do that," she said quietly.

"Did Kash ever ask you?"

Sable stopped, surprised, and faced Kate curiously. "Ask me to marry him?"

"Yes, by quietly going to Nairobi without anyone knowing."

Sable's eyes searched her sister's. "Yes, but I said no."

Kate looked knowingly at Sable. "I thought he might have—years ago."

"He didn't think Father would agree, and he didn't want to come back here to live. He wanted us to make it on our own— in South Africa."

Kate was silent, and they walked on in wordless understanding.

"The whole time I was in Toronto I was sorry I didn't do

it," murmured Sable. "I kept asking the Lord, did I make a mistake? Would it have been so wrong?"

"Maybe not wrong, but you'd have disappointed the family." Kate sighed and swished a fly. "Sometimes a person has to, though. They always wanted a big wedding for us both, and to have their new son-in-law move into the old family house and take his seat at the family dining table prepared to carry on, if not in deed, at least in thought. Well," she said wryly, "they've ended up with two single daughters who are anything but typical."

Sable smiled. After a moment she said, "Kash always said I thought more of what the family expected than I cared about him." An old ache she thought had healed returned, as strong as ever. Maybe he'd been right. Maybe Kash had been trying to find out how much he meant to her. . . .

"Sometimes I think his suggestion we marry in Nairobi was a test," Sable went on.

"Maybe. With Kash it's hard to know. He did ask me if I thought you were serious about marrying Dr. Adler."

"And what did you tell him?"

"I told him yes, if you became engaged. That you weren't the frivolous type. He knew that already, of course." Kate looked at her gravely. "Are you in love with Vince?"

Sable sighed. "I wish I hadn't come back."

"You don't really mean that. If you're like me, that's where our faith comes in. We honor Him when we leave our tomorrows with Him and decide He'll give us the very best, even if it looks like a wilderness in comparison to what others may have. 'He makes streams in the desert . . .' " she quoted from Isaiah, " '. . . and the wilderness a pool of water.' "

Kate left her outside the tent entrance, and Sable watched her sister walk back toward the Maasai women and children awaiting her care.

For the first time in weeks, Sable's heart warmed with a strange joy and peace. *I'm proud of you, Kate*, she thought.

Nine

❦❦❦❦❦❦❦❦

Sable was unpacking her overnight bag and putting her things in Kate's small closet when Mckibber's friendly voice called, "You got company, Sable."

If Mckib was here, then Kash would be, too.

Sable smoothed her hair and, pushing aside the tent netting, stepped into the sunlight. Mckibber was already walking away toward his jeep as Kash stood nearby waiting for her.

She scanned him, rugged-looking in Levi's and canvas shirt. "You're in time for lunch," she said airily. "Kate's expecting you."

"I'd like to talk to you alone first, if you don't mind." He gestured his head toward the long, low kitchen tent. "Vince here?"

"He's in Nairobi trying to hire a guide."

Kash seemed satisfied. Sable, too, wished to hear what he had to say in private. There were so many things to ask him that could not be discussed at the lunch bench if the others were there. Still, she hesitated, judging the appropriateness of being alone with him in a tent.

"All right, but wait a minute." Stepping back inside, she pulled the curtain divider across the sleeping section, leaving the "sitting area." She quickly arranged the canvas folding chairs, then came back to where he stood and announced loftily, "I suppose it's all right to come in for a few minutes. The sun is hot, and Kate won't mind."

She ignored the faint amusement showing in his smile. "Thank you," he said with grave dignity. "It's encouraging to know the young woman I once held in my arms trusts my honor to remain a gentleman—at least for a few minutes."

"Never mind the past."

He laughed lightly, deliberately disregarding her oversimplified dismissal, and entered.

Sable refused to dwell on the fact that his presence made the small space feel stifling. He reminded her of a panther—lean, strong, and graceful. Despite the insects, she drew back the netting and allowed the noonday heat unhindered access. As he tossed his hat down and remained standing, she snatched hers up and fanned her face.

"We've much to talk about," she managed in a businesslike tone. "Where would you prefer to start?"

The silent moments slowly, agonizingly, ticked by, and she impatiently turned to face him so as to elicit some response. But despite her efforts at directness, there was no holding back the foolish warmth that began its ascent upward into her cheeks.

Kash looked at her as she stood in the center of the tent illuminated by the sunshine streaming in. The silence between them became strained. It was Kash who finally broke the tension by pulling out a canvas chair for her. "You've been away from this heat too long. Better sit down."

Sable did, consenting to her defeat, and he walked to the tent opening and looked out across the plain. "There aren't enough hours in the day to discuss the things that need to be said between us." He looked over at her intently. "Did Zenobia mention the Mombasa shipping?" The strong cobalt color of his eyes shadowed over.

She didn't think he wanted her to know yet, but she had to be truthful. "Yes, because I found the ivory in the gift shop. It wasn't in keeping with Gran's love for animals, and I asked her what it was doing there. In the process of explaining, she told me about your grandfather and the Australian gold pieces."

"Would you believe me if I told you Vince was using the

shipping to supply ivory and skins to a Far Eastern cartel selling on the black market?"

"You've mentioned his involvement in poaching before, and my response remains the same," she said tiredly. "He would have no cause."

"Money," he stated flatly. "Not for himself, but to finance a cause he believes in as strongly as you do about showing the *JESUS* film."

She shook her head. "He's a wildlife conservationist. It makes no sense to think he'd be working with such groups."

"People don't always respond logically when they feel themselves backed into a corner. One thing I've learned in my business, they always fight to survive."

His "business"? What was Kash's business if not working with Smith and Browning?

"It's true Vince is a fighter," Sable said, "but not for personal agendas. He cares deeply."

"Yes, I know, you told me. He broods over man and beast. A noble man, Vince."

She stood. "I can see there's no use our discussing Dr. Adler. Shall we go to lunch?"

"If he fights for any cause, it's for his work with Dr. Willard at Lake Rudolf."

"Dr. Willard is a colleague, and so is Katherine Walsh, but Vince isn't involved at Rudolf."

"He wouldn't admit it yet because he knows their philosophy clashes with Christianity. Yet he doesn't believe in the Bible himself. I don't know how you could ever think he did. His past philosophy was evolutionary, and he's working with and privately funding a dig at Lake Rudolf. Vince is adamant he'll unearth a find that will make him more famous than Leakey."

She drew in a surprised breath, staring at him. "That can't be true, Kash, but even if he's associated with a search at Lake Rudolf, that doesn't prove Vince is committed to evolution or to using money from illegal poaching to fund it. He could have friends there," she said defensively. "Why not? It's no secret he has worked for years for a private research lab outside Toronto."

"Have it your way. You want to believe in him, and you will. Even facts won't change some minds."

"And just where are your 'facts' about his involvement? Or are your accusations as wild as his are about you?" She stopped, for she hadn't wanted to alert him that Vince knew of Kash's suspicions—that Vince was somehow involved in Seth's death.

Kash walked up to her, standing so near she could feel the heat emanating from him. "Did he mention Seth?"

She turned away. "Yes," she said quietly.

"He denies it, naturally. What would you expect of him?"

"I expect both of you to be wiser with your allegations." She turned, her eyes searching his and finding a spark of restrained anger.

"When will you stop treating me like a little boy in your Sunday school class? I always thought men were to be the spiritual leaders."

"They are, if they're ready," she snapped, then felt unfair for having said it.

"There's no question Dr. Adler is your type of leader. In the end you may find the so-called experts have the same hold on you that other false leaders have on their adoring followers."

Sable whirled, ready to flatly deny his charge, then confronted by a steely gaze, she clamped her jaw and remained stubbornly silent.

"I realize any spiritual warning coming from me is unwanted and unexpected. However, I'm protective enough of your noble ambitions to want to see them guarded against charlatans like Adler."

Charlatans! "Thank you. But I'm wise enough to know a charlatan when I see one. And Dr. Adler doesn't come close. Have you anything else to say? Because I don't care to discuss him or his work any longer."

Kash lifted both palms as if surrendering. "Far be it from me to force such an independently minded young woman into discussing a subject she refuses to deal with." He settled into a canvas chair, and as she watched him cautiously, he dug into his shirt pocket and pulled out a folded envelope, holding it up between thumb and forefinger. "From your father."

So he did have it. Sable reached for it with excitement, but he held it back. "Not yet. Please sit down."

Her lashes narrowed, but she did so with deliberate elegance. "Gran said you delivered the letter over a week ago. She thought she had placed it in her office, but when she searched, it was gone. Did you take it back or never give it to her?"

"The day I arrived with the letter Vince came in. I decided to wait and give it to you myself. Zenobia is easily distracted, and she assumed I'd given it to her."

"I suppose I don't need to ask why you didn't want Dr. Adler to see it," she stated.

"No. It would have ended up in his pocket, then in shreds."

The idea seemed preposterous, and she wondered why Kash persisted. "That's absurd!"

"Is it? I suggest that's what happened to the letter I sent you in Toronto. Yes—I know you didn't receive it. Zenobia told me so on the phone this morning."

She turned away, refusing to discuss it. "When did you see my father last?" she asked, keeping her anxiety over her father's condition quiet. She was not willing to bring up what Vince had told her about Skyler's strange behavior. Yet if it were true, Kash would surely know it.

"It's been two months," he said. "I stopped at the camp with a friend of mine. He flies a Cessna for the Missionary Aviation Fellowship."

"I'm surprised you'd know anyone working with MAF." She expected him to defend himself, but he did not. "How did you meet this MAF friend of yours?"

"Why do you want to know? Are you interested in me, or just in maintaining your unflattering opinion of me?"

She shrugged. "It's odd, is all."

"Odd that a missionary pilot and a poacher would have anything in common?"

Her eyes reluctantly came to his warm blue gaze. "I didn't say that."

"You didn't need to. You forget how well I know you."

"You don't know me at all—you never did."

"I know you better than Vince does. No—don't protest, and I don't want to hear another speech on his wondrous merits. I happen to think he has few that will stand up under scrutiny, but never mind that now. I've said enough for the moment."

"Maybe too much."

"Maybe. Every time we get to within feet of each other you get as prickly as a thornbush."

Sable gave a laugh and folded her arms. "I don't think that's true at all. It so happens we have a great deal to discuss, but leave Vince out of it."

"I can hardly do that when his big footprints are everywhere. Skyler's one of the most knowledgeable men I've met when it comes to elephants. And Vince knows it, too."

Why did he bring that up, and what was he suggesting now?

"Do you know what's in the letter?" she asked.

"I was there when he wrote it."

"If he trusted you to deliver it to me, then. . . ?" She held out her hand.

Kash smiled. "He also trusted me to deliver *you* to him."

Sable looked at him blankly. "What do you mean?"

"Most ordinary guides won't touch the area with the fighting about ready to erupt again. He hired me to bring you to Samburu, but," he admitted nonchalantly, "I've since changed my mind."

So Kash Hallet was the safari guide her father had contracted out of Tanzania—the man Vince had mentioned last night who'd changed his mind and returned the money to the safari organization. Did Vince know it was actually Kash? And why had Kash changed his mind?

He appeared reluctant to hand the envelope to her. "I admit I'll be very pleased if you'd realize you're making a mistake going there."

"Does Vince know my father hired you?"

"No."

"But he knows Father hired someone," she protested. "He told me last night the guide had returned the money."

Kash looked thoughtful. "Then he does know about the association I'm with in Tanzania."

"Was it supposed to be a secret, at least from Vince?"

"Yes, and I'd prefer you wouldn't let him know you told me."

Her curiosity grew. "Why is it a secret?"

The blue of his eyes softened, his hand rising to touch a wisp of her hair. "You ask too many questions, but never the right one."

Sable's heart beat like a drum. She leaned back.

"Change your mind about Samburu," he said gently.

She shook her head. "I can't . . . please don't ask me to. Kate won't stay away either."

"I know. Dean can be counted on, though, and they share the same vision."

"Dean?" she inquired, searching his eyes.

"The MAF pilot. He flies in and out of Tanzania and Rwanda. He'll be flying to Samburu as well. Kate can always call him on the radio if she needs him."

It never dawned on Sable to ask why she, too, couldn't make use of the radio set if she needed help, or why Kash didn't seem to think it was enough where she was concerned.

"What of Mckibber? He's willing to help me."

"Mckibber's working with me and Dean." He looked innocent. "He didn't explain that?"

She smiled ruefully. "No. Was he supposed to?"

"Not exactly," he admitted, returning her smile.

"When are we leaving?"

Kash stood and walked over to the tent opening, looking about the camp. "I didn't say I'd take you. I returned your father's money to the safari operators."

"I'll pay you again," she insisted, rising from her chair to stand next to him.

"You don't have enough. My expenses run higher than most. And . . . you're in debt up to your neck"—he smiled—"to me. Have you forgotten I now own half of Dunsmoor shipping?"

Sable hadn't but hoped to avoid discussing it just yet. She remembered the wells and how she had entertained the thought of borrowing the twenty thousand from Kash against some of her shares in the company. With his present attitude, he probably wouldn't cooperate.

"You can't let us down now, Kash. What of my father and the elephants? And Kate's work?"

"All true, but what's your reason for following Vince up there? You're not a nurse."

"I'm not following Vince. I'm expected to help Father with his research. He wants me there. He hired you to bring me, and . . . I've other plans. I've brought a *JESUS* film, some Bibles."

He scanned her, his lashes narrowing. "That's what I thought."

"You don't agree? About the film showings? It's going to be difficult to arrange, I know, yet I'm going to try."

"I agree wholeheartedly—if it were Dean doing it."

Or you, she wanted to breathe. *Oh, why can't it be you?*

"Your cause is very commendable, but very risky," Kash went on. "Many of them are Moslems. Do you want to be run out of a village under a bombardment of rock throwing?"

"Are you saying I should retire to a nice safe hotel room and knit?"

He smiled. "Only when you're expecting a bundle of joy."

Taken off guard, she walked away, her back toward him. He had made it sound as if *they* would have the "bundle of joy."

"I wish you wouldn't bring up matters like that!"

"Why not? You wanted to marry me once, remember?"

"It was you who walked away."

"And I've come back, haven't I?"

"Have you?" she whispered. She turned. "Or is it only that you don't want Vince to have me?"

"I don't want any man to have you except me," he gritted.

Sable walked to the tent opening, composing herself. "If you care, as you say, you'll bring Kate and me to my father's camp in Samburu. You'll show me proof of all these evil charges against Vince. Until then, I can only think you're after him and will even use me to do it."

He watched her, looking frustrated but restrained. After a long moment he said evenly, "All right. I'll accept your challenge."

Sable was surprised. She'd expected him to back off. Her eyes looked directly into his now, uneasy at the determination she saw.

"I'll bring you to your father's camp."

Her lips parted. "You're serious?"

"You want to go, don't you?"

"You know I do."

"Then you've got what you asked for. And after Samburu, Sable, I'll expect you to keep your half of the bargain."

She tried to still her beating heart. "Only if what you say about Vince is true."

He seemed to look not at her but through her—to her very soul and heart. Sable shivered despite the heat.

"And if I do prove Vince is guilty, will you break away from him?" Kash demanded.

She swallowed, her throat dry, and no words would come. She nodded softly. It seemed to be enough for him.

He briefly scanned her and snatched up his hat. "You've got yourself a bargain."

She wondered if she might not regret her haste, but Kash didn't look sorry and settled his hat on his dark head.

"When are we leaving for Samburu?" she asked. "When can I tell Kate the good news?"

"I'd prefer you wait until after the conference at the lodge. I want to hear what Vince will tell the conservationists."

"Does your interest have anything to do with the elephants in the north? Do you know if there is some sort of problem?" she asked worriedly.

"That's what we want to find out" was all he said. "I intend to stay the night. Do you have any objections?"

She folded her arms to show casual disinterest. "Should I?"

"Only you can answer that."

"As a matter of fact, I was rather hoping you wouldn't rush off. . . ."

He lifted a brow.

"Do you remember the Maasai manyatta inland from here?" she asked.

"Yes. I know the chief. Why?"

"Could you bring me there this afternoon? I'm looking for the right locations to build two water wells for the Maasai. Kate thought this location would be good, but I also want one farther inland. It's a memorial to our mother and her work with the tribe."

If Kash was surprised by this, he didn't show it. Kate must have already told him, she decided.

"It would be better to locate the wells closer to an encampment where the families are located," Kash suggested. "When do you want to hire the construction team?"

"I had intended to do it before we left for Samburu."

"You sound as if you've changed your mind."

She hesitated, unwilling at the moment to bring up the matter of the missing money. "No, but unfortunately the project must be delayed. Still, I do want to settle on the locations."

He looked at her with interest. "Delayed? Why?"

She drew in a breath. "It seems the twenty thousand Kate and I raised is—well, not here waiting, as I had expected."

Sable briefly told him what had happened but carefully omitted any mention of the possibility that Dr. Adler had taken the money. She must first talk to Vince. She was certain he could explain. Evidently Kash was ahead of her, for he asked, "Who has access to your funds in Namanga?"

She avoided his gaze. "If I told you Dr. Adler, you'd immediately suspect him."

"Perhaps with good cause."

"If he did need to appropriate it for another project, you can be sure it wasn't deliberate on his part," she said quietly. She remembered what Kash had said about Vince's "personal cause" at Lake Rudolf. Would he *dare* use it to fund an evolutionary project?

"You mean he didn't know you expected to build two wells?" he asked smoothly.

"Of course he knew—" She stopped, trapped.

"So he did know. Then he used your money despite your plans."

She turned, exasperated, and looked at him. If her emotions troubled him he didn't show it.

He half smiled. "I wouldn't trust a man who could put a pin in your dreams and see them burst, all for a cause of his own."

That's what you did to me, she wanted to say but was no longer certain of even that. He had said he returned, that he had even written her in Toronto.

"You're rushing to judgment again," she accused. "I don't know for sure he took the money, and neither do you."

"You're right, I don't. But it should be easy enough to find out. It had to be transferred from Namanga to the Nairobi bank. They can inform you who drew it out and where it went."

Sable remained silent and stepped outside the tent, feeling the hot sun.

Kash followed. "Unless," he said, watching her, "you prefer not to know for personal reasons."

"I want to know the truth," she stated. "Why shouldn't I? The wells, the evangelism work, the film—they're the reasons I've come home. Nothing must interfere with that. Not Vince, not anyone."

In the descending silence, he stood watching her, and Sable said again, looking toward his Land Rover, "Did you say your MAF friend is contacting a Maasai manyatta near here?"

"Dean? Yes, about twenty miles away. Why?"

She hesitated, glancing at him musingly. "Do you have friendly contact with the chief there?"

He watched her cautiously. "Somewhat."

She looked back toward the Land Rover and sighed. "I wish I had a small truck."

He scanned her. "Would you mind telling me why?"

She began carefully. "I want to show the film on the life of Christ. It's all in Swahili—but I'll need help setting up the equipment and the permission of the chief. I'm sure he wouldn't give me permission for several reasons—but he might for you and Dean."

"I see. And you think a poacher and an adventurer with no regard for man or beast would be the right kind of man to help you perform so lofty and noble a project?"

The question was double-edged, but she realized he hadn't come out and refused.

"And if I get you this permission, would it make you happy?"

She was surprised by his unexpected warmth and cooperation. "Why—yes! Yes, it would, Kash!"

Sable walked slowly toward him, her eyes looking directly into his. In a soft voice, she continued, "I'm beginning to be happier now than I've been in years."

His gaze held hers. "Then you mustn't be disappointed."

She looked at him, excitement bubbling up into her smile. "Then you're serious—you'll try?"

His languid gaze flickered over her face. "Why not?"

"I don't know . . . I just didn't think you would."

"There's no guarantee the chief will grant permission."

"But you'll try to arrange it?"

"Anything for Sable Dunsmoor. I'll bring you out to the encampment this afternoon to meet Dean. We could try to arrange a film showing before the conference."

"Hey, you two!" called Kate, standing with Mckibber beside the dining tent. "Lunch is ready."

Still holding her father's letter, she placed it in her pocket and walked with Kash toward the tent. It would need to wait, but now she knew its contents—that her father had hired Kash to bring her to the NFD camp. And she wondered how Kash could be suspected of poaching if her father so trusted him.

⊙⊞⊙

After lunch, Sable hurried to Kate's tent to change, ignoring her bag still packed with her boots and safari clothes. Kash was near the tent, loading the Land Rover with water for the twenty-mile drive inland to the Maasai manyatta.

Kate had decided she was too busy to go with them, while Mckibber insisted on returning to the lodge to load the film equipment and bring it back to the Maasai manyatta.

Kash came to the tent as she was grabbing her camera. She turned and saw him standing there, scanning her. He lifted his sunglasses. "If that dress is for my benefit, it's not necessary."

She blushed. "You suppose wrong. It is definitely *not* for your benefit."

"Then I won't ask who else you're expecting on the way, except a lions' pride."

Her lashes narrowed as his gaze took in her light sundress and knapsack, where she kept her sunscreen, sunglasses, and lip balm. "Don't you think you should wear boots and safari khakis?" he persisted smoothly.

"I'm tired of them," she admitted. "I feel cooler."

"You won't for long."

She put on her hat. "I know what I'm doing. I was Kenya-born, too, remember?"

"Ah yes! Who could forget the old and great colonial names of Dunsmoor and Hallet? In the young colony it meant something—it doesn't anymore."

His words unwillingly reminded her about the shipping in Mombasa and the shady deed of her grandfather. They would still need to discuss the serious and uncomfortable matter that Kash owned half the company and wanted it all.

She glanced at him to see if his remark was intended to open the door to that unwanted topic, but his handsome expression showed nothing as he watched her from shaded eyes, toying with the Land Rover keys.

"You've forgotten what it's like out there in the open country. Two years in Canada has civilized you." He smiled and gestured to her bag of safari things. "Bring them just in case. If you don't, you can stay here and give yourself a manicure."

"Your bossy ways haven't changed through the years."

His smile was electric. "They're not likely to either." He

snatched up her bag and gestured her politely past. "After you, Miss Canada!"

She smiled and brushed past, leaving a whiff of her favorite perfume.

Ten

Leaving the medical camp, they started inland on the twenty-mile journey. Crossing a ridge, the Land Rover bounced and jolted over the rough track, with an inevitable dust cloud trailing behind in the stifling afternoon, the sky blue and brilliant.

The track narrowed to two wheel marks bordered by thick acacia thornbush. For an hour they slogged through heat and dust, and on either side of the Land Rover, the dense scrub raked the sides with a screeching that set Sable's nerves on edge. Her light cotton dress was covered with a fine layer of dust, and her back was sweaty against the leather seat. Kash looked over at her and smiled. She turned her head away. He handed her the canteen. "It's lukewarm," he teased. "You left your ice cubes in Toronto."

"I don't like ice water," she retorted good-naturedly, out to prove she hadn't forgotten, and unstopped the canteen to drink, but it tasted miserable.

Sable lifted her field glasses from her lap and scanned the savanna. There was much game to be seen at this time of the day, for in the hot noonday the great herds of zebra and gazelle that grazed across the open ranges in the early morning would retire to the shade of trees, and in the late afternoon, especially in this dry season, they came in herds to the water holes.

Noticing she was searching, Kash motioned to a grove of acacias. Sable turned her head quickly so as not to miss the sight as Kash slowed. A troop of baboons howled, leaping and dancing among the branches as the Land Rover passed.

Sable looked at Kash and laughed. "I never get over seeing them. I used to think of all this in Toronto and wonder if my memories were merely nostalgic."

"And," he said quietly, looking ahead as the speedometer climbed, "now that you're back and have seen it as it is again, does it live up to your memory?"

Why did she think he was including himself in that question? She busied herself with the field glasses again. "Yes, it's as I remembered it to be," she said casually.

Kash made no comment at first. "So, in spite of everything, you're glad you've come back to Kenya?"

He was being rather direct. "Why shouldn't I come back? I always intended to. Kenyatta's my home—at least until the lease with the government runs out again and they decide on another game warden. . . . I can't even bear to think it might happen."

"Most likely it will," he said with nothing in his voice. "You'll need to get used to walking away from your loves . . . like the rest of us."

"I don't think I'll ever get used to it." Sable's mood had changed from one of exhilaration to concealed despondency.

He looked over at her. "I didn't mean to ruin your outing."

"I didn't think I was openly sulking."

"You weren't. But I read you like a map."

"That sounds dangerous."

He smiled. "Anyway, I wasn't asking if you were sorry you'd come home, but about the situation you found when you arrived."

Oh no, now it's coming, she thought. *He's going to bring up the shipping and my grandfather.*

"What do you mean?" she asked innocently. "I don't find any situation so troubling."

"You wouldn't fib to me now, would you? You know the situation I'm talking about—your father, Zenobia—Seth, Vince, and me."

Seth. Sable looked at him contritely. "Oh, Kash, I am sorry—

about Seth, I mean. I didn't mean to sound so indifferent—"
She stopped. "I wanted to say something sooner. You know
how much I thought of him."

"Don't be sorry. I doubt he is."

"But you are," she said gently. "That's what matters. The
two of you were so close. How did it happen, Kash?"

"Ask Vince," he said coldly.

They were back to that again. "He says the same thing of
you."

Kash looked thoughtful. "Does he? He'd like to find out
how much I know. Did he ask you to question me?"

She was on the verge of denying it. "Yes," she admitted. If
she had held back the truth, Kash would have suspected, and his
trust in her would have suffered.

"You can tell him to come to me about it."

"Then, if you won't discuss it, I'll ask Mckib how Seth's
death happened. He'll explain the truth."

He didn't deny Mckibber would know, nor request that she
refrain from asking him, and they drove in silence for a few uncomfortable minutes.

As far north and south as she could see, there was little except thornbush, grasses, and heat. Then Kash slowed the Land
Rover and consulted a map.

She couldn't resist. "Don't tell me the best safari guide in
East Africa has lost his way?"

He smiled. "No, I need to confirm visual checkpoints." He
drove on over mostly flat grass savanna and past occasional
stands of sparse flat-topped trees and bushes, then the Land
Rover crested a small ridge. Spread before their eyes was one of
the last watering holes of the dry season, which hundreds and
even thousands of animals would visit before the rains replen-
ished the reserve.

Herds of wildebeest grazed on the dry grasses of the now
dusty riverbed where there was blue water in the wet season. The
African sky was stacked with brilliant white puffs, and as the sun
was getting low, they glowed flamingo pink.

Sable stirred with excitement and snatched up her field

glasses. A herd of giraffes was approaching. In tune with her mood, Kash cut the engine, and they watched and listened. A jackal wailed with a quavering voice, and from far away the bellow of a lion rolled in, fierce and authoritative. A lone kestrel hovered, its wings silhouetted against the evening sky.

Grunts and snorts sounded from a herd of at least three thousand springbok, small gazelles with horns a foot long that turned inward at the tips. Their faces were boldly painted with a white-and-black bar running from their mouths to their eyes, and also along the crest of their back to the tip of their mulelike tails.

A black-backed jackal with a sly, foxy face and a saddle of black hair over his back trotted between the thornbushes on a hunt.

Their hoofbeats, thousands of them, shuddered the afternoon. The herd was charging alongside the water hole. Sable saw the reason why—a pride of female lions with the male standing off in the bush. Working as a team, the young lions had already decided on the yearling that would become food for their young. The lioness bounded in a powerful sprint after the springbok, which zigzagged sharply but was met by the second lioness in the hunting party. The dust flew. . . .

Sable lowered her field glasses, not wishing to see more.

Kash reached over and took her hand, offering a tender squeeze, and she felt the empathy he shared with her.

Death, blood, and suffering—the result of Adam's sin on all of God's creation—was clearly on display in Africa. She thought of the verse in Romans: *"For we know that the whole creation groans and labors with birth pangs together until now."*

A moment later, Sable looked at Kash cautiously and decided it was time to face the matter of Dunsmoor shipping head on.

"Gran told me about my grandfather . . . and the Hallet property after the Mau Mau Emergency."

He looked off toward the water hole.

"I talked to Gran last night about Dunsmoor shipping," Sable said.

"Yes, I know. She told me on the phone this morning. Looks

like we have a business deal to talk over, doesn't it?"

"I suppose I should apologize for my grandfather."

"No need. He made his own decisions long before either of us were here. Zenobia, too, had nothing to do with it."

"You're angry with us. I don't blame you."

"I'm not angry at the Dunsmoors, but at your grandfather's audacity. The early colonizers thought they were a law unto themselves. His decision to use the wealth that wasn't his permanently affected my life and Seth's. We were two penniless orphans, and things could have gone differently for us if our mother had known about the gold her father had found in Melbourne. Instead, she considered herself a pauper and married my father—a good man in his own way, I'm told by Mckib, and her cousin, but an embarrassingly uneducated Englishman and penniless."

Sable wondered if Mara had actually been in love with Thomas Hallet from South Africa, a young man who had been disowned by his family. Mckibber had mentioned to her once that Thomas had been a wanderer who couldn't keep a job because of his drinking, which ended in fights and petty thefts.

"And if she hadn't gone with him that day to South Africa to try to reconcile with his parents in the hope of moving in with them—she wouldn't have gone down on that plane. . . ."

Kash didn't finish. She knew what he meant. If his mother hadn't left Kenyatta with Tom, she wouldn't have died with him. And if Grandfather Dunsmoor hadn't helped himself to the gold, there would have been no need for them to leave. His parents would be alive. His mother would have married a better man, and the gold would be invested wisely in the Hallet name. Yes, everything could have been so different.

"One man's deed can affect an entire generation," he said thoughtfully. "I never understood how Adam's sin could affect the entire human race," he stated, "but I do now. Our actions become links in a chain that can reach down to our great-grandchildren and create the environment that they're born into."

"But there is victory in Christ, Kash. We're not bound to stay in the environment created by parents and grandparents," she countered. "We make our own individual decisions. We can get out. We can change things."

"Sometimes we can. Other times the chains that bind are too strong to break."

"But Christ can break those chains!"

He looked at her, the warm blue of his eyes deepening. "Yes, I know He *can*. But our circumstances are still affected by decisions made in the past by others."

"And so you're angry with my grandfather."

Sable could have pressed the point that God was in control and that we could trust in His good plans for us when we did not understand, but she feared she might come on too strongly. They had already tangled on that point before they'd broken up years earlier.

"I've thought," he said, watching her, "that matters between us would have turned out better if I hadn't been the son of an uneducated short-term overseer working on Kenyatta for your father."

She pulled off her sunglasses and turned in the hot leather seat to confront him, her voice shaking with emotion. "I never once mentioned what I wanted you to be or expected of you."

"You didn't need to spell it out. It was plain whenever we were alone."

"You're wrong, Kash, about me, and what I expected of you. I never wanted more than what you dreamed about—managing the land, the wildlife. If I wanted more it was your commitment to *me*, to the Lord, to Kenyatta. It was *you* who refused, who walked away from everything."

"Not everything."

The old pain came back, gnawing at her. "If you're as wrong about Vince as you are about me and what I expected of you—"

"Let's not discuss him now, shall we? You asked about the shipping, whether I was angry or not. If my resentment would serve any worthy purpose, I could be angry with the entire lot of you, but there's only one man responsible—your grandfather. And even he had conscience enough in the end to see that the truth of what he'd done was made known, including a confession in his legal papers."

"You insist you're not bitter, but you are. Look at you—you're a walking storm, just ready to break."

"You mistake frustration for bitterness. When I think of how it could have been growing up on Kenyatta and what it was actually like, I don't want to think about it for long."

"Was it so bad? You worked for my father. Was he a tyrant? He thought well of you and Seth. You were the sons he never had and always wanted."

"You don't understand. I wanted you when we were young, but I had nothing! I had no self-esteem to claim you."

Sable gave a giddy laugh that bordered on tears. "That's laughable."

"Don't laugh," Kash gritted, reaching for her arm.

"I'd never do that—but *you?*—no self-esteem? It's absurd. Kash Hallet! Fatally good-looking, capable, strong, talented—why every girl in church wanted you. And you say you didn't have anything to offer."

All I ever wanted was you, she wanted to say, but how could she say it now when everything came too late?

"If I'd known Dunsmoor shipping was built on Hallet money, it would have made all the difference where you were concerned."

"Well, it's all yours now," she said quietly. "The entire business in Mombasa, if you want it. You can overwrite the name *DUNSMOOR* with the bold black letters of *HALLET!*"

"So Zenobia explained that I want to buy you out?"

"She told me."

He watched her. "Are you interested?"

"No," she admitted dully. "I'm not."

"I won't be partners with Vince."

"You're not."

"You mean, not yet."

"Please leave him out of this."

"How can I?"

She drew in a breath. "You make things very difficult for me."

"I'm sorry, that's not my intention. So you're not willing to sell out to me?"

"Not exactly . . . but I am willing to sell you some shares I own. Gran says you have money now from your business in South Africa."

"Maybe. How much do you want?"

She glanced at him from under her hat. "Twenty thousand dollars."

He scanned her thoughtfully. "Why? Do you need a new Paris hat?"

She smiled ruefully. "I want to pay for those two wells before we leave for Samburu. Mckibber could bring me into Nairobi before the wildlife conference to talk with a construction company to have the wells built."

He was thoughtful. "Why not ask Vince to return the original twenty grand?"

"You're so sure he's guilty."

"Yes."

"Are you willing to buy some shares or not?"

"Depends. I already told Zenobia I wanted to buy you out completely—unless you wake up in the morning a wiser young woman than when you arrived. Like I said, I've no intention of becoming a shipping partner with Vince."

"Buying out the Dunsmoors will bring you personal satisfaction, is that it?"

He drew his hand back and leaned against the door, watching her moodily. "Not when it means taking it from the one Dunsmoor I care about."

"You're impossible, Kash. When I wanted you to say that, you refused and went away. Now when I'm older and expected to marry Vince you—"

"I never walked away from you. I made that much clear on the road. I wrote you in Toronto. Had you answered, had you made the slightest overture that you wanted to give us another chance, I'd have come."

"I told you, I never received a letter. As far as I know, you never wrote it."

"Except I've told you twice I did, and that Vince found the letter and destroyed it."

Sable looked at him, but his gaze was as mysterious as ever. "I don't understand you," she whispered. "And I once thought I knew you so well, but in reality I didn't know you at all. You had emotional hurts I didn't see and probably wouldn't have understood if you'd explained them to me. Maybe all I was capable of seeing was my own needs, and that they weren't being met. I wanted you to—" She stopped and looked away.

"Love you?" he asked softly. "I did. But at the same time, I couldn't handle how I felt. I thought you rejected the core of what and who I was. I knew I couldn't meet your expectations."

Rejected him? She stared at him, her sense straining against what she believed to be absurd. How could he suggest it?

"You wanted to make me into a Vince Adler," Kash went on.

"That's ridiculous."

"Is it?"

"Yes, positively!"

He leaned toward her. "Then answer me—when you left for Toronto with your mother and Vince, what did you insist I do?"

She masked a wince and shook her head. "I don't remember."

"Shall I refresh your memory?"

"No."

"I will anyway. We discussed getting married, remember?"

Of course she remembered. She ran her restless fingers through her hair.

"If you meant it, I said, we'll get married now in Nairobi. Seth, Mckib, and I were going to start our own safari business, remember? Shall I tell you what you said?"

"Stop it. I don't want to go on like this."

"You told me it wouldn't do."

"I never said that, never."

"In so many words you did. By insisting we wait until your

family made all the plans. I would live at the lodge in Kenyatta, my job would be with your father, even the ring would be supplied, since I couldn't afford anything appropriate for the grand wedding."

Sable closed her eyes, trying to shut out all of her foolish mistakes. "You misunderstood me. I only wanted to help you, to help both of us."

"I wanted you, Sable, but not your family running our life, or our marriage, providing you the things I couldn't afford. There would be no house except the one I provided, no promotion with the Kenyan government unless I earned it. If Nairobi wasn't good enough, and a safari business with Seth and Mckib—then your love wasn't love at all."

She blinked back the tears so he wouldn't see them. "That's not how I felt, but I'm sorry I hurt you. I didn't understand. Why go on like this? I've changed—we both have. The past is over. We'd both be wiser if we'd let our yesterdays remain buried."

He was silent. The wind stirred the serengeti grass. Somewhere a lion roared.

"Is that the way you want it?" he asked.

"Yes."

Her gaze came reluctantly to his, but she didn't find agreement in his eyes to let things lie buried as she suggested.

"Some of it perhaps, but not all. I told you this morning I was going to learn the truth about Adler and his work. And if you insist on standing with him to protect him, you'll end up getting hurt again."

"And all this is on your terms, of course," she rushed.

"Where Adler is concerned, yes. The game will be played my way."

"What 'game'?" Sable challenged, frustrated. "What do you expect to prove? That he actually killed Seth? You don't think *that*. You couldn't!"

"Not quite as dramatically as you suggest. He was involved in his death, perhaps unwittingly, but partially responsible just the same."

"Then you still insist he's selling ivory and horns and skins on the black market."

"Yes. I told you, to a Far Eastern cartel working out of Indonesia and Taiwan. Seth found out about it by accident while working for a new hunting organization in Tanga. He called me at Nairobi and told me what he'd stumbled upon. Smith and Browning was a cover for a bunch of poachers."

"But you work for them now, like Seth did."

"They don't know who I am. Actually, I'm working for the Kenyan government, but that's between me and you. Even Mckib doesn't know. When Seth called me, he was working with them in Namanga. He told me he was going to stop a kill. I asked him to wait until I could get help out to him, but by the time I arrived with a few rangers, they'd already pulled out. We tracked them into the Lake Manyara region. But they must have found out something because they arranged his death with a rhino. They moved in—and left him to face the charge alone."

Sable was trembling. "It's horrible. What if they know Seth made that call to you?"

"They don't. And they're not very smart, just good shots," Kash said with restrained disgust. "And sometimes they're not even that."

She remembered how Moffet had suffered. "But even if all this is true, what part could Vince have played? He's not a hunter. I've seen him—he can't even handle a rifle well."

"He doesn't need to; he can hire poachers. And you're forgetting what I already told you about his cause at Lake Rudolf. He needs money to help Dr. Willard."

She stared at him, her heart beating uneasily as she thought of the twenty thousand dollars that were missing. Every part of her rebelled against the idea.

As though understanding her struggle, he said, "Seth's death wasn't planned by Adler. Seth simply got in the way of the program. But that doesn't change the fact."

The intense conviction in his gaze, restrained yet passionate, convinced her that there was more to his allegations than dislike or jealousy.

"I wish I knew more about this work at Lake Rudolf," she said.

"It's the main reason I'm going to Samburu." He reached over and squeezed her shoulder. "You can help me, Sable, if you'd stop believing in Dr. Adler."

She lowered her head, toying uneasily with the field glasses in her lap. "Is that why you've changed your mind about bringing me there?"

He slowly drew his hand away and leaned back, playing with the steering wheel. "Yes."

She tried not to think that she was disappointed. She had wanted him to believe in her work, to believe in *her*. But wasn't that what he was also asking? That she believe in him and what he was trying to accomplish?

"I . . . I don't know if I can turn against Vince. But what is it you want me to do?"

"Simply going to Samburu is enough. Adler wants you to go as well. I told you yesterday that he expects your father to make contact with you if you come. That's what Vince wants. To locate your father."

"Why? He mentioned the need last night after you brought Patches."

"For the very reason you just mentioned—elephants."

Sable shook her head. "I don't understand."

"You will if I'm right. I can explain more after I hear his lecture at the wildlife conference. In the meantime, if you won't believe everything I say, at least be careful about what you tell Vince."

"But he already knows you think he's to blame about Seth. And if he learns you're the guide to bring us to Samburu. . . ?"

"It's a chance he must take. There's not a man in Nairobi who would risk the job for the kind of money the organization can pay. Even if there were, I've made certain no one will respond; so has Mckib. He's friendly with the safari businesses. He worked with most of their fathers."

"If you need me to bring my father out of the wilderness—

and Vince does, too—why did you try so hard at first to keep me from going?"

Kash's eyes narrowed under his dark lashes. "Don't you know by now?" He reached a hand behind her neck and gently eased her face toward his. "I'm protective about what matters to me. I didn't want to place you at risk or see you emotionally hurt."

Sable almost allowed herself to sink into the warm smothering tide drawing her, but she turned her head and leaned away. She wouldn't look at him, and the question he'd asked was charged with explosives. She didn't want Kash to know that she'd already delayed the engagement, and she wasn't ready to answer him yet.

Without a word of argument he flicked the keys in the ignition, and the Land Rover pulled away from the freckled shade and across a long stretch of open country sparsely populated with candelabrum trees, thornbushes, and thickets of wild olive.

"Isn't there any road?" she asked.

He smiled, amused. "Even if there were, you wouldn't notice much difference from the open plain."

⌒⫘⊙

The herds had quieted down after the lion hunt and were again grazing in a line stretching across the path of the Land Rover. Driving no more than three miles an hour and stopping when the animals began to show alarm, Kash drove near the water hole.

Clumps of acacia and ziziphus trees looked like small round islands in the river of dried grasses. Farther away, giraffes browsed on the leaves of taller trees. Sable knew that the large concentration of herd animals meant that predators were in the area: leopards, lions, and spotted hyenas.

Sable laughed at a giraffe that did the splits to drink from the water hole, but for the giraffe it was a grave matter. In such a position they were vulnerable to predators, but none were nearby.

They drove inland from the water hole, and after another five or six rugged miles of bouncing in the seat, she saw that they were nearing the Maasai manyatta.

"Dean's here," he said.

Sable followed his gaze and saw the dusty airplane parked in the flat grass savanna.

Kash drove near the encampment but, out of respect, parked well outside the grounds of the manyatta near the plane.

"You never explained what he's doing," she said.

"He's engaged in some evangelism of his own," he said casually, cutting the motor, "but without progress. There's one Maasai evangelist who's teamed up with him to reach the different manyattas. That film of yours just might hold the answer."

She swallowed the amazement she felt over hearing Kash speaking so casually and knowledgeably about evangelizing the Maasai.

He smiled and stepped out. "I'll do what I can to get permission for the film."

She started to get out, but he stopped her. "Better wait until I see Dean. We'll need to speak with the warrior chief first."

As she watched him enter the circle of low huts, she found herself reliving an experience she'd had at age fourteen, when she and her mother, Kate, Kash, and Seth had driven to the border of Tanzania to visit another Maasai encampment, with Mckibber driving the vehicle. She wondered if Kash remembered. On that trip Julia had taught them about the tribe before they arrived, although Kash's knowledge had probably been equal with her mother's, since he and Seth were friendly with a group of young warriors in training at the manyatta.

Sable had been surprised to learn that the basic diet of the Maasai consisted of milk. Kash had added a detail her mother did not:

"They also drink blood in times of drought and food shortage. They draw it directly from the cattle and mix it with the milk. The cattle are rarely killed except on important ceremonial occasions. And sometimes groups of warriors called 'moran' are allowed to drive a fat cow from their father's herd off into the bush to a temporary shelter. Here the cow is killed, and the moran gorge themselves with meat, probably thinking it will make their bodies strong."

While Kash and Seth had brought their uncle Mckibber to visit the warriors, Sable and Kate had stayed with their mother to watch the Maasai woman milk the cows directly into gourds.

"Look," Sable had whispered to Kate, "she's putting smoldering sticks into the gourds."

"They're wild olive branches," explained Julia. "It gives the milk a flavor all its own."

As their mother looked on, Sable and Kate cautiously tasted the Maasai milk.

"It has a smoky olive flavor," said Sable, refusing to wince, although it was strong tasting and upsetting to stomachs not used to the flavor. Julia had assured them that to the Maasai palate it was a delight.

Now as Sable thought of Kash gaining permission from the Maasai warrior chief to show the film, she tried to quiet her beating heart in more ways than one. She prayed that it would be granted and that the rebuilding of her relationship with Kash would not come shattering apart in a disappointing emotional letdown. It was difficult to leave her heart's desires to the Lord, for they wanted to insist on their own way.

Please, Father God, bless this opportunity at the manyatta with the Maasai. . . .

But the request seemed to lodge like a lump in her heart, pounding with concerns and needs of her own. She couldn't stop her mind from honing in on her own desires and needs, like bumblebees landing on bright yellow flowers thick with pollen—

Father, I don't want to be hurt again. . . .

She closed her eyes, which were smarting from the hours of strong sunlight, heat, and dust, and let the salty tears wash them clean. *If only I could wash my heart clean.* As the silent tears dropped and made a stain on her once clean sundress, her anxious mind quieted enough for God's Spirit to bring to her memory a Scripture verse from the book of Matthew: *"Seek first the kingdom of God and His righteousness, and all these things shall be added to you."*

"Things," she thought, *is the all-encompassing word describing what can become my distraction. I must first seek His kingdom—that is the key. Only then will I find the very best in life to enjoy.*

In an act of her will, choosing to obey, Sable opened the Land Rover door and got out, feeling the dust and heat rise to her feet and ankles, and spoke aloud, "I claim this Maasai manyatta for you, Lord. I give myself first to your heart's desire—the precious souls of the Maasai."

And suddenly—as if in mockery and opposition—she felt a painful bite, not just one, but a score. She cried out, looking down at her sandaled feet. . . .

She was standing on a moving brown trail some four inches wide. Giant safari ants! She screamed hysterically, running from the track and trying to knock them off as they bit painfully.

"Sable?" Kash came running, followed by a young European man and several tall Maasai warriors carrying spears and wrapped in blankets, but she hardly noticed as Kash knocked the large brown ants from her legs, then carried her toward the manyatta.

A babble of voices resounded about her, but the hot swelling was now so painful she couldn't concentrate on understanding the Swahili. Kash was speaking to the Maasai, standing with her in the center of a large compound encircled with bomas—four-foot-high huts built of pliable green branches plastered with a mixture of hardened mud and cow dung.

The next thing she knew, she was being carried into one of the huts, through a small entrance room where animals were kept. Dean threw a blanket over some straw, and Kash stooped and laid her there. A calf was penned next to her, and she heard it moving around. The boma had no windows or chimneys and was incredibly dark and smoke filled in order to repel the flies that swarmed in vast numbers around the cattle.

"I've a medical kit in the Cessna," she heard Dean telling Kash.

As he started out, Kash called, "See if you can dig up a light."

"I'm . . . I'm all right now," said Sable, trying to sit up, her teeth chattering despite the stifling heat. The strong smells assaulted her nostrils, and she sneezed.

"Didn't I tell you to wear safari clothes and boots?" gritted Kash.

"You sound like my father."

"I assure you I'm not. Lie down. We'll soon get some medicated ointment on those bites."

"I don't want any fleas and ticks," she whispered so her voice wouldn't carry.

"You can just lie there and scratch. It's better than standing in the center of a line of safari ants. How're your legs?"

"Swollen and painful, if you must know, and stinging horribly."

"And we're twenty grueling miles from Kate, and eight more from the lodge! Not very good timing."

"If you cared at all you wouldn't make me feel worse by sounding so critical."

"I'm sorry," Kash said softly. "Thirsty?"

She smiled ruefully. "Can you get me an ice-cold Coke over ice?"

"How does lukewarm boiled milk sound?"

Sable moaned and scratched a flea bite. "I'm ready to go home now. . . ."

"Ah yes, the daring, rugged missionary, who's anxious to trek into Samburu with far worse conditions, is now ready to fly home to Canada."

"Last Christmas I went skiing . . . the snow was wonderful. Can you ski?"

"No, I carry revolvers and drive dusty Land Rovers over drought-stricken East Africa. But I have climbed the snow and ice of Kebo," he said of Kilimanjaro's highest peak.

"I didn't know how to ski, either. I wonder if you'd like it."

"I might, if you were there. Was 'dear' Dr. Adler there to keep you company?"

"No . . . I was all alone, mourning Mother's death and thinking—" She stopped. *Of you*, she could have said. "But I wish Vince were here now!" She winced, touching her swollen legs and imagining the hideous sight they must be, all red and inflamed.

"Cheer up. I can apply ointment as well as he can."

"No one is applying anything, thank you. I can do it myself. Dean's back. . . ."

A lantern was lit, and Sable grimaced at the sight of her ankles.

"This will help," said Kash, handing her a tube of ointment and uncorking a bottle of pills. He handed her one with the canteen of water.

"What is it?" she asked.

"Just swallow it and ask questions tomorrow."

"Tomorrow!"

"We can't very well drive thirty miles at night. The sun's about to set, and it'll be black out there on the Serengeti. Dean and I are staying in here with you, so no need to worry." He turned to Dean, a stocky, muscular blonde around twenty-seven, in Levi's and a dusty black shirt.

"What can you dig up to eat?" asked Kash.

"Boiled milk."

Kate would like him, Sable found herself thinking as the two men stepped outside while she applied the ointment. Minutes later she lay down and surrendered to the provender. At least the blanket had come from Dean's plane.

She listened to Kash and Dean talking in low voices outside the room. In the sweltering heat she felt her brain buzzing—or was it a mosquito? She looked over at the liquid-eyed calf in its pen staring at her, then as the buzzing grew louder, she found her brain growing heavier until her eyes shut wearily. *I'm sorry . . . Lord . . . I didn't mean to complain. . . . Thank you for the Maasai, for this nice boma, the bed, the boiled milk. . . .*

It was late, but how late she didn't know. She raised herself to an elbow, listening to Maasai voices outside the boma. Something was going on. She struggled to her feet and examined the swelling in her ankles. The lantern was still glowing, and she looked about for Kash and Dean. Dean was in the next room, and Kash was on the other side of the pen where the calf was kept. He was still awake and must have heard the Maasai voices outside at the same time she did, for he pushed himself up from the dirt floor and came around the pen.

"What is it?" she whispered. "What do you think they want?"

By now Dean, too, had come awake and followed Kash outdoors. Sable tried to distinguish the voices and caught snatches of words. . . .

"Warrior dances?" she whispered to herself, heart pounding.

Dean came back inside, smiling at her. "It's midnight, and they've invited us out to learn some of the Maasai warrior dances and to take part in jumping contests."

A rare experience! "I'm coming," she told him. "Give me time to put my boots on."

Kash stood in the doorway as she was digging into her bag for her safari clothes. "You'll never get those boots on now."

"The swelling's gone down. I've got to come, Kash! I remember when you and Seth told me about the dances."

"Kash got the warrior chief to agree to the film showing next week," Dean said, offering his hand to help her up. "I guess you know how rare a privilege it is to have permission to come back and show the film in a warrior's initiation camp."

Sable smiled with delight and looked at Kash. "All we need is for Mckib to show up tomorrow with the equipment."

"Not much chance of that, but you've got your open door," said Kash.

Her eyes sought his. "Thanks to you," she said quietly.

He swooped her up into his arms. "Any woman brave enough to get those boots on deserves to be carried in style."

Eleven

Sable sat between Kash and Dean, watching the Maasai warriors parade out like ebony giants. More dry brush was cast onto the flames. While the white moon enveloped Mount Kilimanjaro, the Maasai warriors began their ancient dance, their spears held straight up toward the black sky. The firelight illuminated their extremely tall and lean bodies garbed in what looked to Sable like red tablecloths. With their black hair intricately woven and adorned and their faces painted with red ocher, they wore fixed grave expressions, gripping the long spears that were as famous as the moran themselves.

They stepped out with a deep guttural voice in unison: "*N-ga-AY!*"

Then, one by one, they began the long, leaping Maasai trot used in war and cattle raids that once brought them three hundred miles or more running over the plains.

At the spectacle, Sable stiffened with a chill. Kash leaned toward her, taking her hand. "The Maasai have legs that can run forever. There's a saying: No one can outrun a Maasai."

She watched, transfixed. One by one, the warriors leaped straight up—the highest jumps she'd ever seen—then came down landing lightly, firm and flat on their feet, not a muscle twitching. "*UM-ba-AY-uh!*" came the deep male voice, almost a hum blending with the rhythm of a few drums. Then two stepped out together, spears glinting. Their chins shot out with grave dignity; they arose tall, then shot up, coming down again and stamping the dusty ground with the right foot. Then all the warriors in the main body began to jump straight up and down, and on each leap the spears twirled. The chant grew heavy, low, and repetitive: "*AH-yea-AH-y! AH-yea-AH-y!*"

The dance grew more complex. Their entranced faces, painted with ocher, glistened with sweat. They formed circles and then circles within circles, continuing to leap so high off the ground that Sable caught her breath. The metal on their forearms gleamed in the light; the beads clicked with the rhythm of their voices. Sable felt fear, exaltation, and the underlying sense of mournful loss.

As she sat with Kash and Dean near the fire, watching the dance unfold before them, Sable thought about the noble Maasai people she had grown to care about so deeply. She remembered the stories her mother had often told her—of their history and customs. A semi-nomadic people who depended exclusively on their cattle, the Maasai believed that all cattle on Earth belonged to them, and it was their right to take them from others. It amazed Sable that for the most part predators seemed to bypass the Maasai cattle, as though they knew their own preservation depended on cooperation.

She had always been impressed with the Maasai because they did not kill wild animals for any purpose except to protect their cattle or their people and for a few ceremonies. The one exception was the lion, which they used to kill in order to prove their bravery, but the practice was now forbidden by the government. Sable had learned from her father that, because of the great respect the Maasai showed for wildlife, many of the best parks and reserves in Kenya and northern Tanzania were located either within Maasai country or on their borders.

"There's no doubt the Maasai are an especially attractive and interesting tribe," her mother had said. "In colonial times the Europeans had a saying that they had 'caught a disease called Maasaitis,' meaning only that they had become fond of the tribe. They are a dignified people who are courteous and friendly to those who treat them on equal terms. But however much we respect another people's culture, never think it is sufficient in itself to save them. The Lord tells us not to forget how lost any people are without Him. Since we admire the Maasai from afar, we must also come close to their hearts with the Light. The Maasai are open to the gospel," she had said, "but they reject our Western ways."

Her mother had taught her that the Maasai's present importance was as nothing compared to their former glory. Perhaps four hundred years ago they had pushed south from the Lake Rudolf area and by 1850 had established their rule over all the open country in what is now known as central and southern Kenya and northern Tanzania. For fear of them, the slave traders avoided the Maasai, and they were never captured or sold.

"Most other tribes lived in fear of the very tall and exceptionally fast-running Maasai warrior," her mother had told her. "The other tribes confined themselves to the forests, where the Maasai fighting tactics were less effective."

The extent of past Maasai rulership was clear to Sable by the place names they left behind in East Africa, even in areas where they no longer lived. Nairobi itself was a Maasai word. It was taken from the expression "*ngare nairobi*," meaning "cold water," and probably referred to the Nairobi River.

As if reading her thoughts, Kash leaned over and said quietly to Sable, "It's important you understand them if you would share the message of Christ."

She looked at him in the flickering firelight and carefully listened to his explanation, amazed at his concern for the souls of the Maasai and how she should approach them. Dean smiled his encouragement as Kash went on.

"They're a democratic group with no actual source of hereditary temporal power, but there are certain men called 'laibon,' believed to have supernatural powers, who advise when a particular action is needed to be carried out. In the old days, Europeans would call them witch doctors, but the Maasai found this insulting. Showing respect is the key to gaining their audience.

"All Maasai males pass through three main stages," Kash told her. "First he's a boy, then a moran—a warrior—then an elder. Boys are circumcised between the ages of fourteen and eighteen—the actual time for each generation is decided by the laibon. The older half of a circumcised group is known as the 'Right Hand.' On reaching warrior status they used to become the front-line troops. The younger half is the 'Left Hand.' They used to form the reserve. Today the warriors are forbidden to attack other African tribes or to kill lions—but it still occurs in secret. In an effort to dampen their warlike nature, the black, white, and red buffalo-hide shields have been taken away from them by the Kenyan government—probably more out of fear than reason, although they still carry their spears as a defense against wild animals."

As the campfire crackled, Kash, Dean, and Sable envisioned the early days when stately files of Maasai raiders in black ostrich plumes and lion headdresses, spear points gleaming, crossed the plains with confidence. Kash continued to explain: "On the morning of the circumcision ceremony each boy goes out very early and lies on the open ground in order to become cold. Cold water is also poured over him. While the operation is being carried out, the candidate must not flinch or cry out or he will become an object of ridicule. Immediately after the operation he remains in his mother's hut for four days, and on emerging for the first time he wears female clothing.

"Once the wounds have initially healed, all the circumcised boys blacken their bodies with charcoal and make a white pattern in chalk on their faces. Two ostrich feathers form a headdress, and the boys roam the countryside in a group. They shoot birds with bows and arrows and mount the feathers on a wooden frame to make their own headdress. They also shoot blunt arrows at girls of their choice. Gradually during this period their hair is allowed to grow, until it is sufficiently long to do up into plaits and weave the characteristic elaborate styles. At this point the young men become full moran and remain so for about eight years.

"Today, the moran have no duties apart from defending their people and cattle against enemies and wild animals. In the past, on suitable occasions, they sometimes took the offensive.

They were a formidable standing army that was responsible for the military dominance of this tribe, but now the role of the moran has lost much of its significance.

"During their period of warriorhood the moran live in a manyatta, like this one. Each moran takes with him some of his father's cattle and a senior female relative to look after him. After seven or eight years as warriors, the moran have their heads shaved and are allowed to settle down, marry, and take their place as elders of the tribe. At this time two are elected from the group to act as the leaders and representatives of their generation."

Sable continued to listen to Kash and watch the dancers, until her head began to nod against his shoulder and the sounds of the night blended with her dreams. She felt Kash's strong arms lift her and carry her away from the fire into the darkness. . . .

The next morning Sable awoke feeling miserable from a reaction to the safari ant bites. Kash had already spoken to Dean about flying her back to the relief camp, where Kate could better treat her, but Sable wanted to stay at the manyatta until Mckibber arrived with the film and equipment.

"That could be a few days," said Kash. "You need treatment now. There's little else I can do with this medical kit."

Disappointed, she finally gave up and allowed him to bring her out of the manyatta to where the Cessna was tied down.

Dean was walking around the plane, apparently checking everything on the outside, while Kash helped her into the passenger seat.

"I'll wait for Mckib," said Kash once she was seated.

Dean then climbed into the pilot's seat and began methodically going through a checklist while turning all sorts of knobs and levers. After checking to see if her seat belt was secure, he pulled the starter switch. The propeller turned slowly at first, then the engine sprang to life. He checked instruments and controls, then taxied to the end of a clear area and applied full power. The small plane gained speed on the rough surface until her seat tilted back and the ground fell away.

The plane banked twice, and Sable looked out the side window at the figure of Kash becoming smaller as he stood near the Land Rover.

I can't help it, she thought, swallowing the lump in her throat. *I'm still in love with you.*

⌘

Dr. Vince Adler was waiting with Kate at camp when Dean landed the plane on a flat strip some distance from the tents. As Sable managed to get out of the seat and step down to the ground by herself, Vince and Kate came hurrying toward her. Kate was composed but became concerned when she noticed Sable was walking very carefully. Vince wore a thundering brow, the wind tossing his thick dark hair.

"Nice of you to return," he stated curtly. "I've worried ever since Kate explained where you'd gone with Kash Hallet."

Sable refused to feel guilty or to allow his searching look to place her on the defensive.

"I was in perfectly good hands. Kash is one of the finest safari guides and hunters in East Africa." Then she added, thinking it a rare opportunity to begin to prepare the soil of his mind, "We could use a guide like him and his uncle to bring us to Samburu. Did you find anyone in Nairobi?"

"No," came his toneless voice. "I'd almost think a vendetta was out against my hiring anyone."

Sable masked her expression, remembering what Kash had said. She turned to Kate, explaining the thrilling news about receiving permission to show the *JESUS* film at the manyatta. "But I had a reaction to some ant bites, and Kash decided I should come back."

"He was right," said Kate. "That can be serious. I'll need to get you to the medical tent and find out what happened. By the way, Mckib stopped by. He had the film equipment and was

• 158 •

on his way back out to the manyatta. Too bad you couldn't stay there and be a part of it, Sable, but you'll have more opportunities in the NFD."

"It's disappointing," admitted Sable, "but Kash and Mckib will see it through, and Dean is returning to help now." Sable turned and introduced him to her sister. "Dean's an MAF pilot and a good friend of Kash. Dean, this is Kate Dunsmoor, my brilliant and dedicated sister, a nurse with the family-owned mission begun by our mother."

Sable noticed that both Dean and Kate appeared a little shy as they exchanged pleasantries and decided it was a good sign.

"You're working out of Nairobi?" asked Kate.

"I'm flying in and out all the time. It's funny I haven't met you before. I come by here at least once a month. I'm flying in supplies for the relief workers on Tanzania's border with Rwanda."

As Dean and Kate continued their conversation, Vince appeared impatient with the entire situation and took Sable's arm. "Can you walk? We'd better get you into the Lab." He always called the medical tent the "Lab," and Sable walked with him across the field, settling her hat to keep the sun's hot rays from her face.

She had expected Vince to make more of her trip with Kash to the Maasai manyatta, but he was silent as they waited for Kate to come and prepare an injection.

"You'll feel better tomorrow," he assured her. "We'll talk then."

Later, when she went to Kate's tent to bathe and tumble into bed, she wondered about Vince. If she had thought Kash could be unknowable, she was learning that Dr. Adler could be a stranger. And to think she had come to Kenya to seriously consider becoming his fiancee. What had ever possessed her? But it was only being fair to herself to also say that in Nairobi and Toronto, when she was under the duress of her mother's prolonged suffering, he had portrayed himself a much different man during that time.

Still, I didn't see him under enough different circumstances to really learn what he can be like when displeased by my actions, she told herself. For one, Kash had not been present to throw confusion into their relationship. Nor had she done anything to disappoint or try him. But things were different now. She was acting independently of Vince, and he didn't like it. And he certainly disapproved of Kash Hallet.

As Sable fell asleep she prayed, thanking the Lord for her difficulties. Her recent trials and troubles and her encounters with Kash had shed new light on Dr. Vince Adler. Had those trials not come she might have learned too late.

Thank you for your faithfulness to me, Father. I've so much to learn about waiting on you.

⟲∭⟳

The next morning, expecting a difficult time with Vince, Sable was surprised when Kate came to the tent bringing coffee and telling her that he'd driven back to the lodge without her. "I'd say he's rather displeased with you," said Kate, handing her the cup.

Sable sighed. "Did he say why he went back to the lodge?"

"The wildlife conference starts on Monday, and he needs to work on his speech. He's taking Dad's place. The conservationists are already arriving."

"Then I've got to get back to the lodge, too. Are you attending? It will do you good to get away from here awhile."

"Yes, and so are Dean and Kash. They're due in this afternoon. I can't wait to hear how the film showing went."

Sable watched her over her cup. "What do you think of the MAF pilot?"

"Oh, I thought he was very amiable."

"Amiable! Is that all you can say about Dean?"

Kate laughed. "You don't expect me to say I'm already falling for him?"

Sable was grave. "After my mistake in nearly becoming engaged to Vince? *No!* I'm glad the thunder and lightning haven't hit you so quickly. I've known Vince for over two years, and I'm just seeing him as he really is for the first time."

"I'm not so sure. If you want my opinion, I always thought he was brittle, the kind that feels so intensely about things that he'll go off the deep end if they don't work out or if something ruins his sand castle."

Sable remembered what Kash said about Vince's commitment to the work at Lake Rudolf.

"You never told me you thought that way."

"I couldn't. You wouldn't have accepted it, but I told the Lord plenty of times and have been praying for you ever since you and Kash broke up."

Sable looked at her and smiled wearily, thinking how blessed she was to have a sister like Kate. "Thanks."

"It may be you're just now able to see with clearer vision," said Kate. "I don't want to sound odd or anything, like a know-it-all, but it seemed you were in a state of denial about Kash and how you still felt about him. It took coming home again and running into him like this to light the candle."

⁂

It was afternoon when Dean flew the Cessna into the camp. Kash and Mckibber had left the manyatta earlier that morning and would soon be arriving by Land Rover and small truck, bringing the film equipment back with them. Dean had flown past them on the way in.

The news of the film showings was more exciting than even Sable had hoped and prayed for. There had been several showings of the film, and afterward a number of Maasai warriors had indicated decisions to receive Jesus Christ as their Savior. A Maasai evangelist friend of Dean's would do the follow-up work of teaching. Dean was already enthusiastically developing plans with him to show the film at other Maasai encampments in northern Tanzania. Learning that Sable had also brought Bibles in Swahili and bicycles for the native missionary evangelists to get around in their work, Dean was anxious to return with her and Kate to the lodge, where Mckibber said these particular supplies had all arrived by truck from Mombasa. The rest of the supplies for Samburu would be arriving the next day.

As Sable thought about her private Christian work in Amboseli Reserve and Kate's short-term medical work here coming to an end, she rejoiced in knowing that the film, the Bibles, and the bicycles would remain, and that the work would be carried on by Dean's evangelist friend and the other native missionary evangelists from the church in Nairobi.

"It's on to Samburu," said Kate, smiling thoughtfully. "Did you tell Vince who our guide will be?"

"Not yet. From the mood he was in, he won't be pleased."

"If he wants to get to the NFD he'll soon change his mind and be thankful Kash is willing to risk it." She walked to the tent entrance and looked about outside. "I'd feel happier about leaving if there was someone to take our place. Folding the tents and slipping away to new horizons doesn't solve the Maasai's problems. They desperately need a permanent medical clinic— and water wells. So many basic health problems could be solved if they had a good water supply."

Sable's mood was sobered by reality. The victories she rejoiced in were worthy of celebration, but they only scratched the surface of spiritual and material needs.

"We are transients sowing seeds of grace," she said, "but the needs are permanent. May the Lord of the harvest bless a hundredfold what was sown."

Kash and Mckibber didn't arrive that afternoon as expected. Dean had already left for his flight back to Nairobi, and evening shadows had fallen. Sable, curious and beginning to worry, had already loaded the vehicle to drive back with Kate to the lodge tomorrow. Then she heard the welcome sound of the Land Rover and a truck approaching the camp. . . . No, several trucks, she thought. Had Vince arranged for the supply trucks to wait here until they were ready to leave for Samburu?

She heard the sound of Kash's boot steps approaching, and

drawing back the insect netting, she stepped out into the twilight.

"Where have you been? I was beginning to worry."

"Nairobi."

He'd gone to check on where the twenty thousand went, she thought uneasily, wanting to know the truth, yet concerned that Kash might use the incident in a personal cause for revenge against Dr. Adler. "I wish you hadn't."

He glanced at her casually as he beat the dust out of his hat. "I've brought you an early Christmas present."

Confused, she looked at him. Christmas present?

He gestured, and Sable looked past his rugged form to where construction trucks from Nairobi were parked nearby, loaded with equipment and men.

"I didn't have the heart to leave you disappointed over the wells. They'll be drilled after all. I thought it would make things easier for you, since you'll need to trust me explicitly for the next several weeks."

Stunned, she caught her breath.

"Oh, Kash . . . what can I say?"

"You don't need to say anything."

"But . . . how can I thank you? You don't understand what this means to me—and Kate. . . ."

"I do. That's why I did it now. But there is something you can do."

Sable's eyes swerved from the Nairobi trucks to meet his gaze. He smiled. "Mckib and I are starving. We haven't eaten since last night. Have you learned how to cook?"

She laughed, tears coming to her eyes, and reached to throw her arms around him tightly. "Come on, I'll empty the kitchen for you!"

As they walked toward the tent where the lanterns glowed and the smell of food and coffee drifted out, Kate was laughing with Mckibber in front of the trucks, talking to the drilling team.

Kash has a tender heart for the Maasai, thought Sable, warmly pleased. She looked at him and smiled, and as she did, her steps slowed until they paused outside the kitchen tent. Her smile faded into a look of longing as his eyes held hers and his hand took warm possession of her arm.

Mckibber's voice rang out, interrupting the moment: "Say now! Can't two hard-working men have a tin of good Kenya coffee?"

Twelve

Sable drove her grandmother's Land Rover from the relief camp in a brighter mood of heart than she'd known for a long time. Kash's unexpected action of returning Patches, followed by the effort he'd made to show the film at the Maasai manyatta and arranging for the wells to be built, had thawed her heart and stirred an abandoned love song.

"Yet, I must be careful," she told herself. "I'm getting emotionally involved."

Kenyatta Lodge came into view with its two giant acacia trees on either side of the driveway, and Sable turned into the yard with Kate following in her jeep piled high with personal boxes and trunks that would next accompany the two sisters north to their father's Samburu-Isiolo camp.

At the sound of the vehicles, Grandmother Zenobia came out the screen door and stood on the wide porch in her bright and loose-fitting red dungarees, her silver-gray hair braided and pinned on top of her head. Her three golden retrievers had come bounding across the yard from behind the lodge, barking their greeting to Sable and Kate, their whiplike tails beating their excitement.

"Down!" cried Sable, laughing as Ginger stood up with both paws gently resting on her arm and breathing hotly in her face. The other two circled and whined about her safari boots, excitedly sniffing the smells of "an adventure" that still clung to her slacks, before moving off with a rush to greet Kate.

"Dr. Adler is here," Zenobia told Sable as she came up the steps.

Sable caught the subdued concern in her grandmother's voice and made a quick search of her unsmiling face, but her clear brown eyes revealed little else.

Was Vince still upset over the excursion she'd made with Kash to the manyatta to show the *JESUS* film? Or was there something else? "Where is he?"

"He's taken to the Treehouse to work on his speech. Why don't you go speak with him? I'll send Jomo over with something cool to drink—unless you'd prefer tea or coffee?"

Sable thought of a confrontation with Vince and hesitated, wondering why her grandmother appeared anxious to have her see him now. Sable turned to look off in the direction of the mini "lodge" built in the giant acacia tree as Kate came up and planted a kiss on Zenobia's cheek.

"If Vince is working on his speech, then the conservationists must be arriving soon," said Kate. "Any word yet from Dad?"

Zenobia sighed and shook her head. "No message, and I don't expect one, even though the conference begins tomorrow morning."

"Dad is bound to wonder whether Sable arrived and if we can get the supplies into Samburu, so it seems he would be contacting us."

Zenobia frowned. "You know Skyler. He's all taken up with the elephants right now. The last Vince heard, your father was off in the wilderness tracking them and doing research—oh! Did you ask Kash about the letter, Sable?"

"Yes, he gave it to me."

Kate turned, surprised. "A letter from Dad? Where is it? What did he say?"

"It's inside my handbag—here," she said, handing over her bag to Kate. "He said Kash would bring us to Samburu, is all." She looked at her grandmother. "Where did the Mombasa trucks leave the supplies?" she asked, concerned for their proper care in the interval. She also wondered where Kash expected to get trucks to haul the goods into the NFD.

"They're out back in storage. Don't worry, dear. I saw to it the truckers were careful when they unloaded the boxes and crates."

Once again Sable was alerted to the note of restrained concern in her grandmother's voice when she stated, "I believe Vince has some news on the trucks and crew bringing the goods north."

Has Kash already been in contact with Vince about the safari? wondered Sable. Something was wrong, but what? She had best go speak to Vince now.

"Count me out," groaned Kate. "The first thing I'm headed for is a long, cool soak in the tub! I'm going to splurge, Sable. Where's your fancy bubble bath?"

Sable smiled. "Look on my dresser . . . I brought you a whole box of luxuries from Revlon. Too bad Dean isn't coming to dinner tonight. . . ."

Kate's eyes flickered. "He was interesting, wasn't he? Who'd ever think I'd meet someone like that out here, committed to showing the film? I thought all the best men were already nabbed."

Sable laughed at her exaggerated interest, and Zenobia pricked up her ears. "What's this? A man? A *single* man?"

"Yes," said Sable in a conspiratorial whisper, "and not only a man but a *Christian* man. Ah! That makes all the difference in East Africa!"

Zenobia widened her eyes and pursed her lips, looking at Kate. "Then I do believe in miracles after all."

Kate, appearing to grow suddenly shy, gestured to Sable. "But it was Kash who arranged the film showing."

"Yes," said Sable rather dreamily. "He did . . . he and Dean are good friends," she explained to the interested Zenobia. "Dean is working with MAF, helping Christian nationals in Nairobi."

"My, but things are getting interesting," said Zenobia. "I must invite this Dean what's-his-name to dinner, along with Kash, of course." She leaned toward Sable, lowering her voice. "But don't tell Dr. Adler it was my idea. I'm already having enough trouble with him over the Mombasa shipping. Run along, Kate, go soak. And you go see Vince," she urged Sable. "I'll tell Jomo to send over some refreshments." She turned and hurried into the house, muttering to herself, "Goodness, but today has been busy! I haven't had time to go visit the orphans since the conferees arrived yesterday. By the way, dear," she called to Sable over her shoulder as she disappeared toward the kitchen, "Baby Patches is doing wonderfully on his BIG bottle!"

⟨∞⟩

The Treehouse was perhaps a quarter mile from the main Kenyatta Lodge—visible from Sable's bedroom window—and she took the Land Rover instead of walking since the main track skirted the lake and there were several black rhinos, along with huge crocodiles, on the bank.

She drove slowly to keep the dust down. From this main track there were numerous side tracks leading off and down to the shore, where pink flamingos gathered. There was a small observation post mounted high in one of the trees from which visitors could scan the lake with field glasses and use their cameras. The lake attracted hundreds of birds of various types, many of which Sable could identify. She recognized large white spoonbills with their long black bills shaped like spoons, smaller black-and-white wadey birds with their long and delicately upturned beaks, and of course the graceful pink-and-white flamingos that always attracted the tourists' cameras.

There were game here, too, close to the lake. Waterbucks, bushbuck, and impala were seen feeding on the yellow grassland in the park, and Sable's favorite: the reddish brown Bohor reedbuck, an antelope about thirty inches tall at the shoulder that galloped in a rocking-horse motion she found colorful and enjoyable.

Perhaps the most interesting sight for the tourists around the small lake was the colony of hippos that congregated in the spring-fed pools at the northeastern corner. The huge but lovable monsters would lie with their cavernous mouths draped open while little birds picked their teeth clean of vermin. The amusing sight always brought a laugh from the tourists and a clicking of cameras.

Sable parked the Land Rover in the speckled shade and climbed the wooden steps to the Treehouse.

The Treehouse, a large wooden structure situated in a giant acacia tree, had been built by her grandfather before Sable was born and was modeled after the famous Treetops in the Aberdare Game Reserve. Although smaller than the original, the Kenyatta Treehouse was a comfortable game-viewing hotel with several small sleeping chambers and a communal sitting and dining room. The evening meal was usually a rather elegant affair served by Kikuyu and Bantu waiters who held service jobs at the lodge. When growing up, Sable had heard the story from Kash of how one of the Bantu waiters carrying a dinner tray of roast duck had walked the track along the lake and met up with a hungry leopard. Needless to say, the man dropped the duck in exchange for his safe return to the lodge. After that, Zenobia had bought several vans and hired drivers to ferry the waiters and trays back and forth from the kitchen to the Treehouse.

The Treehouse was built on piles, with a flight of steps leading up into the sturdy, reinforced branches, and there was a circular pool of muddy water in front. Salt was thrown down to attract the animals, and sometimes fresh meat was put out to lure the leopard, one of the most difficult and rare of the big cats to see on the reserves. When a leopard put in a stunning appearance, it was the talk of the breakfast table the following morning. And, of course, the other animals came to the pool as well: black buffalo, hyena, silver-backed jackal, and elephants.

Knowing that poachers continued to hunt the rare and endangered leopard for its skin infuriated Sable.

She had climbed the steps to the unpainted door and, finding it unlocked, stepped inside, closing it silently behind her.

The rustic sitting room was done in Maasai colors of clay and ocher, with blue bead work and leather on the walls as decorations. The small sword called a "simi" in a red sheath, a spear, and a tribal headdress in black and white ostrich feathers decorated the plain wood wall. There were also lion and elephant crafts made from sisal rope that Zenobia had bought from one of the shops in Mombasa, and some Turkana tribe dolls from the NFD region, suitably dressed in leather aprons and beads. And a large sesame-wood chest, which had also been bought in Mombasa from one of the Arab dhows that came in with the monsoon winds to sell their goods, stood in the far corner of the room, now scarred from seasons of use since the days before the Second World War. Arrangements of dried grass and flowers were in old Maasai milk containers, and a grinning baboon made of coconut shells sat on the floor holding a tray of real fresh fruit that the waiter had brought this morning. Vince sat at the window behind the 1940 vintage rolltop desk. When she entered the room, he stood, removing his pipe from between his teeth. He wore a wrinkled but clean short-sleeved white shirt unbuttoned at the throat. Tall, lean, and tanned, he was keen-eyed and unsmiling as she walked to the center of the room, where shadows from the tree branches made moving arches on the wood floor.

"Hello, Vince. Hope I'm not interrupting your work," she said quietly.

"Your presence is a joy that never interrupts. I saw you arrive with Kate." He gestured his head toward the window. "I assume Kate's arrival means the camp was closed down?"

Sable nodded, aware of the heat, of the shadows that danced, of the buzzing insects on the fly screen. "They were taking the tents down when we left early this morning."

A line of concern was etched on his face over some thought that made him uneasy. "Who's seeing to Kate's medical dispensary—Markingham?"

"Yes, and a driver, I think, a man he called Bigsby. They were packing things in crates when we left."

As though satisfied, he walked over to the desk, where his work was stacked. "I regret not being there these last few days. I'll miss doing research on the Maasai's customs. They're a noble tribe, closely related to the Samburu. I've feared your evangelistic tactics might be considered by them to be insulting."

Startled, she looked at him, trying to judge by his expression whether or not he was serious.

"I don't understand. You're not implying that my showing the *JESUS* film is in any way detrimental to the East African tribes, are you?"

"No, no, nothing like that. It's just that I have gained an appreciation of their pristine culture—well, it doesn't matter now. We're leaving soon. However, I doubt you'll find the Samburu and Turkana tribes of the NFD much interested in your film, not that I don't think your intentions are well meant."

"I hope you'll permit me to disagree. Wherever the film is shown in the language of the people, they respond to Jesus because of who He is: the Son of God. Jesus isn't Asian, European, or Armenian. He is the Savior of all people. He speaks their language, you see."

Vince smiled uncomfortably. "I'm sorry, dear, I've gotten you riled. I didn't mean to. I think what you're doing is commendable, even if it is rather 'missionary.' "

"I've always thought 'missionary' was a term deserving my highest regard, but I don't represent any organization. What I'm doing, I'm doing on my own. I've paid for the film and equipment myself. So far I haven't embarrassed anyone."

He laughed. "We'd best change the subject before you refuse to have dinner with me tonight. I wouldn't want you at Hallet's table with that energetic MAF flyer friend of his either." He changed the subject smoothly. "About Kash Hallet thinking I was somehow involved in the accident of his brother—were you able to find out anything?"

His question set her on edge. She couldn't tell him what Kash thought. "He believes Seth's death might have been arranged. Of course, there's no proof."

"There wouldn't be, naturally. The entire matter was an unfortunate hunting accident. Did he say why he thought otherwise?"

"He believes it had something to do with poaching," she said carefully.

"A vile situation that's not likely to change anytime soon, but I hope Hallet realizes how committed I am to the reserves."

Sable's thoughts were darting about like nervous swallows. She didn't particularly like the way he spoke about Dean and Kash, or the idea that Christian missionaries were well-meaning but naive to be somehow infecting the "pristine native culture" with their own biased values. The gospel, she thought, is not cultural, neither did it originate with any man. The *JESUS* film was not a cultural message, but taught the life of Christ by enacting the Gospel of Luke.

Bringing Jesus to the world didn't destroy cultures or wholesome customs; it brought them the only Savior of mankind and the love of the wonderful Shepherd. She remembered how the Lord saw the people as "sheep without a shepherd." She felt her calling to be a high and holy privilege, one she wouldn't change for anything.

She watched Vince thoughtfully, troubled. What would his response be when he found out that her father had hired Kash to bring them into the NFD? She walked slowly to the window and looked below at the pool of muddy water. Some birds were pecking the ground looking for dung beetles.

"Neither Kate nor I like closing down and moving on, but the Amboseli camp was only temporary; we all knew that. Kate feels permanently called to the camp at Samburu, and despite your misgivings"—she turned and looked over at him—"I feel motivated to show the film there, and even in Somalia if I can."

She thought of Kash arranging the showing at the manyatta and wondered with concealed excitement if she might not gain his support for some of her other ventures. . . .

"You're smiling," said Vince, relighting his pipe that had gone out and watching her with his keen dark eyes.

She sobered. "Was I?" She touched her hair, tucking a mussed strand into place rather self-consciously as she covered her thoughts. "It's not about leaving Amboseli with so many needs still unmet, I can assure you, but we've learned others will take our places. Some Christians from the Nairobi church are going to be coming out. Some have come to know the Lord, and the children seem especially responsive to the film." Her enthusiasm grew. "Oh, Vince, it's wonderful to see the impact that it's making. The nationals hope to raise money to build a small clinic and even start a church near Namanga. And now that the wells will be drilled, the Maasai will have even more cause to understand the depth of goodwill in the name of Christ—"

"The wells will be drilled, you say?"

He had showed mild tolerance for her private endeavor in using film evangelism, and it wasn't until her mention of the wells that he came alert. The frank curiosity in his eyes told her he hadn't expected the announcement.

"Where did you get the money to drill?" he asked, surprised.

"Oh—so Kate already asked you about the mix-up with the funds?"

"Kate? No, she didn't tell me," he admitted quietly, and a frown showed on his dark brow. "I knew about it before you arrived." He looked at her, then drew in a breath. "Sable, I've a confession to make to you and Kate both about the wells intended for the Maasai. I misunderstood your intent where the money was concerned and thought you had allocated it to me to use for the research we're doing up at Lake Rudolf."

So he admitted it. And Kash had been right. At least about Vince taking it for the work at Lake Rudolf.

"You haven't told me anything about your project, Vince. I'd be very interested to know what it's about. And when you say 'we,' who are the people involved?"

The change in him was dramatic. She'd never seen his eyes glitter with such excitement or his energy level shoot up like a volcano. He came to her, smiling. "I'll take you up to the camp as soon as we get into Samburu. Katherine is there now, and Dr. Willard from our research lab in Toronto. I tell you, the possibilities are astounding." He gripped her arm in his lean hand, giving her a tiny exuberant shake. "We have found a new source of knowledge. We're on the verge of a discovery that will exceed anything yet unearthed at Olduvai Gorge. Dr. Willard has a new method of discovering man's origins—a way that could make present methods obsolete."

A deadness settled over her soul as her eyes searched his. "Is that what you did with the money meant for the Maasai wells? You sent it to Dr. Willard and Katherine Walsh?"

"I thought you knew about the research work going on there," he said quietly, his hand releasing her arm. "I thought Skyler told you the money was meant to fund the project for another year. I'm sorry, Sable, but I'll get the money back to you as soon as possible. But meanwhile, I'll make sure you won't regret the investment."

Kash had been right. . . .

"You never told me you were an evolutionist."

He gave a short laugh. "Sable! I'm not—not in the way you think."

"I'm serious, Vince. You should have told me."

He waved his pipe and walked to the desk, reshuffling his papers. "I'm an anthropologist, Sable. I examine all avenues, all possibilities, to explain man's origins. I deal with *facts*, not stories. What don't you understand?"

"I thought you were a Christian—that you believed God uniquely created man in His image. Are you saying that you can't study man's beginnings without being an evolutionist?" she accused.

"Let's not get into that can of worms. I told you, I'll get the money back as soon as—"

"It's not just that, Vince. You did tell me you were a Christian when we dated in Canada. You carried a Bible to church, you evidently approved of my interest in returning to East Africa to work with my father, to show the film about Christ to the tribes—"

"If it makes you happy, I approve! Why not? I am a Christian . . . in my own way, but don't insist I come through your little wicket gate."

"It's not my little wicket gate. It was Jesus who said 'I am the door.' The truth of Christianity isn't a smorgasbord open to picking and choosing what you want on your plate."

"I believe most of the Bible. But don't expect me to believe the myth of Adam and Eve in the Garden of Eden biting an apple and sending creation into a nose dive. I believe Jesus was sent by God, but—"

"Are you telling me you're a theistic evolutionist?"

He bit his pipe and gritted, "No, I am not. I used to be. I'm not sure I'm an evolutionist at all in the way you mean it. I can best explain what we're doing at Rudolf when I bring you there to meet the team. Look, my dear, let's not fall out over this. It's not as drastic as you seem to fear, nor anything serious enough to come between us. As for the money, I'll write Toronto today and see if you and Kate can be reimbursed. And I'll take you on a tour to Lake Rudolf. Once you meet Dr. Willard and Katherine, you'll see our work is certainly worthy of your respect."

Sable sat down slowly, watching him.

"I thought you and Dr. Katherine Walsh were working with my father at his camp in Samburu. Now you say she's at the digs at Lake Rudolf with Dr. Willard. Just what is the connection with my father and his work?"

He walked to the window, smoking his pipe, one hand shoved in his khaki trousers.

"There's no connection, actually."

"No connection—" she began, astounded. "But I was under the impression you were working with him."

He looked over at her above his pipe. "We were first working with Skyler. Katherine inscribed the data he wanted to include in his book. But we were always much involved with Dr. Willard at Lake Rudolf. She's his niece, as I think I already told you. On weekends Katherine and I would hire one of the bush pilots to fly us up to Rudolf, where we met with the Toronto group."

"Is Dr. Katherine Walsh also from the same private Toronto group?" she asked uneasily. "Does she also believe in evolution?"

He waved a hand as though the question were irrelevant. "Please, dear, Katherine and her personal beliefs have nothing to do with us."

"I'm beginning to think she and Dr. Willard's beliefs may

have more to do with your interests than I ever imagined." She stood. "I'm glad you want to show me the work there because I now wish to know all about it."

"And you shall, just as soon as we arrive. I've no cause to keep secrets from you, Sable. I used the money, yes, but I was under the impression you meant it for the research. I've nothing to hide, and there certainly isn't anything sinister going on." He walked to her, his eyes pleading. "Once you give us a chance to show you, to explain, I'm sure you'll be enthusiastic."

Sable's heart beat painfully slow, and her frustration mounted as his gaze insisted on the impossible.

"Vince," she said softly, "you can't serve two masters."

He laughed. "You're never more charming than when you play the little evangelist."

"Don't make fun of me. I'm serious. There aren't two Gods—one humanistic and secular, and the other the God of the Bible and special creation. You may walk the Christian path for a while, but you'll soon come to a fork in the road. It's inevitable. You'll then need to choose. Will it be this world's system, which seeks to deny its Creator and Savior? Or will it be the God of revelation?"

"I will do what truth demands of me. Is that sufficient to soothe your worries?" He strode to the desk and opened a drawer. He produced a black Book and held it toward her, his eyes glinting. "I read the Bible. And I find much wisdom and good in its pages." He put it back and watched her evenly. "I suppose Kash Hallet has suddenly become a saint? You think he took you out to the manyatta and showed the film because he cared about the souls of the Maasai? He did it to impress you. He's a poacher and a scoundrel."

Sable turned away. "He's never claimed to have dedicated himself to the service of the Lord, but he did arrange the film showing with the warrior chief. And the wells are going to be built—and Kash is arranging it—out of his own bank account. I think that speaks well of him."

Silence enveloped the room, and nothing was heard except the branches of the tree scraping the side of the Treehouse. A moment passed before Vince walked up and turned her around to face him. His jaw was tense, and his black eyes flickered with emotion.

"There's something else about Kash you better know before you canonize him."

"Will you stop it?" she breathed, pulling her arm away. "I'm not setting him up as a saint, nor anyone else either, including myself. We're all human, with faults, weaknesses—and sins! I'm not making excuses for him—or you. But I know what I believe, and I don't want to compromise to please you."

"Good, because I don't want you to," he assured her. "Yet you can't fault me for wanting you away from him. Then again, even in Toronto you never did actually say you loved me. An odd thing, considering we discussed an engagement. All rather businesslike, wasn't it? I wonder how businesslike you and he were when you considered marriage—"

"Please, Vince, don't start that now. You agreed quite willingly to leave the future until after Samburu, and I took you at your word. If every time we meet to talk you bring up Kash, it's going to interfere with our work there."

He sighed. "You're right, the work is far too important to suffer because of personal issues, and I've no intention of compromising either my calling or yours to wrangle with Hallet again. If I bring him up now, it's because we're going to see much more of him than even I expected."

Sable cast him a glance. Did he know? He couldn't.

He studied his pipe as though he had never seen it before. "About the supplies—I think we have the trucks we need. I received a telephone call yesterday from the safari outfit in Tanga."

She tensed. Vince walked up to stand beside her at the window, looking out and watching a warthog at the water's edge.

"I didn't know it the other night when we talked," he said, "but Zenobia did."

"Zenobia knew what?"

He looked at her. "That Skyler hired Hallet to bring you to Samburu."

"Zenobia knew?" she asked, surprised.

"She admitted it today when she found out about the telephone call." His eyes were shadowed where he stood and she couldn't tell what his reaction was, but she was certain he was displeased. It would be best to make as little of the matter as possible.

"Yes, Kash told me at the Amboseli camp that my father had hired him. He refused at first, of course—you know Kash. He's dead set against my going there, but he finally relented." She smiled. "You should be pleased, actually. Without him and Mckib we might end up being stuck here until the rains come, then I'd never get to tour your group's work at Lake Rudolf. You did say you couldn't find any guide in Nairobi."

His mouth was humorless. "Then you're pleased about Hallet?"

She must behave honorably, cautiously. "I'm pleased we've a safari outfit at last, and whatever you think personally about Kash, even his enemies will admit he's the best."

"Yes, so I've heard. You've no other reason to be pleased?"

"That's an unfair question, Vince. If there are other reasons as you suggest, you'll allow me the dignity to sort them through on my own and in private."

He smiled unpleasantly. "Why is it I suspect there's little need of sorting anything out for long? You've already made up your mind about us. He's already come between us."

Her tension made the heat in the room seem suffocating, and she moved closer to the screen, wishing for a breath of air to stir things. The afternoon sun was high above the Treehouse now.

"That isn't quite true. I haven't made up my mind about anything except the need to wait and pray, something I should have done more of before I ever permitted either of us to discuss an engagement. I was wrong to imply I was ready."

"You're quite certain that praying about things makes a difference?" he asked with a small smile.

Sable traced the crawling fly across the screen with her finger. "You did know about Kash and me in Toronto. I told you about the past, how I had felt about him. . . . I didn't try to mislead you, and . . . I'm sorry. I wanted to be fair."

His expression softened unexpectedly. "You were fair, my dear. I'm jealous, is all. You won't fault me for being a man?"

His eyes showed sincere helplessness, and a quick dart of guilt pierced her conscience like a thorn. "Vince, I didn't want any of this to happen. I hope you'll believe me about that. I . . . I never expected to see him again."

He caught her hand from the screen and squeezed it, looking deep into her eyes. "I do believe you. You're too fine a woman to play a man cheaply. I believe you told yourself you were over Kash Hallet, that you'd never see him again. You wanted to build a new future, and I was the man you were willing to consider. I still find that a compliment. And now . . ." His words faltered.

She couldn't end his discomfort by rushing to deny his fears. Her heart weighed heavily in her chest. If he hadn't meant to intimidate her with feelings of guilt, he had, nevertheless, succeeded. She began to think whether or not she'd been completely fair to Vince. She'd told herself in Toronto that she'd gotten over Kash, but that was now obviously untrue. She hadn't forgotten him. Perhaps she never would.

Vince surprised her with his next words. "There's still something more you should know about Kash Hallet."

She stepped back, folding her arms and meeting his gaze. "All right. I'm listening. What is it?"

"For one thing, he's a poacher with the worst outfit in Tanzania or Kenya. He's working for Smith and Browning out of Tanga."

She could have rushed to defend Kash, to try to explain his reasons for doing so, but she knew she couldn't without betraying his cover. How could she tell Vince that Kash was working undercover for the Kenyan government?

"He brought the young elephant calf to you simply as bait to win your trust. Do you think a cold-blooded hunter with his skills cares anything about elephants? If he wants to bring you to Samburu, he has a crass reason for doing so. He intends to hunt ivory.''

She knew that wasn't true. Her eyes swerved to his. Vince looked sincere in what he was saying, even if the charges were wild.

"He knows Skyler is doing data on the elephants up in Marsabit. What better excuse to get in the territory and cover his tracks with the authorities than to be the guide for a Christian relief group?''

She stared at him. He was repeating the words Kash had spoken of Vince, she thought, sickened, praying that they were both wrong about each other. She was unnerved because she found that what Vince was saying fit Kash in some ways even better than it did Vince. Vince had never been a hunter, and his entire work was centered in natural science and conservation. She nearly admitted to Vince what Kash had said about him but caught herself.

"I suppose you wonder why I'm making these charges against him," said Vince quietly. "In this case it isn't dislike based on jealousy. He needs an excuse to enter the NFD in order to track the big tuskers," he said. "There's a report of an old elephant up in Marsabit with tusks several hundred pounds in weight! Imagine. . . . Do you know the money that much ivory would bring in the Asian markets?''

"No," she breathed with alarm, "and I'd rather not think about it. If greed can kill and wipe out an entire species like the elephant—then those to blame are less than animals! Some things can't ever be replaced. And the unique creation of God is one of them.''

"You needn't convince me, dear," he said softly. "I'm well aware of the danger.''

She turned abruptly and faced him. "How can you suggest Kash would do this? What proof do you have?''

He sighed. "I have no hard proof. If I did I'd go to the authorities with it. The hunting outfit he's bringing with him in the guise of truck drivers and safari crew is proof enough.''

The distaste in his tone alerted her. "What do you mean? What crew?"

"Smith and Browning."

Sable couldn't move. The words echoed in her mind, conjuring up images of Moffet and of the rude truck driver she'd come up against on the road to and from Namanga.

"Kash wouldn't hire them," she insisted.

He walked over to the desk and picked up a piece of paper on which he'd written a name and phone number and showed it to her. "I received a telephone call from Pete Browning this morning. He called to ask when Kash wanted the zoo trucks delivered to Kenyatta to load your supplies for Samburu. True, he claims the trucks are being used simply to deliver, but I've my own ideas in the matter. It's a clever way to get the hunters and trucks up to Marsabit. From Marsabit they can cross the border into Ethiopia or Somalia and get away without getting caught."

Sable was remembering back to the dusty trailer trucks parked in the camp across the Tanzanian border and the loathsome blond-headed hunter she'd confronted over getting the calf back. Was this the crew Kash had in mind to bring them to her father?

Far worse than the anger she felt over the zoo hunters was the disappointment over Kash. Did he actually expect to use a crew and trucks known to be involved in poaching?

He'd told her he was working with Smith and Browning as a cover to bring about their arrest, but why would he risk allowing them access to the last big-tusk elephants in Marsabit? Even if he was innocent, he was making a dreadful mistake. The crew of Smith and Browning were more than fifteen; he was only one man. And what if Vince was right after all and Kash was a poacher?

"I can think of only one reason why he'd be using their crew and trucks," said Vince.

They have the best cover possible in getting into the restricted area, she thought. But out loud she said, "There's got to be some mistake."

He sighed and looked out the screen. "Maybe. I hope so. For his sake." He looked at her over his pipe. "Skyler wouldn't hesitate to shoot him if he thought he and his poachers were going to wipe out the herd."

Her throat went dry, and the droning flies were too loud. She could have cried, *But Kash has never really worked as a hunter for Smith and Browning. It was Seth who hunted for them. But Seth opposed the poaching when he found out, and he was killed in an arranged hunting accident.*

But she couldn't say anything. She wasn't supposed to know about it. For a moment her faith in Kash slipped and took a tumble, hitting rock bottom, but . . .

No, he couldn't be planning to hunt the elephants in Marsabit. It wasn't in him. He loved the animals of East Africa too much to destroy them needlessly. He wouldn't work with Browning. The two men were opposite in nature and had different goals. And yet—he'd been in that trailer camp when she arrived, and Browning had called Kash the "boss."

Hadn't the apostle Paul written that the *love* of money was the root of all kinds of evil? For money, some would do anything, compromising their standards and convictions.

Kash was not a compromiser. That was not one of his flaws. He wouldn't lead Smith and Browning to the elephants at Marsabit . . . he wouldn't let them kill them . . . he wouldn't. . . .

She stood looking at Vince, also a man whom she had believed to have convictions.

"You've had a rough day, dear," he said quietly. "And now I've added more worry to the burdens you already find heavy." He held her hand in his. "Don't think about Smith and Browning. I'll speak to Kash about it myself when he arrives. Who knows? Maybe there's some sound and reasonable explanation for his hiring them."

She could have told him that his speaking to Kash about it was what she feared he would do, and that the conflict between them would expand.

"I'm all right," she said, pulling her hand away and sinking into a chair with a weariness she tried to hide. "As you say—

there must be a fairer explanation to all this than what we've come up with. Fears can imagine the worst."

"Yes, of course, you're right." He looked at her, troubled. "The truth is, regardless of who owns those trucks or the past reputation of the outfit, we need both the vehicles and the men if we expect to reach your father's camp. And it looks like we're stuck with Kash Hallet."

Sable made no comment as Vince paced and went on. "The wet season is coming soon. Did you see the clouds? Once it starts, the roads will be impassable in the NFD. And with the possibility of a new outbreak of fighting in Somalia, we've got to take advantage of the lull to get in. If we don't, we might as well admit defeat."

The notion of defeat was unthinkable.

"We can't change our minds now and quit," she told him, standing and pacing the overheated room. "If my father trusted Kash to bring us into Samburu, then I won't turn him down because of suspicion." She turned and looked at him, rather surprised to see a brief look of pleasure before it faded behind his original frown.

"But he'll need to explain about the hunting outfit," she said, "even if we do need their trucks."

"Yes." He turned back to his sheaf of papers. "And that answer had better be good enough to convince the conservationists tomorrow."

"You don't mean Kash would have the audacity to show up with Browning tomorrow at the conference?" she asked. "Everyone knows the reputation of the outfit."

Vince shook his head with apparent disgust. "Browning is coming with the trucks. At least he can meekly say he's a 'reformed' poacher now. After all, he's working for Hallet, a man hired by Skyler Dunsmoor, who has an impeccable reputation and credentials when it comes to wildlife protection."

Sable considered, then turned away, relieved when there was a knock on the door and Jomo arrived with a tray of iced lemonade and a pot of hot coffee.

Thirteen

The breathless air reeked of satiated wet earth as the morning dawned sun-bright and humid after an unexpected, although brief, rain during the night. A few voluminous clouds lingered above the Kenyatta game sanctuary like sentinels as the first day of the East African International Conference on Wildlife Conservation began with breakfast.

The delegates had traveled from Europe, America, Canada, and Australia. After a breakfast served in the dining commons on tables with crisp white tablecloths and tan stoneware appropriately engraved with animal motifs, the conference opened with various short speeches by respected naturalists and zoologists, all giving grave reports of the future prospects for the wildlife of Africa.

Mini-seminars followed, and after luncheon, a sober-faced discussion panel led by Dr. Vince Adler predicted a bleak twenty-first century unless public opinion could persuade the lawmakers to enact further protection for the elephants and game animals.

The afternoon had passed under its own cloud as the somber mood expanded, with conservationists documenting on video the diminishing numbers of the endangered animals across Africa's reserves.

"Unless something can be done internationally to put an end to poaching by penalizing those who *buy* as well as those who pull the trigger and set merciless traps—then within the next decade we will be adding several more species to our list of extinct animals."

The panel ended the grave discussion for a much needed coffee, tea, and fruit break, with the next main lecture to be held after dinner that evening. The speech was to have been given by Sable's father, Skyler T. Dunsmoor, but since everyone seemed to know by now that he wouldn't be coming, they had opted to ask Vince to fill the podium.

Throughout the day and during the breaks, Sable heard her father's name quietly mentioned among the gathered delegates, but she pretended not to notice how their voices noticeably fell off whenever she entered the vicinity. She had overheard one American professor speaking to a delegate from England: "Whatever the rumor concerning his mental balance, I'm not convinced. I met him last year, and Skyler Dunsmoor isn't the sort of individual to crack under pressure. If he's in seclusion somewhere in the Northern Frontier District, there's got to be a logical reason for it."

"I quite agree. The entire scenario of his turning into a recluse, talking to elephants, is a bit strained if you ask me. Then again, old boy, Vince isn't known for his exaggeration, either. Seems to me he's in a position to speak on the subject with some credibility. He and Dr. Katherine Walsh were with Skyler in the NFD when he disappeared into the volcanic region while tracking elephants."

"Dr. Adler's the best man to speak on that. He's arranged for a guide to bring him up into the Marsabit region—one of the best, I hear, raised right here on Kenyatta."

"You're speaking of Kash Hallet. He'll be here tonight. If it's true, I must say I'm rather surprised. Hallet's been staying fairly aloof from the conservationist route lately—ever since his brother was killed. There's a bit of nasty business about that, I'm told."

The long day ended with an elaborate dinner and a delay in the evening lecture. Delegates began to drift from the dining commons to refresh themselves in their rooms or to get a breath of fresh air in the steamy night out on the game-viewing veranda overlooking the water hole.

The night was heavy with the pathos of Africa. Stillness wrapped everything with a dread of the strong preying on the weak. In this case, to Sable, it was fallen man who was the enemy, out to mar and destroy the image of an awesome creation that bore witness to God's handiwork. Thoughtless killing to the point of extinction seemed to her a profane behavior that insulted the great Designer.

A breeze stirred from somewhere, gently touching the hem of her long slim-style dinner dress of draped cream-colored silk. Her hair was worn up with casual elegance, and two small glitter combs winked like genuine diamonds.

Kash's place setting at the table next to her own had stayed empty, and she wondered what might have happened to delay his arrival. He had commented earlier that he wanted to hear the lecture Vince would give to the delegates in place of her father. She glanced at her delicate silver herringbone wristwatch. The lecture was already five minutes behind schedule.

Below, the floodlights fell on the circular water hole, which shone like a pale gray looking glass, but so far no animal life stirred.

Perhaps there are no big game animals left alive, she found her strained emotions thinking, exaggerating the depression everyone apparently felt at the conference. The threat had been brought to its worst possible conclusion by excellent speakers, but those who needed to hear it the most were busy elsewhere in the world, either oblivious to the danger or uncaring.

They just don't know, she thought, and because of her deep feelings for the reserves, she couldn't envision anyone *not caring* if they knew, especially Christians who delighted in the work of their heavenly Father, and who would be grieved that elephants and lions were so few in number.

Some of the wildlife conference delegates had already spoken throughout the day, and the news and information brought for the international group was bleak. There were few one-horned rhinos left in the world, the leopards were endangered to the point of extinction—as well as lions, tigers, elephants, rare birds. . . .

The list of God's magnificent creation went on: five left here, maybe twenty somewhere else. And always the danger increased. *"The poaching continues. Skins, ivory, horns—still being ruthlessly taken with no regard for animal preservation of the greatest large animals of the world. Within a decade there may be no more elephants, no lions, no cry of a bird in either Africa or the rain forests of the world."*

How can anyone who worships the Creator not weep for such carnage against His handiwork? Sable thought.

She stood on the veranda, staring down through the night's blackness and thinking that the small hope her father would arrive to speak to the conference delegates was growing slimmer by the hour.

As she stood there, the big circular pool showing pale and flat, she thought of all the tourists who had sat on this veranda through the years of past generations, lolling with ice-cold drinks, watching for elephants and leopards, as well as all the small creatures that had come like shadows out of the African night to quench their thirst at the floodlit water hole. Things had been different in Gran's day, the lodge so carefully planned and the water hole like a stage set. Now it seemed to Sable that fewer and fewer animals came, and they had to leave bait to lure the few remaining leopards.

"A wildlife conference without wildlife," she murmured to herself.

The voices of some of the delegates farther down the veranda were raised among themselves in disagreement: "Killing, you mean. Let's call it by its real name. Shooting endangered animals for sport is killing for pleasure!"

"The hunters wouldn't agree with you."

"I don't expect them to, and their self-righteous indignation doesn't impress me either. To kill for food is one thing, but to kill the few remaining animals of a species so you can impress your cronies back home about what a big mighty sportsman you are is not sport, but the love of killing for the 'hunt's' sake. The animal doesn't have a chance against a powerful hunting rifle! Some of them would kill the last of *anything* if it meant boosting their egos."

"One day the world will wake up and find their grandchildren discussing elephants and lions the way we do dinosaurs. They'll only exist in books and movies. Doesn't anyone else out there care but us?"

"Calm down, Udall. We're all on the same side here."

"Are we?"

"What do you mean by that?"

"Are you certain we all agree with Skyler about the elephants at Marsabit?"

"Are you suggesting otherwise?"

"That's what I'm suggesting!"

"Now, Udall—"

"Quiet—! Someone's coming."

Sable stood rigid, heart throbbing in her temples. A figure appeared out of the hot night, his safari shirt reflecting the light. *Kash!* He came up the veranda steps from the grounds, and someone murmured, "What's he doing here?"

"I've heard he's working with Skyler to protect the elephants."

"You're not serious?"

Sable was interrupted from listening when footsteps sounded from behind her. She turned to see Zenobia standing in the lighted entranceway of the dining commons.

"There you are, Sable. Kate's looking for you."

"I'm coming now. . . ."

The dining tables with their pristine white linen had been stashed away now, and the chairs set out neatly in rows, transforming the dining commons back into a conference hall. Sable silently took her seat beside Kate, glancing off to the darkened veranda to see where Kash had gone.

The international delegates filed in two and three at a time, carrying leather portfolios. A few brought laptop computers for taking notes; others held portable tape recorders. Their somber faces reminded her of soldiers who'd survived an attack by the enemy and remained hopelessly outnumbered but determined to die rather than surrender.

Kash entered after the others had taken their seats and opted for an unobtrusive position at the back by a decorative fireplace, but his virile presence never went unnoticed in a group. By now everyone must have heard that he was heading up Smith and Browning, and glances were shot his way from a few of the aggressive conservationists.

Kate must have noticed, for she leaned toward Sable and whispered behind her lecture program, "Conroy Udall is quite direct about his disapproval, isn't he? He may not shoot game, but he looks ready to draw a six-shooter on Kash."

Sable moved uneasily in her chair as she watched the challenging glower that Udall threw toward Kash.

"He's the kind to stand up and say something that embarrasses everyone," continued Kate. "I wonder if you shouldn't head him off? Maybe introduce Kash as the guide bringing us to Samburu at Dad's request?"

"I would," Sable whispered, "but Kash asked us not to say anything until after tonight. Vince will announce how Father hired him. Anyway, I overheard a few of them talking on the terrace. They already know Father's hired him, but they still disapprove."

She wondered what would happen when Smith and Browning's trucks arrived in the morning!

Kate glanced toward the podium, curious. "Where is Vince? He's supposed to take Dad's place as speaker tonight. I haven't seen him since dinner. He behaved oddly, don't you think?"

Sable hadn't noticed, so taken up was she with her own concerns. "Did he? Gran said he was going over his speaking notes, that he was quite upset over the information he's going to bring the delegates."

"Here he comes now . . . looks like he's going to deliver a eulogy."

This was a moment in the spotlight that Vince had wanted for himself, and he was making the most of it as he glanced about at his audience. His own mood was brimming over with what Sable knew Kash would find both boring and "pseudo-intellectual." Whether or not Vince was aware of Kash could not be ascertained, since he didn't seem to take note of his presence at the back of the room.

Vince allowed the effect of his silence to gather like thunderclouds over a mountain while he slowly prepared his notes on the lectern. He looked directly down at Kate, then Sable.

"We all know Skyler Dunsmoor to be a wildlife conservationist we hold in highest regard for his many unselfish years of research on the elephants of East Africa—especially in the NFD region of Samburu and Marsabit. He regrets he cannot be here with us tonight. He's asked me to convey his warmest greetings to what he considers the best team of fellow conservationists yet gathered here at Kenyatta Lodge."

Her father had "asked" him? When had Vince spoken to her father?

"I apologize for keeping you all waiting tonight. You will understand why when I tell you that I've just been on the telephone with Skyler."

Sable was fully alert, sharing a surprised glance with Kate. Their father had spoken with Vince but had not asked to speak even a word of greeting to her or Kate?

A ripple of surprise and interest ran through the audience.

Vince's voice sounded clearly as he stood on the platform answering questions put to him from the delegates.

"Has Skyler any idea how many elephants are left in Marsabit?" asked Udall.

"We know they've been killed for years," said another delegate. "The forest is being burned for grazing land, trees giving way to shambas, cattle and goats replacing game animals. The villages are multiplying, war, unrestricted poaching—there can't be many."

"What does Skyler hope to accomplish single-handedly?"

Vince shuffled his notes. "Skyler tells me he's in contact with officials in the Kenyan government. The question is, do we have time to stop the rebel factions from culling the elephants?"

"Some of the elephants may have migrated to a safer area

that the poachers have not yet discovered," said Udall. "Does Skyler know where it is?"

"To learn that, we must wait until I meet with him at Samburu. The information he asked me to share with you is all here, documented as well as time and the situation will warrant. My assistant, Miss Dunsmoor, will distribute the handouts."

His assistant? Sable, realizing that Vince was smiling at her and that heads turned toward her anxious for the information, stood, masking her surprise. She walked to the podium and took the handouts from Vince and began to pass them out as he continued.

"The news, ladies and gentlemen, is brutally frank, as truth sometimes is. I will in no way try to shield your emotions from the tragedy now playing out in the region. The last great herd of giant-tusked elephants in the NFD region is facing extinction, not by poachers as we had thought—but through interfactional war. The rebel factions, faced with a food crisis, are slaughtering the elephants to feed their soldiers and selling the ivory on the black market for weapons. Unless the Kenyan government risks sending troops in to put an end to the slaughter, there is little we can do to stop it."

Sable was stunned by the news. A horrified silence engulfed the room. As the conservationists read through the information sheet trying to understand the full meaning of the news her father had sent to Vince, Sable had reached the back of the room where Kash waited by the fireplace.

Her eyes searched his for confirmation as she handed him the sheets, but it was not dismay she saw in the midnight blue eyes, only anger. He scanned it while she waited, heartsick. His jaw flexed. "He's lying."

Lying! She stared at Kash, at first unable to respond. As Vince's voice echoed in the background, her insides twisted into a knot.

"Lying about speaking to my father? Or the army killing the elephants to feed their soldiers?"

He pretended to be busy studying the handout. "Both," he stated. "He hasn't spoken to Skyler. He doesn't know where your father is, and Vince is the last man he'd get in touch with. And as for any fighting between the rebel factions, it's centered in Somalia, around Mogadishu, where U.S. Marines landed some time ago, not Marsabit."

Seeing Kash's expression as he watched Vince, she felt a chill touch her skin. The disdain was masked with restraint, but knowing Kash so well, she couldn't miss it.

Sable felt an odious chill run down her spine. Kash believed Vince could be so deceitful as to stand before conservationists and bemoan the state and future of the elephant population in the north, all to cover his true involvement.

"Why would he lie?" she whispered.

His eyes came back to hers as if to discover the reason for her protest. "You know the answer by now."

She watched Vince, remembering what Kash had said: Vince had another cause that meant even more to him than wildlife preservation. The work at Lake Rudolf, and his associates who formed some sort of alliance for research.

"It's far easier to blame the rebel factions for slaughtering the elephants than a hunting cartel supplying a Far Eastern market. Some of the businessmen he wanted Zenobia to permit to buy into the shipping are middlemen selling the goods."

She remembered something else—Browning and the trucks that were to arrive tomorrow morning. "Those despicable zoo hunters work for you, not Vince."

"Do they?"

Alert, she scanned his face for a deeper meaning to the suggestion. "You mean to say they don't?"

"I won't argue whether they do or not. We're leaving in the morning, that is if you won't wisely change your mind and stay with Zenobia. Let me and the others handle the problems in Samburu."

"What about Browning? The zoo trucks? What better way to get into the elephant reserve than working with the respected conservationist Skyler Dunsmoor?" she asked dully. "Your crew of hunters will have a cover by transporting two women doing Christian relief."

His eyes flickered, but his expression didn't change. "Is that what you think? Or did Adler tell you that?"

When she made no comment he added, "I told you in the Land Rover on our way to the manyatta what I was doing working with Browning."

I do trust you, she wanted to say, but just then someone entered the room from the veranda steps. Her eyes fell on a brawny blond-headed man in Levi's and a jacket. His cool gaze circled the room of conferees until it fell upon Kash. Then Browning, seeing Sable, smiled unpleasantly and gestured his head in exaggerated deference.

Her gaze came to Kash for an explanation, but while his gaze narrowed, he didn't apologize for Browning's presence among wildlife conservationists. Their eyes held. When it was obvious he would say no more, she turned to walk across the room to take her seat beside Kate. Kash caught her wrist and she paused, her back toward him.

"A woman who trusts a man whose heart she claims to know shouldn't need to ask those questions. If you're still doubting the kind of man I am, then we haven't left first base."

He left with Browning through one of the side doors, and Sable looked after him.

⌒⟁⟁⟁⌒

The day dawned hot and bright with the rumble of truck engines and voices below in the front of the lodge. Gran's dogs were barking and a horn blared. The bedroom door opened, and Kate swept in with exaggerated fanfare, bringing a tray with a mug of coffee and a steaming bowl. "Are you still sleeping?" she teased cheerily. "I've been up an hour, had my devotions, and a hearty and healthy breakfast."

Sable groaned. "Can't be morning already."

"It is. And if you don't want Kash to know what a lazy little creature you really are in the mornings, you'd better get a move on. He's an early riser and would love to give you a rough time of it. What are you going to do when you two get married? He's the kind to throw you in the shower."

"Oh yeah! Let him try! Thanks for the coffee—what's that?" she asked with a grimace, staring at a bowl of mush.

"Oatmeal and wheat germ. It's good for you."

"First thing in the morning? You're kidding. Just coffee please, black."

"Mckib's already loading the supplies." She rubbed her palms together with delight. "This is the day, my girl. We're headed for Samburu!" Her eyes were alive with excitement. She was dressed in a traditional safari habit, her newly shampooed dark hair glinting in a long ponytail that made her look eighteen instead of twenty-eight. She whistled a happy tune and went to Sable's closet to haul out her traveling clothes.

Sable exaggerated a groan. "Mother should have named you Tweety Bird instead of Kate. One would think Dean was going to bring us on the journey instead of the dude who calls himself a 'zoo' hunter."

"Never mind Browning. My stomach churns just looking at him. How Kash can put up with him, I don't know. He's got a crew of a dozen hunks out there all lounging around with hunting rifles. The conservationists are blue in the face. One thing's clear—not all the crew appear to be loyal to him."

Sable grew serious as she drank her coffee. "Kash couldn't be partners with him." Then she looked at Kate curiously. "What do you mean, not all are loyal to Browning? What makes you think so?"

Kate shrugged. "I noticed some of the men seemed quite different, more like Kash. They keep to themselves."

Sable wondered and threw aside the sheet. Grabbing her robe, she slipped it on and carried her mug of coffee over to the open window.

Below, the vehicles were parked and the men were loading them with crates. She saw Kash near one of the trucks, talking to Mckibber.

"Kash says Dean will be flying into Samburu to help you show the *JESUS* film," said Kate on her way out.

Twenty minutes later Sable was dressed in expedition slacks

and safari boots and came down the porch steps with her hat in one hand and carrying case in the other. Noise and excitement filled the yard as the crew worked, calling orders above the noise of barking dogs. Zenobia came from the direction of one of the trucks, a pert figure in her usual dungarees.

Sable set her case down and wrapped her arms about her grandmother. "I'll call you from Samburu, Gran."

"Do what you must, dear, then come home with Kash. This is where you both belong. Did you get the shipping business settled yet?"

"Yes and no. . . ."

"Well . . . it won't matter much once you're married. You'll have a big wedding, of course. We'll invite everyone we know from Nairobi. You'll make a beautiful bride."

Sable laughed wryly. "I think we're getting ahead of ourselves, aren't we? I don't know about any wedding in the offing, and if Kash heard you talking like that he'd disappear to the wilds of Tanzania again."

Zenobia looked across the sun-drenched yard in his direction and merely smiled. "Bring Skyler home, too, will you? I miss him dreadfully."

Sable kissed her cheek. "I'll do my best."

When Zenobia went off with the three dogs trotting beside her, Sable watched her until she went up the porch steps into the lodge, then picked up her case and looked toward Kash. He stood by a Land Rover, the attractive and exemplary image of the traditional safari hunter-guide.

With the harsh cry of birds filling the air, Sable picked up her case and walked up, debating whether she wished to ride in the white van with Vince and some of the others. Kash settled the issue by taking her case and placing it in the Land Rover.

He opened the passenger door. "We have a good deal to discuss," he said easily, and Sable wasn't inclined to disagree.

Fourteen

Mckibber, who had decided to accompany Kash at the last moment—probably due to his nephew's prompting—sat in the back of the Land Rover, two rifles and a water bag beside him and cartons of ammunition at his booted feet. Along with the supplies they would deliver to Samburu, camping gear, boxes, and jerry cans were stashed in the two trucks, and some of the crew were seated on the heap of stores. Browning was driving one of the trucks, and Sable commented dryly, "As reckless a driver as he is, he'll probably end up running off into a ravine somewhere and ruin our supplies before we ever get to Samburu."

They drove through Nairobi and took the road northeast to Thika, climbing steadily.

"This is great old settler country," Mckib told her longingly. "Mostly citrus groves and tea plantations."

Sable glanced at Kash, knowing how he felt about owning land in Kenya, but his expression showed none of his disappointment. She saw plantation houses built by the British set well into the shade of jacaranda and capre chestnut trees in bloom. The once fine houses were now aged and tired looking with peeling paint, and the gardens looked to her to be filled with workers' huts and overgrown with weeds and filled with rubbish. African children ran and played everywhere.

Mckibber began, "Now, if I could go back fifty years—"

"But we can't," Kash smoothly interrupted, "so let's not

talk about our losses. Hand me the map, will you?"

Mckib leaned forward, passing it to him with a wink at Sable. "Think he really needs this? Look at him. Best guide in Kenya and he's got to read the map just a few miles out of Nairobi."

Sable laughed. "Deceptive, isn't he? Poor Mr. Browning may think his 'boss' doesn't know the route to Samburu."

Beyond the township of Thika she began to get glimpses of Mount Kenya, its summit like a great medieval fortress—black rock against perpetual crystalline snow and deep sky. They were into more open country now, with the Aberdare mountain range closing in to the left. Just before midday as they passed the turnoff to Nyeri, Sable read the signpost of a tourist mecca: "Treetops." Visitors often stopped here and had lunch at the Outspan Hotel. The daughter of the king of England had spent a night in the treehouse lookout on vacation one year and climbed down the next morning to learn she was the now Queen Elizabeth.

"Great tourist stuff," said Mckib. "They love the story."

"The Mau Mau burned it down," said Kash, "but it's been rebuilt."

They made camp before sundown. They were just north of the equator by the western slopes of Mount Kenya, and a white cloud had formed over its peak.

⟨⟨⟩⟩

By afternoon of the second day they had reached Nanyuki, its street thronging with people. Browning accelerated his truck around the Land Rover, bumping over potholes that were only half filled with gravel. He slammed on the brakes and came to a halt, dust flying in front of a small building with faded lettering: "The Settler's Store."

Sable looked at Kash and saw his restrained irritation as he had to brake the Land Rover while glancing into the rearview mirror to see if the next truck would stop before plowing into their back end.

"What got into him?"

Browning swung down from the cab, patting his bare belly while his shirt draped open.

Kash's eyes narrowed as the dust blew against them, and Sable covered her face with a handkerchief.

"What are you doing?" Kash gritted. "I didn't plan on stopping here."

"Ah, c'mon, Hallet! Loosen up! I gotta 'ave ma' beer. We're dyin' of thirst, me and Mateo both!"

Mateo was Maasai and had graduated from Nairobi University. Mckib had told her at the camp the night before that Mateo had once belonged to the Kenya Rifles military. Sable had mentioned seeing Kash talking to him alone several times on the safari. "Are they friends?" she had asked.

"Not in public," said Mckib, giving her a wink. She understood this to mean that Mateo was not one of Browning's men. There were several others who didn't look to be so either, men of quiet and rugged demeanor whom she'd noticed stayed to themselves, were alert, and seemed to look to Kash for instructions.

Outside the store, she saw Mateo look over at Kash before following Browning and several others of the crew into the store.

Kash wore a bored expression as he got out from behind the wheel. "Wait here," he told her. "Browning needs his bottle."

Kash followed them inside the market, and Sable turned to Mckibber. "He doesn't like Browning, and Browning seems to know it, so why do they work together?"

Mckib got out to stretch. "Browning owes him money. He's got no choice but to put up with Kash. You're right, the feeling is mutual."

A while later she glanced into the store and saw that it was still busy inside. This was probably the most business they'd had in weeks. She asked hurriedly, "Did Kash buy into the outfit to keep tabs on Browning?"

Mckibber turned his head, his eyes keen beneath his silver brows. "Always did know you'd see the truth 'bout Kash eventually. It's Adler and Browning who are the unlikely teammates.

Adler needs his foul hunters to poach ivory."

Sable was careful to not show her emotions in case some of the crew noticed them talking. "It was Dr. Adler who warned me about Browning and his crew," she said. "He seems to think Kash and Browning want to hunt elephants in Marsabit."

"Bah. The devil was a liar from the beginning. That's what Adler's doing. It's him that's paying Browning to try for the elephants. But we'll stop 'em. Your father's involved with us, too."

"Why didn't you tell me sooner?"

"I ain't supposed to tell you at all. Kash told me to keep me mouth buttoned."

"Kash bought in with Browning to keep an eye on him?"

"Yep. When Seth died, the outfit was in debt at Tanga. Kash used the opportunity to buy in. Browning didn't know who he was till it was too late. He knows now . . . Vince told him, to be sure. So he's as restless as a tiger walkin' on coals."

Sable had long ago begun to suspect as much after Kash told her he was working for the government, but she had refused to believe that Vince could be involved. She still had her misgivings, but they were growing weaker by the hour.

The dusty white van came up beside them, and the driver left the motor running as Vince wound down the window and spoke, his eyes flickering with impatience. "Why did Browning stop? What's he doing now?"

If Vince was working with the outfit, it wasn't because he liked Browning either, she thought.

"He's thirsty," said Sable with a wry smile.

Vince said something under his breath and climbed out, going inside the store.

Sable walked up to the side of the van, where Kate sat fanning herself with her hat. "I'm not getting out unless they have ice for sale—or a bathroom with running water."

"Don't waste your time," said Sable.

Kate groaned. "That's all Browning needs is something to fuzzy his brains. He can't drive straight as it is. And this driver isn't much better. He's got a cassette player with hard rock music, and Vince is about to have a nervous breakdown." She climbed over the baggage. "I'm riding the rest of the way in the back of the Land Rover with Mckib."

The store had once belonged to an East Indian merchant, Mckibber told them. "Safaris used to load up here with tinned foods and fresh vegetables before entering the NFD. This is the last spot before Samburu, and the desert is next."

The store had been Kenyanized long ago, and the shelves were mostly empty except for local vegetables and some sacks of maize flour called "posho." Sable checked the fresh fruit but decided against the melons, since they were overripe from sitting out in the heat. Flies were everywhere, crawling over the fruit and root vegetables. She looked off toward the open country near the northern slopes of the mountain and saw huts and patches of abandoned cultivation.

"After the settlers left, the land was given to the Meru and Samburu," said Mckib.

Sable, however, saw little sign of people, cattle, or prosperity.

A minute later Browning and some of his crew came out of the store with warm beer and a bag of cigarettes.

Kash settled his hat and reached in back for the water, watching Vince walk up and speak to Browning. Sable noticed, too, but said nothing as they got back into the Land Rover. Kash backed up and drove in front of the truck and headed for Mount Kenya, where the track would bring them to over six thousand feet.

They were now snaking down the switchback path on the shoulder of Mount Kenya toward the brink of the Northern Frontier District, a burned-out plain reaching into an infinity of desert in which towering buttes of pale red rock stood like castles shattered by wind and sand. Dust devils whirled. Sable squinted, seeing no horizon. The deadness of the country lost itself in a haze; the land and sky were the same opaque sun-blistered white, and away to the left the blurred shape of mountains arose like ghosts on the edge of visibility. She found it appalling, yet breathtaking.

"Can elephants cross this vast desert to reach the mountains of Marsabit?" she asked Kash.

"Yes. Take a closer look. You'll see this isn't like the great Chalbi Desert. There are trees and scrub, and the elephants know where the water is."

Sable felt a little better and settled back, trying not to think about the heat and hot wind. Both she and Kate had worn long-sleeved blouses and wide-brimmed hats and slathered on mounds of sunscreen before they left camp that morning, knowing they would face the blistering desert.

They coasted down into the oven heat of the desert and drove late into the afternoon, until the terrain began to change—more trees, shrubs, and doum palms.

"Kash likes to camp at Lolokwe," said Mckib of the great bare-topped sugarloaf mountain that stood out on the plain north toward Maralal.

Sable looked off, shading her eyes, and saw the sides of the mountain looking crimson in the sunset.

That night when they made camp, Sable and Kate washed in the small stream. Kate had finished first, and the twilight was turning purple as Sable hung her laundered blouse on a thorn-bush to dry during the night. She retrieved her bar of soap from the stream and was hastening her way back the short distance to the camp. A fire was already burning, and the refreshing smell of supper clung to the air. As she started for her tent, she saw Kash and Mateo talking in low tones. Another man joined them, a soft-spoken European whom Kate had pointed out as a curiosity the day before.

"That man can't be one of Browning's. Look at him—he even poured my coffee this morning and said, 'Did you sleep all right, ma'am?' "

Sable had remained thoughtful. Kate had been right. At least a half dozen hunters with the outfit were too polite and polished to be poachers for Smith and Browning. Then who were they? And what were they doing?

Seeing Kash and Mateo talking with a man who'd quietly joined them, she grew more curious. Kash must have felt her stare, for he looked toward her. She expected to see his surprise or concern at being found in a huddle and wondered why he showed no response. He said something to the other two, who glanced her way, and then she walked on as if going farther downstream to wash.

Kash walked toward her carrying a towel and a clean khaki shirt, his revolver stuffed in his belt.

"You shouldn't be away from camp alone. It's getting dark. This is lion country."

She wanted information about him. "Those two men—they're different from the others."

He acted casual and lifted a brow. "Different?"

Her half-smile suggested she saw through his evasive behavior. "Some in your outfit are loyal to you, others to Browning."

He smiled, disarming her. "Are they? Hunters are loyal to whoever pays them the most."

"Those two men—Mateo and. . . ?" She waited for the name of the second man.

"Jim."

"Yes, they're different from most of the others. They even eat differently. Jim used a knife and fork. And Mateo did an unusual thing: when Browning handed him a mug of coffee and walked away, Mateo smelled it first before drinking it."

He rubbed his chin as though seriously considering. "Let's hope Vince and Browning aren't so observant."

She took him in briefly, trying to ignore her feelings. "Then I was right. They're working for you; they're handpicked."

He threw the towel over his shoulder and glanced toward camp as if to see where Vince and Browning were. She followed his gaze and saw them standing by the campfire.

"They're loyal to me, yes. They're working for the government to crack the international poaching ring."

The news was exhilarating because it also meant Kash had told her the truth about himself and what he was doing with zoo hunters. She wanted to smile, but under his steady gaze she opted to look away, not wishing to alert him to her feelings.

"I wonder if you noticed anything else," he asked quietly,

and when she looked at him curiously, he commented, "Vince and Browning had a late powwow in one of the trucks last night. They thought we were all asleep."

She was bothered by this. "I fell asleep early and heard nothing until this morning."

The cobalt depths of his eyes showed impatience over Vince.

"Considering what I've already told you about Adler, you should know he's raising money for the work at Lake Rudolf by selling ivory."

The evidence continued to stack against Vince, and she could not continue to avoid the obvious. He was involved in something unpleasant.

"Browning's been working for Adler for over a year," he said.

"So that's why you bought into this outfit?" And when he frowned a little, she explained, "Mckib told me you loaned them money."

"I think I've said before that he talks too freely."

"Don't be mad at him," she soothed. "I have to know sometime about what you're up to, don't I?"

"Seth was killed while he worked for Browning, as I told you at Amboseli. Now I know why."

She waited tensely, hoping he would explain. He seemed to consider. "Seth was on to Adler and Browning. He guessed that a photographic safari wasn't on the up and up. He was to lead them into Norongoro, but he knew it wasn't to film the rhino but to kill two that they knew were feeding in the area. Seth led the safari and sacrificed those two rhinos to obtain footage of the kills—and those involved. He felt he could do more to stop the cartel in the future by going along with it. He got what he wanted—the kills on film—and on that film he got footage of Vince, Browning, and another man named Macklin in the background with the Africans."

Sable stared at him. "You . . . you mean they *knew* Seth had them on film, and they killed him for it?"

Kash was thoughtful as he watched Vince set up his canvas chair beside the van and sit down with his supper. Browning sauntered up, leaning against the van, talking to him.

"I'm now sure it's the reason Seth is dead."

She glanced behind her toward camp, feeling afraid for the first time. Poaching she despised; murdering men was something else! And Kash actually believed the cartel—with Vince and Browning's cooperation—had arranged Seth's death to silence him and—

She turned quickly, her eyes searching his hopefully. "Do you have the film Seth took?"

Kash looked moody. "No. Seth's camera is missing. Either Browning took it, or Vince. I looked through Browning's things back at the trailer camp at the Tanzanian camp. It wasn't there. If he was smart he would have destroyed it, but Browning isn't smart. And that's what I'm counting on."

She struggled to speak the words. "Would Vince have taken it?"

His eyes came to hers and searched, and she looked away. They both understood that this was the first time she had admitted he was probably involved.

"Vince doesn't have it. I've already checked his room at Kenyatta, and before that in Nairobi. He might have buried it somewhere, but I'm thinking he never had it. There's a chance Browning still has it somewhere—or the hunter named Macklin."

She had never heard of Macklin, but the way Kash spoke his name told her the man was clever and dangerous.

Sable remembered the camera equipment she'd seen in the truck that Browning drove. She looked at Kash, but he was watching the camp. She noted the determination of his handsome jaw and suddenly feared for his life. If the hunting cartel knew he was on to them, they wouldn't hesitate to eliminate Kash in the way they had Seth.

She feared to tell him of the camera equipment and debated her silence during supper that night. She must tell him, she thought, as soon as they arrive at Samburu.

As the Africans got busy gathering wood in a panga for the fire, the tents were set up beneath Lolokwe. Colonies of weaver birds darted noisily in and out of the wait-a-bit thorn trees, their nests looking like clusters of coconuts hanging in the bare branches. Kash had once told her about an experiment that had shown that the knowledge to weave their spherical basket nests was programmed into their genes by the great Creator; it was not a trial-and-error sort of adaptation that was learned and taught to their offspring as the evolutionists believed. He had helped a scientist raise five generations of weaver birds without any nesting material in order to prove that any learned skill would become entirely lost. It was found, however, that as soon as nesting material was reintroduced, later generations of birds began skillfully weaving. The scientist had also stated that since the genetic makeup of each parent bird is fixed at conception, any skill that it learns cannot be genetically passed on to its offspring. The scientist was entirely without an explanation as to the origin of the weaver bird's abilities. Kash had said the scientist had disallowed the best explanation of the experiment's result—"that it was an awesome testament to the designer, creator, encoder, and programmer of the DNA molecule."

Silver-breasted blackbirds watched curiously but showed no alarm at the presence of humans. The campfire was blazing, and Mckib oversaw the making of supper with the help of the old African Kumba, who went about his business preparing a grill with chopped pieces of wood.

The dusk was brief, the night solitary and inky black. Above, the stars were distant and brilliant. Everything was suddenly silent with the birds quiet and the night animals not yet on the prowl.

Kate's voice was nearly a whisper as she sat close beside Sable. "Are you nervous, camping out like this in the heart of wild Africa?"

"No," she said, but as their eyes met they suddenly laughed quietly, for they were both aware of the dangers that lurked.

A faint breeze was coming off the mountain and Mckib sniffed the air. "Rain," he said.

Vince looked taut and weary as he came up and sat beside Sable, drinking his black coffee. "Tomorrow we'll be at Skyler's camp," he said. "Once Kate is situated there and the supplies unloaded, we can arrange a flight to Lake Rudolf to meet Dr. Katherine Walsh and Dr. Willard. Kash has offered to bring us there."

Sable was rather surprised that Kash would have mentioned it to Vince, since he wouldn't want Vince present when he brought her there.

Kash came up and stooped on his haunches, facing them, the fire behind him. "Don't leave your tents once we get you inside for the night."

"No warning necessary," said Kate good-naturedly, but Sable was curious.

"Do you expect lions?"

He smiled. "Maybe."

"It's snakes and scorpions he's concerned about," said Vince. "Is that right, Kash?"

One could hardly tell the two men were enemies, she thought.

Vince looked at her. "They're likely to be crawling about in the cooler night."

Kash moved a few feet away and, using a twig, turned over the sandy dirt. Sable's skin prickled when a scorpion with front pinchers extended crawled out, irritated at being disturbed.

"They burrow just beneath the surface," said Kash lightly. "There are hundreds of them in this area. Just be careful where you walk."

Sable needed no further warnings.

After exceptionally tender roasted strips of beef and a potato that the cook had baked on the grill, they ate fresh fruit, then enjoyed coffee and tea. Sable, aware that Vince appeared to be watching her, tried not to look at Kash. She was expecting him to tell her news about her father, but as yet they hadn't been left alone for even a few minutes. When supper was over and the dishes and cooking utensils cleared away into one of the smaller trucks, Kate yawned and stood, said good-night, and headed for her sleeping bag. Sable sat by the fire hoping Vince, too, would retire and leave her and Kash alone.

Vince, however, seemed in no such mood. Sable glanced at Kash, but his expression gave nothing away. After a moment he stood and threw the dregs of his coffee into a shrub and looked up at the stars.

"It's been a long, hot day," he said and looked toward the river.

Sable laughed. "You're not serious. . . . What if you meet up with a crocodile?"

"I'll stand guard," said Mateo from the quiet background, and she looked toward the Maasai rather surprised. She hadn't even seen him, he was so quiet as he stood near a doum palm.

"How about you, Vince?" said Kash tonelessly. "Water's delightfully cool."

"Thank you, no. I'll rough it."

Kash whistled as he went out to the Land Rover and caught up his bag from the back, and minutes later went off with Mateo.

Sable thought of a cool swim to get rid of the dust and perspiration that clung to her and frowned to herself. Men had everything easy. Among twenty men, there'd be no bath for her and Kate until they reached her father's camp. Not only that, but Kash's disappearance with Mateo left no moment for her to speak with him alone. Unless . . .

Did he expect her to follow? She glanced about. Vince must have decided it was safe to leave, since his threat to her attention had walked off into the African night.

Sable hesitated. It wouldn't look proper to go trailing after Kash after he'd made it clear he was going for a swim.

She stood, rather irritated in mood, and felt her soiled clothing sticking to her skin. She swatted at a mosquito and, turning her back rigidly toward the river, picked her steps carefully across the camp to the tent she shared with Kate. Kate hadn't worried about smelling sweet; neither would she.

Sometime in the night she awoke to the patter of rain on the canvas and the dripping sound it made on the sand. Still fully clothed, she raised her head and listened. . . . There was another sound outside the tent. She tensed and looked over at Kate, who was not there. What had Kash said about not leaving the tent at night? Where was Kate! She was far from foolish and would never take needless risks.

A little groggy from lack of sleep and the smothering heat, she fumbled to find her flashlight and crawled through the tent opening. Was Kate ill?

The rain was warm and plopped on her head, wetting her face. Kate would never be foolish enough to decide to take a bath in the river while all the crew were retired to the trucks and tents, would she?

Sable moved cautiously across the path until she stood in the middle of the camp, glancing around for some sign of the direction her sister might have taken. A flashlight flicked on and off in the distance but looked to be coming from above the ground. Sable began walking toward it. She came within sixty feet of a half-dead acacia tree and stopped. "Kate?"

"Don't move!" rasped Kate from up the tree.

Sable stopped abruptly. From somewhere beneath the tree, she heard a growl, and a large dark form spun around, scampered across the sparse growth, then crouched not more than ten feet in front of her, its golden eyes fixed on her provocatively, its ropy tail slashing from side to side in the tall grass.

Kash had once told her to never put a lion in a compromising position, never to threaten it. Had she already broken a rule? A bolt of fear sent her heart thudding, and she broke into a nervous sweat.

The lion's vocalization had shown surprise, but it turned threatening when its hindquarters crouched down. It could easily lash out and tear her open from shoulder to waist.

"Lord Jesus," gasped Kate from the tree branch, "please help us—"

Sable could not move even if she had wanted to. Her legs were rubbery.

Where was Kash? Vince? Anyone! Then she realized no one would come, since Kash had warned them not to leave the tents and wouldn't be expecting an emergency.

The lion was keyed up, its ears perked forward, body held low, tail thrashing up dust. Then—with a loud straining grunt, the lion sprang into the air as Sable's throat constricted. It whirled around and, playfully hoisting a simple chunk of wood between its teeth, strutted down to the riverbank from where it had come and disappeared.

From the tree branch, Kate burst into relieved tears, and Sable sank slowly to the grass and simply sat there, too weak to move.

Kate scrambled down from the tree, ran to Sable, and grasped her. Helping Sable to her feet, they clutched each other and stumbled back into the small dark tent.

"I'm sorry—" said Kate, trembling, her hands cold and clammy as she stroked Sable's bent head. "I . . . I had to go out."

Sable only shook her head and rocked to and fro, the lion's golden eyes still staring at her from the darkness of her mind.

Kate fumbled to produce a waterskin. "Here—take this." She gave Sable a small white pill.

Sable asked no questions. Her fingers were shaking so badly she could hardly get the pill into her mouth.

Kate lowered Sable to her sleeping bag, then sitting beside her, rubbed the tension from between Sable's shoulder blades.

"Kash will never speak to me again if he knew what happened to you."

"If . . . if the Lord hadn't been with us, I'd be dead now," whispered Sable. "No one could have made that lion turn around and sprint away except the One who had kept Daniel."

Silence enveloped them, and the rain was still plopping on the canvas.

"Yes—" said Kate with sudden enthusiasm, and then, as if overwhelmed by the experience that had turned into deliverance, she laughed.

"Remember that Sunday school song—the one you used to

sing all the time and I used to hold my ears 'cause I didn't like it?" Then she began to sing it in a shaky voice tinged with both laughter and tears—

"Dare to be a Daniel, dare to stand alone, dare to have a purpose firm, dare to make it known—"

Sable laughed, too, and sniffed back her tears. She had wanted Kash to come and save her from the lion, but the Lord had been there. His deliverance, His awareness of every detail of her life—even blundering into a dangerous situation in the dead of the African night—was now far more precious.

The pill began to make her relax, and she closed her eyes, the name of Jesus sweet as honey on her lips.

"I'm going to show the film in Samburu. . . ." she murmured sleepily. "Nothing will stop me."

Fifteen

The next morning they drove to Samburu, taking the track north from Meru. Soon they were climbing among the acacia trees that were lifting their flat heads over the plain. Thorn trees and scrub grew thickly together, and in the distance outcrops of red rock looked down upon them from an elevated position with stark raw beauty.

"Look," said Kate from the backseat, "over there."

"Elephants," said Mckib.

Kash slowed the Land Rover. Sable counted five fully grown elephants, two with very small calves under their bellies. There were seven youngsters in all, some of them half grown. The largest elephant, the matriarch, guarded the others from behind, and she paused as though uncertain whether to enter the clearing when she picked up the scent of humans and noise coming from Browning's two trucks. The elephant turned and faced them, her ears fanned wide, her trunk elongated, feeling the air. The trunk moved to and fro, testing. A small breeze stirred the leaves. The adults had surrounded the calves, trunks waving, all of them undecided.

Sable glanced back at Browning's hunters and felt an angry frustration settle in her chest as though she might expect them to be stroking their hunting rifles and drooling to themselves. She glanced at Kash and saw his moody expression. He stepped on the accelerator, and Sable looked behind to make certain the trucks and van followed.

Relaxing a little more, she settled back and anticipated the delight of seeing her father again after so long a time. Perhaps he'd even driven in from the wilderness camp to meet them at Samburu Lodge.

"That's Isiolo to the right of the river," Kash told her, and she followed his gesture to the small township that divided the two game reserves. He then turned onto gravel, and three giraffes stood motionless by a thorn tree, munching the topmost branches. As the Land Rover passed, they galloped off with a stiff but graceful gait that enabled them to keep their heads at a constant elevation. A blue-gray ostrich stood alone, the breeze ruffling its feathers. She saw little else of wildlife now. Ten miles farther on, when Kash turned left at a fork in the track, they slowed as they neared some thatched huts: the entrance to the Samburu Game Reserve.

They drove over the bridge that crossed the river, and on either side, shrubs and trees and wildlife abounded. Doum palm were everywhere, and what was called *mswaki*, Swahili for the toothbrush bush, the leaves of which were used by the locals to polish and keep their teeth white.

The Samburu Reserve was a wildlife park rich in species not always seen elsewhere in Kenya. The thin-striped Grevy's zebra, the reticulated giraffe, and the gerenuk, a graceful, long-necked gazelle that browsed high in tall bushes by standing on its hind legs.

"It's called giraffe gazelle," said Kash, "and gerenuk is Somali for 'giraffe-necked.'"

He pointed out a Beisa oryx with its long, pointed, straight horns. "A predator is unwise to attack an oryx."

There were leopards, too—and they caught a picture-perfect scene of a slim spotted cheetah racing past umbrella acacias and champagne-colored savanna grass while gaining on an unfortunate gerenuk.

Samburu was officially two reserves: Samburu on the north bank of the Uaso Nyiro River, and Isiolo-Buffalo Springs Reserve on the south bank.

"The Uaso is Maasai for 'river of brown water,' and it divides the two reserves. And 'Samburu' means 'butterfly,' " said Kash.

The feel of lush tropics surrounded the river as Sable's delighted gaze fell upon some elephants bathing in the water. The full river flowed past a stand of trees growing thickly on the bank, and the glistening wet bodies of crocodiles appeared greenish as they swaggered out of the water's edge to soak up the sun on the bank. A huge gray hippo with its pink mouth wide open like a cavern stood motionless in the river.

The water looked muddy to Sable as they drove into the main grounds. The lodge was larger than Kenyatta and spread out along the Uaso banks, where the main building reminded her of a round satellite-like lounge. It extended out over the water where guests could watch an occasional leopard come to quench its thirst.

She noticed rooms on both sides of the building, and Kash mentioned that the dining room was decorated in Spanish decor.

As they got out of the Land Rover, big black baboons were scampering about the roof like greeting clowns, and half-tame birds flitted among the lower tree branches, their bright summer shades of raspberry, watermelon red, and shamrock green glinting in the waning sunlight. Hearing the mad, boisterous screeching mingled with delicate, cheerful song was more than her mind could take in, and she laughed as Kate covered her ears. Above, the sky glowed like burnished copper.

So this was Samburu—"butterfly." Deeper into the reserve toward Marsabit was the home of the large-tusked elephants and her father's research camp, which waited with mystery.

Tomorrow they would drive the last leg of the safari to haul the supplies and open the medical and Christian relief camp to serve the Samburu and the Turkana nomadic tribes. While Kate's medical work would win friends, Sable would strive to show the *JESUS* film and in between times work with her father to help document the behavior of the elephants.

"I'd just as soon reach Dad's camp tonight," said Kate. "I wonder why Kash wants to stay at the lodge?"

Sable, too, wondered and stood watching the trucks arrive and park farther down the river. Browning opened the door and climbed down, and soon the back door slid open and the rank members of his crew swarmed about the trucks and van like locusts, unloading their belongings for the day. Sable stared at the truck-trailer belonging to Browning and thought again of Seth's camera and film. Was it in there?

Mckib, returning from the lodge without Kash, informed them they had rooms until the next morning, when they would leave for Skyler's camp.

"You mean rooms—with a shower?" asked Kate with exuberance.

"And sheets," grinned Mckib. "Rest of us be camping out near the river. The crew's got to get set up before it gets too dark. It ain't safe to meander after nightfall. No one in his right mind wanders on foot in lion country."

Sable glanced at Kate, who smiled and, picking up her overnight bag, hurried toward the lodge—and undoubtedly the shower. Sable was prepared to quickly follow when Mckib took hold of her arm and said in a low voice, "Kash says to meet him out here tonight. Bring the things you'll need. You'll be gone a few days."

Sable was surprised. "We're leaving?"

"You and him is."

"Well—what does he want, did he explain?"

"He'll explain tonight, what it's about. Just trust him, he says. Says to meet him after you have supper, around eight-thirty. And not to say anything to Vince or Browning."

⟨∽⟩

A message arrived at their room from Vince, asking both Sable and Kate to join him, Browning, and Kash for dinner.

That Kash would be there seemed confusing, since Mckib hadn't mentioned it. What need to meet Kash on the grounds if he were to be seated at the table during dinner? She didn't think Kash would show in the dining room, and Sable eased her way out of the invitation.

"Browning!" she wrinkled her nose. "I'd rather keep company with a hippo for supper. You go, Kate, and make an excuse for me to Vince, would you?"

"What! You're going to leave me alone with them? For how long?"

"I don't know," she said evasively. "Until I meet Kash as he asked. But don't wait for us."

"I won't want any dinner by the time I've put up with Browning for two hours. Did Kash say why he wanted you to meet him alone?"

"No, but I've learned long ago he'll have his sound reasons. Will you cover for me or not?"

"You know I will, but the old 'headache' routine doesn't work nowadays. What shall I say, and at the same time keep from compromising my integrity?"

Anxious to get away, Sable glanced toward the back stairs that led down from their room onto the lower terrace. She had another plan besides meeting Kash, one of her own.

"Don't explain. Tell Vince I'll be there as soon as I can."

Before Kate could respond, Sable left their room and hurried silently down the wooden steps until she came to the terrace. A few tourists were out with night binoculars and paid her no mind as she passed through the small gate, down two more steps, and out onto the grounds.

Careful where she walked and using her flashlight to scan the path, she went quickly away from the lodge toward the river, where the vehicles were parked. She neared Browning's truck-trailer. As she'd expected, the crew were off somewhere loading up on beer. A small gas lamp flickered in the trailer window, so she knew Browning was still inside getting cleaned up for dinner. Sable concealed herself behind one of the trees and flicked off her flashlight, waiting for him to leave.

Luck seemed to be on her side. A few minutes after eight the door opened, and Browning stepped out in a clean shirt and khaki trousers. In the light that shone down from the string of lanterns suspended over the front grounds of the lodge, she could see his golden hair still wet from his first bath since they had left Amboseli Reserve.

She smothered her feeling of dislike and watched him saunter across the grounds toward the brightly lit dining room, where Kate and Vince would be waiting for him.

When he had disappeared inside, Sable stirred from behind the tree and walked quickly toward the trailer. A glance about the area showed that there were no guards.

She went up the step to the door and tried the latch. As she had hoped, it was open, the light still burning. Evidently he didn't expect to be gone long.

She closed the door behind her, trying to calm her heart. The odor of cologne and stale beer and cigarette smoke affronted her nostrils. Swiftly she began her search, opening cluttered cabinets and drawers on a built-in bureau. Finding nothing worthy of her efforts, she turned to the boxes stacked about the walls. Guns and rifles, ammunition, magazines. . . .

She turned to the small closet and opened the latch. Instead of clothing it was another gun rack, and at the bottom were a pair of boots—

The door behind her opened, and she whirled. Browning stared at her, his shock visible; then the creases in his tan face curled into a nasty smile.

"Well now, hello. Looking for something, sweetie? Maybe I can help you find it."

He stepped inside, his head almost touching the low ceiling, and shut the door behind him. He stood there, watching her with a smile, his eyes unpleasant.

There was no logical excuse to make, and she wouldn't favor him by cowering.

"I'm to meet Kash outside now, so you'd better pretend you didn't find me here and let me pass without a scene."

His teeth flashed in a deeper smile. "Why, of course, Miss Dunsmoor. Would I be rude enough to force you to stay without your consent?"

She took her eyes from his and glanced at the doorknob. His big brown hand clasped it firmly.

She took a step in his direction, but he didn't move.

"You said I could go."

"Sure. After you tell me what you were looking for."

"Maybe I was looking for the key to the truck—to check the supplies."

"Maybe, but you weren't. You haven't bothered to check on them before, why now? 'Sides, you know they're safe. Kash would see to that. And it so happens he has the key, as you know."

She hadn't known, but it would do no good now to deny it.

"What were you looking for?" he asked again, this time his voice as blunt as his unsmiling face.

"Kash is waiting for me by now. Suppose you ask him? He won't like it if he finds out you're holding me here against my wishes. I could scream."

His eyes hardened. He opened the door and stepped aside, and Sable didn't wait. She rushed past, but he reached out and latched hold of her, swinging her around to face him, holding her tightly against him.

"Just one kiss, angel face—for breaking in here."

Sable pushed against him, turning her face away. He took hold of her hair, pulling her head back with a jerk that brought her face up toward his.

His breath smelled and she cried out, frightened now as his grip tightened.

"If I were you I'd turn her loose," said Kash.

Browning's hands dropped, and Sable stumbled back, landing against the closet.

Browning held up both palms toward him as Kash stepped inside the trailer. "Take it easy, man. Stay cool. It was just a little joke is all—I know she belongs to you—" He gasped and doubled, eyes widening, as Kash struck a quick, savage jab into his belly.

Sable's hands flew to her face. She turned her head away, hearing the sickening sounds. The trailer rocked, boxes crashed to the floor, and some cups and plates fell from the small table as grunts and groans filled her ears, ending with a thud and crash when Browning's heavy body landed into the fallen boxes.

Sable didn't move. After a precarious moment of silence she ventured a brief glance, grimacing as she did. One look at

Browning and she jerked her head away.

Kash was searching the trailer, tossing aside the cushions on the bunk. Below the springs was a camera. He grabbed it, latching hold of her arm, and steered her out the door and down the step into the hot, dark night.

They hurried toward the Land Rover parked on the other side of the grounds near the river, and Sable had to run to keep up with his stride.

"I'm sorry—" she began, then in a small voice, "Are you hurt?"

"Scratched knuckles is all. He'll be out of commission for a day. That will give us time."

Time for what? she wondered.

"I've been intending to search his trailer. All I needed was an excuse, but you shouldn't have gone there. Never tempt a swine like Browning; he'll always take the bait."

"I went for the camera, but he came back," she said meekly.

They'd reached the passenger side of the Land Rover, and she turned to look at him. In the moonlight she could see his frown, even as his eyes softened. "You were brave, but unwise."

Under his gaze she hastened to change the subject. "Is it Seth's camera?"

"Yes, his initials are on the case."

"Aren't you going to open it to see if the film is there?"

"In a minute."

Sable looked from the camera to Kash.

He hesitated, as if wrestling with his emotions. "The last time I raised the issue of kissing you, it was totally at my initiative. . . . I think it wise to wait for your cooperation. How long are you going to keep me waiting?"

She swallowed, dragging her eyes from his, and reached behind her for the handle on the car door.

"Speaking of temptation . . . don't you think we'd better get out of here?"

He studied her for a moment in the moonlight, and she saw the corner of his mouth turn. Without a word he leaned over and opened the door. "We're going to Lake Rudolf."

"Lake Rudolf!"

"Vince claimed he wanted you to see the work. So do I, but for a different reason. Dean's waiting with the plane. Let's go."

"And leave Kate?" she cried.

"She'll be safe enough. Mckib will explain, and my men are still here mixed in with Browning's hunters. They have their orders and know what to do. And I've sent Mateo ahead to tell Skyler when we'll arrive. After Rudolf, we'll join him. He's not at the Samburu camp, but north, at Marsabit."

There was a small airstrip some six miles from the lodge, and Dean was waiting with the plane when they arrived.

"I thought you were bringing Kate, too," came the half-disappointed voice.

"She's keeping Vince busy, but don't worry. You can see her at the camp in a few days. Let's go and get this over with. We haven't much time, since Skyler will be waiting for us at Marsabit. He's got the elephant herd under close supervision. I just hope the rest of our men can get through by way of Somalia."

Sable wondered, but Kash was in no mood to explain more now. "First, we meet Dr. Willard."

The night was clear, and the velvety sky was bright with stars and planets. Once seated in the plane, Sable buckled her seat belt as Kash closed the small door. Soon Dean had the motor running, and after his careful routine checks and some radio announcing, they took off.

Sable tried to see over the nose as they gained speed down the center of the small runway. She felt exhilarated as the Cessna left the earth and climbed. She peered down through the window and watched the winking lights of Samburu Lodge growing smaller, like earthbound stars.

⁂

After seeing practically nothing below the plane for over two hours, the lights from Lake Rudolf's lodges were a welcome sight as Dean lost altitude and searched for his visual checkpoints. He located the small airstrip, circled, then entered the landing pattern. "I had a friend lose a plane here," he said above the engine noise. "During the day the winds in this area can be deadly. They can roar through a campsite and toss everything sky-high like a bunch of matchsticks."

Soon they landed on the small airstrip in calm air. A few minutes later Kash stepped to the ground and helped Sable out while Dean went to tie down the plane.

"Is this East Rudolf National Park?" asked Sable, confused by the terrain.

"This is the Loyengalani airstrip," said Dean, "on the east end of the park. You've got to be someone important to the paleontologists before they let you use their airstrip. Strangers are discouraged from visiting their base camp."

"You see," said Kash, "we're not paleontologists, just mere mortals. Anyway, Dr. Willard's camp is not with the others. It's about a one-and-a-half-hour hike from here."

Sable was surprised. Somehow she'd expected Dr. Willard to be part of the East Rudolf paleontologists.

"It's after midnight. We're going to need some rest. We brought sleeping bags. We'll take out the rear seat back, and you'll be able to lie down. Dean and I will camp out under the plane until dawn."

Even though the fuselage was small and her legs were in the baggage compartment, Sable felt at peace as the sleeping bag began to warm up. She felt the plane gently rock with the mild night breezes. It had been a long day. She spoke to her heavenly Father and thanked Him for protecting her from many dangers. . . . Today it was Browning . . . and last night the lion. Now she wasn't sure which was worse. She remembered Psalm 46:1: *"God is our refuge and strength, a very present help in trouble. . . ."*

༺◦◦◦◦◦༒

The morning sun was rising on the reddish gold eastern horizon. She walked between the two men on the three-mile hike to Willard's base camp. The wind was starting up. In just a few hours it would be blisteringly hot and dry as the sun reached its zenith.

Lake Rudolf, called the Jade Sea because of its greenish blue color, covered some thirty-five hundred square miles and was surrounded by a frightening purple lava desert that was once even larger and connected to the Nile. It was a rich archaeological area where various expeditions claimed momentous discoveries of early man.

The Turkana tribe occupied the western shore, and like the Maasai, they were seldom influenced by the outside world. Sable looked upon the warriors wearing elaborate hairstyles and ivory or wood lip plugs. They carried small wooden stools and were experts with their circular wrist knives.

"We estimate around twenty-two thousand crocodiles live in the lake," Kash told her, "but poachers leave them alone. Their buttonlike skin growths make poor ladies' handbags."

Sable noticed zebras here, too, and giraffes.

"For years," said Kash, "a large expedition of anthropologists and African assistants have used Koobi for their base, surveying and digging in a nine-hundred-square-mile fossil-rich area."

Sable knew about National Museum Administrator Richard Leakey, son of the late Louis Leakey and co-leader of the expedition. In the early seventies he had announced finding and *reconstructing* the "oldest complete skull of early man." Known as "1470 Man," the fossil was claimed by evolutionists to be from 2.6 to 2.8 million years old. The skull and complete femur were considered to be important for several reasons: the fossils were among some ninety specimens found at Rudolf. "The skull is claimed to have a cranial capacity of more than eight hundred cubic centimeters," said Kash.

"What's the significance of that?" asked Sable as they walked along together with Dean in the lead.

"For years evolutionists thought that Australopithecus with a cranial capacity of only five hundred cubic centimeters was an ancestor of modern man. The problem they have now is that this fossil is considered by them to be more than a million years older, yet it looks very much like modern man, and the complete femur, or thigh bone, indicates that he walked upright, the same as you and I. They are now calling him 'East Rudolf Man.' Richard Leakey now believes that Australopithecus was not an ancestor of modern man at all, and that presently held evolutionary theories and nomenclature of early man will have to be revised."

"I could have told him *that*," said Sable airily. "All he has to do is read Genesis chapter two to find how God created mankind."

Kash laughed. "Yes, I think you could have, and you would have provided an explanation that harmonizes very well with the fossil record."

"I didn't know you knew so much about the subject," she said, curious and pleased to discover something new about Kash.

"During the long period while I was working on the weaver bird project I started asking 'too many' questions and started examining the library of the scientist who hired me. I began to notice that no matter what species I read about in his evolutionary texts, the same patterns began to consistently appear. Statements like, 'When we study the earliest fossil evidence for this species we find that it already has millions of years of evolutionary development behind it.' I'm no professional, but I've been able to read between the lines. What the statement is really saying is, the oldest fossils that have been found for this species are quite typical, and since the fossil record provides no evidence for its evolutionary development, it is therefore *assumed*. It is still very true, as it was in Darwin's day, that the first appearance in the fossil record of all major classes of organisms are very characteristic of their class. One book on the subject, *Evolution: A Theory in Crisis*, written by Dr. Michael Denton—who is not a creationist—states that one of the most striking characteristics of the fossil record that is widely recognized by many leading paleontologists today is the 'virtual complete absence of intermediate and ancestral forms.' "

"Well, if that's true, why don't more anthropologists reject evolution completely?"

"Their problem is, there are few alternatives once they have disallowed the correct solution to the issue. Without permitting the possibility of the reality of an awesome Creator, they have backed themselves into a corner." He looked down at her. "Does Vince know that Dr. Willard has given up on evolution?"

Her surprise showed. "He's never mentioned it. But I don't understand. If Dr. Willard isn't an evolutionist, why have you warned me against the work that he and Vince are doing?"

"You'll see for yourself when we talk with him."

Sable scanned him, her heart warming. How could she ever have thought Kash to be spiritually lacking? Why had she allowed Vince to deceive her about his interest in the Christian faith?

It must have been nearing noon when Sable looked ahead and saw a camp. They approached a cluster of bomas and what appeared to her to be a large building under construction by African workers and a few European overseers.

"Take a good look," Kash told her, gesturing to the domed building. "That's the choice investment that Vince *borrowed* your twenty thousand dollars to have built." His cobalt eyes glinted maliciously when she frowned. "I see you're not easily impressed. Perhaps meeting Dr. Willard will change your mind."

She looked at him uneasily. "Can you prove it? That he used the money for this building?"

"Would I have brought you all the way here if I couldn't? It's a research house, a meditation house, and VIP lounge all in one. It's here that Willard, Vince, Dr. Katherine Walsh, and a few other geniuses will gather."

"A 'meditation house'?" she asked, a little confused. "What are they meditating about?"

"About the 'ultimate truth.' The new open door to what man is and can become . . . his destiny, his beginning—or should I say, his end? Their eventual conclusions will amaze the common man, who will look into the mirror and claim with confidence, 'I am God!' "

She resisted his half-smile. "Vince would never—I mean, he's not a fool."

"No, and neither is Dr. Willard, nor millions of others who believe the same thing. They're grossly intelligent, yet fools in God's sight. 'The fool has said in his heart there is no God.' When one rejects the Light, what else is there but the spiraling stairway down into spiritual darkness that leads to mental madness? 'Professing themselves to be wise, they became fools,' says Romans. What else can you call a human being who can go down to Lake Rudolf, stand there, look up in the starry universe, and cry, 'I am God!'?"

Sable shuddered as the hot wind tossed her hair, causing it to glimmer like honey. Her eyes searched his, and she knew he was telling her the truth of what he'd learned about Dr. Willard's organization.

"What does it all have to do with Vince, about poaching ivory?"

"Money. I told you that before. Let Dr. Willard explain about Brother Vince. Come, he's seen us."

As they approached the camp, a man came out of one of the bomas and stood waiting for them. Sable assumed the silver-haired man in his late fifties was Dr. Willard. He was a handsome man who could pass for any important head of a big corporation. His hair had grown long, however, and dusted his bare shoulders, and he was as brown as a baked coconut. He wore khaki shorts and boots and seemed packed with energy. His face, as he greeted them, was creased by the sun, and his eyes wore a hard, bright gleam, like clear granite.

"We don't have many visitors, so naturally we're excited to have you," he said, shaking hands with Kash and Dean and smiling at Sable. "Your father is a brilliant man, Miss Dunsmoor. And so is Vince. He tells me you'll be married next year. Let me congratulate you."

Kash gave her a side glance.

"You know my father, Dr. Willard?"

"He's visited us on several occasions with Katherine. Katherine was working with him at the elephant camp in Samburu until recently. She's joined us here now full time, thanks to Vince. She's my niece," he laughed. "He didn't need to do much hard sell. She was an A student and earned her doctorate a year ahead of schedule."

He gestured to the domed structure. "This is our new building. Vince has contact with a group of entrepreneurs in Toronto who are enthusiastic about our work here. They've honored us with a permanent building. It should be completed early next year."

Then Vince hasn't told him the money came from me and Kate.

"Looks as though Dr. Adler wholeheartedly supports your cause," said Kash.

"A brilliant fellow. Without his financial support we couldn't continue. Like the rest of our group, Vince believes our future discoveries will make all past evolutionary hypotheses pale into insignificance."

Sable remembered back to her conversation with Vince at the Treehouse. Hadn't he said something about a great future discovery?

"And just what is your work?" she asked quietly.

"Anthropology, but in a new light. It used to be a search for fossils. At least, that's what we gave our lives to for many years. Recently, we've taken a new and distinct approach to discovering the origins of life."

"Amazing," said Kash. "I suppose Dr. Adler was difficult to convince? I thought he, like yourself, was a hardened naturalistic evolutionist."

"Conviction did not come easily. Like me, he became disillusioned with evolution as we know it."

Disillusioned with evolution? Sable glanced at Kash.

"Come inside," said Dr. Willard pleasantly. "We'll have refreshments and talk if you like. Banyu!" he called to a worker. "Bring something for our guests!"

Seated in the boma and served tea and fruit, Sable was silent as Dr. Willard and Kash carried on their discourse and Kash pretended innocent curiosity.

"So you no longer believe in evolution?" asked Kash.

"I believed in evolution religiously for most of my life. I believe what Darwin said, that 'if evolution is true, the best evidence for it should be in the fossil record.' I studied and categorized the fossil record for years with my colleagues. Until just recently I was diligently attempting to make an evolutionary tree of life. In high school I noticed that the various species in the evolutionary tree were connected with question marks, and I made it my goal to remove just one or two of the question marks! But the more I studied, the more I found that evolutionists were just speculating. Many hypothetical reconstructions are beginning to look more like fantasies than serious conjectures. For example, the only reason an evolutionist says that birds evolved from reptiles is that he can't find anything better than a reptile to use as an ancestor. Birds lay eggs, and reptiles lay eggs, and so this is used as an evidence of common origin. But if this were so, there should be millions of years in which reptile scales were randomly evolving into all sorts of things, one of which was a feather."

"And no such fossil has ever been found?" asked Kash smoothly.

"No. And anyway, it is not even logical to think that a scale can progress into a feather. A feather is a very complex structure that grows from a follicle, and this is the very opposite of a scale, which is a projection in the skin. And to my horror, I found that the fossil record was completely silent on this issue. In fact, it is silent on all other similar issues that one can think of. It has now been over one hundred thirty years since Darwin and the fossil record has been categorized, and many evolutionists have given up looking for missing links."

He emptied his cup of tea and looked at them soberly. "What the record shows is that there never have been any links. In fact, the fossil record is a record of extinction, not of evolution! Every paleontologist knows that at one time there were many times more distinct species than presently exist. This is true for both plants and animals. And not only that, but all species make their appearance in the fossil record abruptly—so that their evolutionary development is firmly grounded upon nothing."

He refilled his cup and leaned back, looking thoughtfully toward the open door. "Evolution has long been standing on a shaky foundation. Many of the best scientists sense this but have nowhere else to go—and no desire to go elsewhere. And so, the face that they present in public speaks with certainty about things that are scientifically 'unverifiable.' "

"Doesn't the word 'science' basically mean knowledge?" asked Sable.

"Quite so. Any scientific principle must be subject to experimentation. A principle is testable only if it is possible to conceive an experiment to demonstrate it."

"So that if the experiment failed—then the principle would be invalidated?" said Sable.

"Yes, scientists say that the principle must be capable of 'falsification.' If it is not, then it is not a scientific theory."

"You mean," asked Kash, "there's no experimental way to demonstrate whether it's true? Therefore the theory of evolution is not a scientific theory."

"Yes, I've known that all along. Evolution has never been observed, no experiment can be conceived to test it. But that never really bothered me because I thought it could be supported in other ways, by showing that it is harmonious with the fossil record. But one day I woke up and looked in the mirror and asked myself this question: 'What one thing do I know about evolution that is true?' After practically a lifetime of study I could not think of anything! It became a new awakening for me. My mind was suddenly free."

"What about the possibility of an intelligent creator?" suggested Kash.

"Some of my former colleagues have taken that route, but to me it is too restrictive. It ultimately means that I must submit to a superior being. I don't see that it is necessary for me to let any kind of god run my life."

"Well then, have you come to any new conclusions?" asked Kash innocently.

"I have indeed. I have experienced a new awakening into the possibility of transcendent knowledge."

"Transcendent knowledge?" Kash asked with apparent naiveté. "How can this be obtained?"

"Through contact with a spirit guide."

Sable leaned forward, looking from Dr. Willard's smiling face to Kash. Kash lifted his tea and drank, watching her over the cup.

"You've contacted a being you think is an angel?" she asked quietly.

"We have, or I should say, he's contacted us. Vince, too, has met our angel," said Dr. Willard.

"Met him? You had a meditation service?"

"That is how we contact our spirit guide. Eventually, once we've proven he can trust us, we expect he'll lead us to a higher form of knowledge than could ever be known by conventional methods. The world will be astonished as we prove the origins of early man. Arcturus has hinted that wiser beings from another planet first began the process of life on Earth. I'm certain that will prove a shock and disappointment to those who take the Bible literally—and to the evolutionists as well."

Sable looked at Kash, but he was unreadable.

"A pity Vince isn't with us," Kash said. "We could have a jolly time as we sit about the campfire tonight discussing Arcturus."

Dr. Willard smiled indulgently. "Do I take it, Kash Hallet, you don't think there's anything to this spirit guide business? I assure you we are serious."

"I believe there's a great deal to your angel, Dr. Willard, but we disagree on his mission and who may have sent him to win your allegiance."

"There are so many things that Arcturus is able to reveal that we need to tread carefully. We feel extremely privileged he has been willing to communicate at all."

"And, of course, Vince also feels extremely privileged to support this endeavor?"

"Without Vince and Katherine, we'd be left to run our research lab on pennies and promises. We owe him a great deal. One day, when our finds are made public and we've a number of wealthy donors, we expect to reward him properly for his faith in our work."

"And do you have wealthy individuals in mind who will be impressed with Arcturus?"

"Oh yes. We have contacts in the entertainment world in the United States and England, not to mention some others."

Sable had excused herself and walked outside to where Dean

leaned against a tree in the shade dozing. "Heard enough?" he asked sympathetically.

She nodded. She didn't think Vince was as beguiled by the supposed spirit guide as he was convinced that a large sum of money might be gained by investing in the growing "spiritual" work of the Toronto Research Lab.

A few minutes later Kash walked up, and she met his gaze.

Dean glanced toward the boma. "It looks like Dr. Willard and his niece could use a dose of truth."

"They've already heard the truth," said Kash gravely. He looked at Sable. "Dr. Willard is the son of a minister. Now, of course, he's proud to let you know that he's way beyond such infantile beliefs. He's on the verge of discovering transcendent knowledge."

Sable was sitting glumly on a rock, fanning herself with her hat. She knew she should feel some great emotional loss over Vince because he was enmeshed in a great deception, yet she had already suspected Kash of being right for days. Now that the facts were clearly set forth before her eyes, she accepted it calmly and felt little emotion except a strange release. Kash watched her, the irony gone from his eyes, as if wondering whether he might have offended her. She wanted to tell him he hadn't, that he had done what was wise. She was secretly pleased that he had been strong enough and determined enough to make her face the truth.

Dean seemed to guess they wanted to be alone and made an excuse to leave them and join Dr. Willard. "Do you believe in sudden repentance?" he asked, looking toward Willard. "Maybe I can make him see the light."

"Go ahead, try," said Kash. "You'll find him as dense as the Dead Sea. 'Arcturus' is as real to him as the god the Maasai believe lives on Kilimanjaro."

When Dean walked toward Dr. Willard, Sable was silent. Kash leaned against the tree, looking out toward the distant lake. For a minute he remained silent, too.

The strangely shaped volcanic cones surrounding the lake looked like statues, bleak and dead, like the belief system that surrounded the small cultic compound. Sable stirred.

"Are you unhappy about Vince?" Kash asked.

She looked at him as the wind tugged at his shirt and dark hair, and she found herself warmed within by the deep blue of his eyes.

She smiled. "Not in the way you ask. I feel sorry for his spiritual confusion, yes, but I'm not sorry I'll never be Mrs. Vince Adler." She hesitated, then said quietly, "I was mistaken to think Vince could ever replace the memory of a *certain man*." She looked at him. "You were right when you said I walked into a relationship in order to forget what we had—what I thought we had lost."

"We didn't lose it, Sable. It's still there, stronger than ever. It's ours for the taking, if you want to try again."

Her heart hammered, and she swallowed, looking at her hands. "Do you?" she whispered. "Want to try again?"

He straightened from the tree and reached down, taking both her hands and pulling her gently to her feet. "Do you need to ask?"

"I just want to hear you say it."

Her eyes clung to his, and she saw everything she had ever prayed for and dreamed about.

"I want you more than anything," he whispered into the wind.

She couldn't speak. Their eyes held, and tears came to hers. Kash drew her swiftly into his embrace, and his lips took hers warmly, tenderly, saying more than words ever could.

Sixteen

*I*t was past noon, and the sun was shining with hot brilliance
as they landed at the small airstrip near Marsabit Town after
a pleasant flight from Lake Rudolf. Dean, however, appeared
anxious. "I've got to get back to Samburu to find Kate," he told
them with a grin that said his heart had already found more than
he'd bargained for.

"Tell her we're safe and we'll join her soon. I'm anxious to
show the film as soon as we can and help Father document his
findings on the elephants."

"Sure." He looked at Kash. "You won't need my help with
Mr. Dunsmoor and the herd?"

"We've a dozen Kenya Rifles militiamen waiting at the outpost near here to assist us."

Dean gestured his salute and climbed back into the plane to
take off as Kash and Sable retreated a safe distance away. Minutes
later, they stood watching as he circled the strip, climbing and
heading south to Samburu.

After visiting the park store for gear, Kash and Sable rented
a Land Rover and drove north from Marsabit Town.

Out on the African plain the desert breeze stirred the feathers of a flock of black rooks that perched on dead-looking limbs
of a thorn tree. A zebra's harsh barking sound awoke some white
egrets, which spread their wings and flew southward while a
small herd of oryx fled in all directions, the hot dust blowing
under their hoofs.

Heading toward Mount Marsabit, Sable saw the odd-shaped pyramids and balanced rocks she'd heard about from her father. The stone appeared to take on mysterious forms in the bluish desert haze among low thorn scrubs, toothbrush shrub, and desert rose with pinkish rubbery stems. Poison sap grew in abundance, and Kash told her it was used by the nomadic tribes to poison their arrows.

Sable pointed to an odd sight—several inches of grain chaff circled a giant hole in the red sand.

"Harvester ants," said Kash. "They gather kernels from the thin grasses and leave the husks."

By late afternoon, the mountain ramparts of the Matthews Range rose up in the west, casting purple shadows, and on the plain among sparse isolated bushes, pairs of dik-dik stood seeking refuge from the sun.

The Merille River ran down from the mountains in the rainy season, but now members of the Samburu tribe were out digging for water in the dry riverbed. Sable saw their tall bottles made of leather, three and four feet high. Other Samburu sat resting beneath a tree near the bank. The young boys' heads were shaven except for one lock of hair, and they wore thin beads and earrings made from river shells. The girls were dressed in leather aprons with a cotton cloth tied at one shoulder.

"Unmarried girls are painted red," said Kash.

"I wonder why?"

He smiled at her. "It makes them easy to locate."

Sable was sure that wasn't the real reason, but she noticed that some had tattoos on their bellies as well and was relieved when he didn't comment. Married women wore what looked to her to be a heavy collar made from the doum palm fiber and decorated with large, dark red beads. Their arms were decorated with coils of silver steel and golden copper. A woman carrying an infant in a sling wore thin green beads. Men and women wore metal anklets, bead headbands, and copper earrings; she noticed a Samburu moran had an ivory ear plug and a string of beads that ran beneath his lip and back behind his ears.

"After all this is over with Father and the elephants, I'd like to try to arrange a film showing here. Do you think we could?"

His eyes teased her with a warm blue glint. "We'll get married back at Samburu, then I'll take you on film-showing expeditions from here to the nomads of the Kaisut Desert."

Sable smiled, her eyes holding his. "I might just take you up on that."

In the distance a Samburu herdsman stood leaning carelessly upon his spear, his ankles crossed in a stance that was characteristic of warrior herdsmen from the Maasai to the desert nomads.

Mount Marsabit arose from the desert with green foothills climbing in steps toward isolated cones. The air was cooler now, and in a meadow, a lone bull elephant stood with lopsided tusks. This was the high oasis Sable's father spoke of in his letters where the elephants congregated away from the threat of man. This was where the big elephant Ahmed lived, whose tusks were estimated at 150 to 170 pounds each—and this fact alone made him a target for poachers.

Mount Marsabit was the place of volcanoes, of the sweet lark song, of red and blue butterflies, and the last home of the great elephants. And far below, the whitish desert vanished into desolate nomadic horizons. There were green meadows filled with copper-colored grass, blue thistle, common blue morning glory, vetch, sweet pea, and the curious insect-simulating verbena with flowers fashioned like blue butterflies, even to the long curling antennae.

Kash told her about one type of cow pea with large curled blossoms. "To each blossom comes a golden-banded black beetle that eats the petals; each beetle is followed by one or more ants that appear to 'nip' at its hind legs to speed its progress in order to obtain a residue from its thorax.

"If you go out the next day," said Kash, "you'll find the flowering is over and the beetles are gone."

The creation of God is truly amazing, thought Sable.

The roads of Marsabit were patrolled by the Kenya Rifles militia, and Kash pulled over to ask the soldiers if they'd heard from Mateo, Kash's Maasai partner.

"He's here now, arrived last night from Samburu."

Sable also learned that a herd of huge elephants including Ahmed had been spotted. Did this also mean her father was in the vicinity?

Later, as Kash and Sable waited by an olive tree with a view of a river, sheltered from the wind and sun, they listened for sounds in the great silence. An amethyst sunbird flitted past; a crimson butterfly landed for a moment on her hand. She breathed wild jasmine, watched the grass ripple, and listened to the music of the coot birds coming from a tall lava crater. They waited, hoping to get a glimpse of Ahmed, who did not appear. Few forests were as still and tantalizing, and the silence intensified the beauty that was endangered by poachers.

The last habitat, she thought, and felt overwhelming grief as she realized how fragile it all was. How quickly it could slip through man's fingers and be no more.

They camped with Mateo and the Kenya Rifles that night and enjoyed their company. The next morning while it was yet dark, Kash left the Land Rover at camp and led her on a walk toward the river. She said nothing as they walked through the grasses and doum palms to the bank, where a boat with oars waited.

Where did the boat come from? she wondered. *Did Mateo arrange it?* She looked at him for an explanation, but as yet he said nothing.

Kash gestured his hand good-bye to Mateo. He would remain behind on lookout, watching the road from Samburu. As soon as Browning's crew and trucks were spotted, Mateo would bring them word at Skyler's camp.

She was sure Vince would be with Browning and the others when they arrived to hunt the elephants.

Kash helped her into the small boat and began rowing between thick, darkly silhouetted trees where the morning stars still shone brightly overhead. He rowed around a bend, and as the river widened and the sky grew lighter, she glanced about and spotted a hippo.

The sun was breaking with sudden boldness, even as it had

set without fanfare, and monkeys screeched, swinging in the branches that extended out over the riverbank. Crocodiles slid off into the muddy water, their jaws snapping, as though irritated by the human encroachment. As they floated past, Sable held her breath, watching uneasily as another gray hippopotamus sought to bury itself in the water and mud, little showing except for its wide-spaced eyes, which appeared to stare at her.

Not far ahead, a motorboat was docked, and a Samburu tribesman was standing guard. Kash tied the rowboat and helped Sable into the larger boat. A minute later the two of them were moving quickly down the river with Kash at the wheel.

Sable, more comfortable now, looked about, not at the hippos, but at the green-black trees growing along the bank.

"Look in that case," Kash called above the hum of the motor. "There should be some things for coffee and breakfast."

"Where are we going?" She knew but wanted to hear the glad news at last.

"To meet your father"—he smiled—"the elephant man."

She smiled at him over her shoulder, then went about to get a propane stove going and the water boiling. "I won't ask you how you arranged all this," she called.

"I didn't—not the boat and food anyway. Skyler did. Mateo arrived earlier and told him we were coming."

When the coffee was done she poured two mugs and brought him one at the wheel. "Breakfast is boiling," she said easily, trying not to notice when his warm hand brushed hers and she felt alert to him. Their eyes met and caressed, then she quickly looked away, sipping the too hot coffee.

"Boiling?" he asked with a lifted brow.

"Eggs—in water," she said with a smile. "That's all there was."

As the boat progressed, she listened to the familiar animal noises she had grown up with echoing through the bush country of East Africa. Strands of her long hair stuck to her neck in the muggy dampness of the morning. The boat wound through the heart of the Samburu and Isiolo game reserves bordering the volatile area of the Northern Frontier District near Somalia.

There'd been tribal unrest in the region over who had rights to the territory, and while matters were generally quiet now, fighting could erupt again.

Walls of green rose on either side of the river, and trees overhung their way, blocking out the morning sun—as though twilight, with indigo shadows, was descending. Then as the river grew wider, sunlight again beat down on them from a clear, brilliant sky.

As the morning wore on, Sable sat tensely, close to where Kash stood at the wheel, and squinted her eyes to look ahead, anxious to see her father waiting at a boat landing.

"Why is the meeting with my father a secret?"

"I'll let Skyler explain," he said easily. "It will be best coming from him."

Her nerves were now taut with expectancy. "Does it have to do with the elephants?"

"Yes."

Sable fanned herself as a hush fell over the river. The heavy, languorous midday brought drowsiness and detachment from reality. Her senses were drugged by the enormous silence, broken now and then by the screech of a monkey running through the treetops or of birds calling harshly. She stood and walked to the warped edge of the deck and held to the rail, its paint chipped and peeling. Kash gestured ahead. "Almost there. Skyler's waiting."

Sable shaded her eyes and looked ahead toward the small boat landing. The trees ended abruptly in a clearing, where some low sambalike buildings had been built, and she saw the familiar penned animals kept and cared for by the dozen or so Africans who worked with her father.

Skyler Dunsmoor stepped from the trees, and Sable smiled warmly and waved as he called to her.

Her father hadn't changed much in two years. He looked like a giant, rough and big-shouldered, with a thatch of silvergray hair and a beard he hadn't bothered to trim recently. Like Kash, he wore a sleeveless safari vest over canvas jeans and boots.

A rifle was on his shoulder and a pistol stuffed into his wide leather belt.

His face was hard and browned by the sun, and his eyes had an ice-blue cast that looked like reflecting snow from Mount Kenya.

As Kash docked the boat to its mooring, Skyler came down the small wooden ramp to meet her, sweeping her into his robust arms with a hug that lifted her off her feet.

"There she is! As beautiful as ever! No wonder you've got two men fighting over you."

"Father, please—" she said, embarrassed, but nothing appeared to embarrass Skyler.

"Kash is worth ten of Vince," he said.

"Only ten?" she asked, arching her brows.

He grinned. "Welcome home, Sable! Sorry I wasn't able to meet you at Kenyatta. I suppose your grandmother is upset with me."

"She's wondering why you haven't been home all these months, yes. She told me to bring you back. She needs you."

He sobered. "So do the elephants. Did Kash tell you?"

"About the poaching? Yes, but—"

"Not just a few poachers," he interrupted. "That's bad enough. But there are hunters in the area; they've crossed over from Somalia. And they're to join Browning and his goons to take Ahmed and the entire herd."

"Can they be stopped?" she cried.

"That's what we plan to do," he said gravely. "But they're on to us. They've been alerted and intend to strike before we're ready. They've already attacked and killed some twenty elephants."

"What about the elephants here? You mentioned Ahmed."

"We'll discuss everything at camp," he said. "We've friends waiting there."

The friends were Kenya Rifles, soldiers stationed at the northern frontier outpost near Samburu and farther north into Marsabit. They carried weapons and had a number of military vehicles and trucks at their disposal. A half dozen tents were scattered around a clearing, and smoke drifted up from an open fire. Sable noticed that the trunks of the trees had polished bases where the elephants had rubbed themselves. Some canvas chairs were grouped around a table under the fly net beside a tent.

Kash told her they intended to catch Browning and his crew, along with the hunting cartel in Marsabit. He and Skyler had been working closely on this for months, along with the Kenyan government, to crack the cartel serving Far Eastern interests with ivory and rhino horn. The game warden in the south near Amboseli was also involved and had been cooperating with Smith and Browning in Tanga.

"Do you expect to go to Marsabit now? Is that why we came?"

"The plans were made with Browning a month ago," said Kash. "I needed more time to prove Adler was also involved. Your father's been our eyes and ears here with the great herd. He's been tracking them for weeks now. They're moving up into Marsabit Mountain region where they think they're safe from the hunters."

"Unfortunately, the cartel has been tracking them, too," said Skyler. "They haven't waited for Browning and his crew. The herd is decimated and trying to reach the main herd in the north. They've a hunter working for them now out of Uganda."

"Macklin?" asked Kash coldly. "They plan to come in by way of Somalia?"

Skyler nodded.

"I was afraid that might happen."

"They're paying him plenty, too. Macklin knows he's up against you and the Kenya Rifles."

"Where are they now?" asked Sable nervously. "What if they find the elephants and kill them before you can stop them?"

"That's what's troubling," said Skyler. "Ahmed has moved up into Marsabit and so have the others. They need time to recoup after what they've been through with the hunters. They need rest, food, and to mate again. Their condition is desperate," her father was saying to Kash in a quiet but steady voice. "They're exhausted, but they keep going, as though they know they must escape. Cows and bulls are traveling together, something rare. The old have been lost, and the young. There's a few left. I think they're trying to meet up with the bigger herd north of us. That's what we've got to do, Kash—see they join the entire herd of big-tuskers headed up to the safety of Mount Marsabit. To do that, the cartel has got to be stopped—here, this week. If we don't succeed, it's all over."

"We have an advantage," said Kash quietly. "You know this country, they don't—not as well, anyway. And I've already made up my mind."

There was something in his level voice that made Sable turn and look at him. His face was determined.

"The hunters will be stopped, even if they become the hunted." He tapped his fingers. "I have the law of Nairobi to back me up this time. And the world's conservationists would cheer. Once the elephants are gone, it's forever."

Sable tensed. "But if the hunters are already in the area killing . . ." Her voice fell off.

Skyler looked over at Kash. "By now Browning knows you've left with Sable. He'll move out with Vince to join up with Macklin."

Sable's hands clenched as she looked from one to the other. Kash looked at her. "Your father knows more about elephants than any man in East Africa. That's why Vince thought you'd lead them to him. Skyler knows something about this herd even Macklin doesn't know. The elephants are smart—just how smart, researchers don't know yet, but Skyler thinks they know when they're faced with extinction. Ahmed is leading the herd to an area Macklin hasn't learned about yet. We plan to make sure the old bull gets through with the others."

"But the smaller herd," she argued, "the one trying to reach Ahmed—you said Macklin's crew has already spotted them."

Her father's face was dark. "He has. And there's a matriarch leading the family. They have a lot of young calves with the herd."

"That means they'll need to move slowly," said Kash thoughtfully. "That gives the advantage to the poachers."

"They're not far from here heading north," said Skyler. "So are Macklin's poachers—and Browning, is my guess."

"What are we waiting for?" whispered Sable anxiously. "Can't we confront Macklin now?"

Kash looked at Skyler, and the two exchanged glances that told her it might already be too late to stop the slaughter of the small herd trying to reach Ahmed.

Kash stood. "We'll do our best."

Ahmed, she knew, was the big bull that was recently shown on television. Hunters had boasted they were out to get him and would this time, irrespective of the poaching laws.

"There are others with big tusks with the old bull," said Skyler. "I counted over fifty. Their tusks will bring hundreds of thousands of dollars in the black market."

Sable stood, unable to control her emotions. "I'm going with you, Father."

Skyler looked at Kash, who shook his head, but Sable came between them, facing Kash. "Do you think I could stand it just staying here and pacing? If you don't let me go—I'll follow on my own."

As her eyes pleaded with his he frowned, but his expression softened. "All right, but you may see a slaughter you'll wish you hadn't."

"I've seen it before," she whispered, "with Moffet. And that's the reason I must be there now. I must be involved. And if they all die—my heart will die with them. There's got to be someone there feeling the tragedy with them. Someone who realizes the preciousness of the Lord's creation."

Kash squeezed her arms, and as if unaware that her father watched, he drew her head against his chest and ran his fingers through her hair. "We'll stop them if we can."

"And we've some good men on our side, too," said Skyler.

Sable looked up at Kash. "You never would admit it, but is that why Mateo was with the others in Browning's crew? You planted them?"

"They'll turn on him and the crew, if it comes to that. We're still outnumbered," he told Skyler. "Macklin will have a crack crew with him. He won't take chances."

"Yes, I know. And that's what worries me. I know these elephants, Kash. They've been hunted to near extinction, and they're nervous and angry. They know, you see. They know what's happening to them. They don't want to charge, but they will if cornered—especially one of them. She's very brave and would die for the remaining herd. But you know what? She was once as gentle as Moffet. Can you blame them for turning on us when we seek their extinction?"

Sable looked off in the distance thoughtfully. The sun looked like an orange in a taffy-colored sky and seemed to melt the mountains on the horizon. A loneliness pierced her soul.

Her father and five of the Kenya Rifles drove in the lead, heading south to meet up with the smaller herd heading to Mount Marsabit. Sable rode with Kash and the other five African soldiers. The track zigzagged between gray-green thickets of wild olive and giant euphorbia, acacia, and some leathery-leaved evergreens that were embroidered with a parasitic growth of rope-thick lianas. The air was still and heavy with aromatic scents. Like winged splashes of color from a rainbow, sunbirds flicked in and out of the trees.

A cloud of insects that Sable hoped was not mosquitoes hung over a muddy stream as Kash drove the Land Rover up the slope. A half mile later he turned off into a row of giant yellow-barked acacia.

This was the area her father expected the smaller female herd to seek on their way north. Kash sent out several Africans to see if they could locate evidence of Macklin's poachers. An hour later they spotted tire tracks—but it was Mateo, not Macklin. Mateo had turned back to warn them that Browning and his crew, along with Vince and Mckibber, had left Samburu Lodge soon after she and Kash had flown with Dean to Lake Rudolf. And they were now on the trail of the elephant herd.

"The elephants are caught between Browning, who is coming from the south, and Macklin's crew north of here."

Sable heard the disturbing sound the same moment her father and Kash did. Kash said something to Skyler, then turned toward her. "Wait here." He ran ahead, climbing the hill topped by the darkly silhouetted thorn tree. But Sable, her emotions boiling, followed and reached the tree as Kash was already sliding and running down the slope with his rifle. He darted behind a thicket, then crawled military style toward the arid plain beyond where a Land Rover was churning a cloud of brown dust and a small herd of elephants was trapped for the kill, bunched together in frightened confusion.

Sable lifted her field glasses to focus on the driver. She stared, one hand clenched in a fist at her side as she recognized Vince! At first she could hardly believe her eyes. The second man in the passenger seat wore goggles and carried a large hunting rifle. There was no doubt what Vince was doing with the Land Rover. As he circled and turned, then circled again, he was trying to redirect the lead matriarch into the line of fire. Sable's frustration rose to an emotional fury. "Stop!" she cried helplessly into the air. "Stop, Vince, stop! What are you doing?"

Her father was huffing as he came up beside her with his gun, shaking his head in disbelief. "Too late," he groaned. "The herd might have made it to safety if—"

Sable's fingers tightened on his arm. "Look, Father! It's Kash—oh no! He mustn't—"

Kash and Mateo had emerged from the thicket and, holding dead bramble bush in front of them for cover, were crawling closer toward the Land Rover.

Sable gripped her field glasses with trembling fingers. "If the elephants get wind of their approach, they'll stampede them." Her heart lifted in prayer to God.

Her glasses lowered, and her eyes swerved to her father. The muscles in his jaw flexed as he held his field glasses steady.

Vince turned the Land Rover again, the sound of the engine dimmed by the elephants' squeals and trumpeting. Then there was only the sound of the engine as the hunted animals clustered together facing death.

An elephant herd most always traveled together as a family unit, with the older matriarch, grown daughters, and aunts leading female calves and young males. They had been created with a deep instinct for loyalty and affection for their offspring. Sable watched the lead matriarch use her trunk to draw her young calf behind her, trying to protect it. Sable gritted her anxiety. The calves were hidden now within the packed mass of gray backs and widely spread ears as the family unit faced the Land Rover and the two hunters within.

Behind them, Kash and Mateo were approaching when a shot was fired from the Land Rover, cracking the air. In the brief moment of silence that followed, the frightened herd stood like majestic sculptured figures in gray marble, motionless. Then an elephant went down on its knees, its ears folding back, its noble head beginning to droop.

Another shot cracked, this one coming from the direction of Kash and Mateo, as the Land Rover swerved out of control.

The elephants swung around, trunks weaving. There was no trumpeting now, and the Land Rover had slowed. Sable turned her field glasses on Kash, who was lying in the dust, the rifle out in front of him. He had blown out the left front tire. Sable heard her father's intake of breath. The Land Rover's engine revved up again, and the matriarch was distracted from Kash and Mateo lying close by. She was making her move, surging out ahead of the family unit, trumpeting her anger. Sable's breath stopped. The next moment the desert dust was rising from beneath the elephant's charge. Her head was lifted, her trunk curled in below the great tusks. The Land Rover began to clumsily seek escape, its blown wheel flapping and catching in ruts, yanking the steering to the left as Vince fought to regain control. The elephant was gaining, closing in on the object of torment. She came fast and powerful, lowering her head and ramming her tusks into the rear of the vehicle. The elephant shoved it forward, and the poacher was turning in his seat with the rifle lifted. The matriarch tore her tusks free, then rammed the vehicle from the side while lifting and overturning it, trumpeting in a fury of rage.

Through the dust Sable could see the rest of the herd and hear their roars, like a panicking crowd. Then the matriarch swung round and made for the herd. The others trumpeted,

flapping their ears as though applauding, and then began running across the dusty plain toward the shelter of distant doum
palms.

Sable anxiously watched the plundered Land Rover, but
though on its side, Vince and the hunter crawled out safely, half
hidden in the cloud of dust.

"They're alive," said her father, no emotion in his voice.

Sable sank to the ground, head lowered as she sought to
steady her emotions. Her father's hand reached her shoulder
and squeezed it.

☾◯☽

When Kash returned with Mateo later that night, Mckibber
had regrouped with them according to plan. Kash was grave as
he spoke to her father alone, giving him the news that Mckib
had brought.

"Both crews are already north of us. Ahmed has been spotted. We must stop Macklin at the river, or we won't stop them
at all. I've got the Kenya Rifles heading there now, but we're
outnumbered. Macklin must have thirty men, and Browning has
ten. Those loyal to us will turn on them, but it's going to be
messy."

Kash walked up to Sable, taking hold of her forearms, and
his eyes searched hers. "I want you to stay here at camp. I don't
want you to see this."

She shook her head, her face damp with sweat and dust and
tears. "No, where you and Father make the last stand—that's
where I'll be, too. And if they all die—" Her voice cracked.

He held her tightly, soothing her with his hands, then kissed
her softly. "Then you'd better ride with your father." He
sighed. "Sable, don't let him do anything unwise when we get
there."

She swallowed, trying to read through his impenetrable
gaze. "What do you mean?" she whispered. "Do you expect
him to?"

"I don't know. He loves those animals. We all do, but his

• 246 •

attachment goes deeper. He feels as if he is personally responsible to save them from extinction."

Any words she could have spoken were lodged in her throat,
and she closed her eyes. Kash gave her a final embrace, then left
her there by Skyler's Land Rover. She looked over at her father.
He was looking off toward the plain where two elephants shot
earlier lay still in the dust beneath the stars.

Her father joined her a few minutes later, his eyes empty.
"You're coming with me, daughter? Then let's go."

They packed up at once and drove out across the narrow
track, lurching and bumping along as they tried to avoid rocks
and holes.

Ahead, the three other Land Rovers with Kash, Mckib, Mateo, and the dozen Kenya Rifles slowed, the headlights searching for elephant tracks. Sable, however, was praying, looking up
at the Southern Cross, which shone brilliantly like a diamond
pendant above the black outcropping of mountains. Uncertainty and foreboding tightened her chest.

Seventeen

By noon the next day the elephants were upwind of the Land Rovers, and before Sable realized what had happened, her father's Land Rover was right among them, and then she understood that he had known they would come this way. She heard branches snapping as the elephants came thrashing their way downriver.

"They're cut off. The poachers are ahead, waiting," said her father, dismayed.

"Can we turn the elephants around?" she cried desperately.

He shook his head sadly as though he'd given up, then on second thought he came alert. "Maybe—if I could get their attention, I could get the matriarch to swing left, away from Browning's and Macklin's hunters."

"Father, wait until Kash gets here. He's coming now—look—"

Her father was watching the elephants. The lead matriarch caught the scent of danger on the breeze and stopped, her trunk lifting in all directions. In heart-stopping silence she stood, and the elephants behind her stopped, too, bunching up together with the young ones protected behind them. The matriarch kept her impressive mass between the threat and the rest of the herd.

"Look—" gasped Sable, awed.

Out from among the green doum palms came a big bull, alone.

"It's him," breathed her father, stricken. "It's Ahmed.

Those tusks—the hunters will go for the prize!"

Ahmed swung his huge gray bulk up onto the bank and stood solitary, magnificent, his trunk lifted. He realized the matriarch and herd were farther up the river, and he turned and started in the direction of Mount Marsabit, as if to lead the herd to safety, but the poachers had spotted him.

Sable's heart constricted as there came the roar of engines. She saw the zoo hunters' trucks and Macklin's Land Rover followed by several others with men shouting, banging on door panels, horns blaring, harassing the elephants into confusion. There followed the squeal and trumpeting of elephants—a cry that tore through the morning air.

"They've got them trapped! They've got Ahmed!"

"The Kenya Rifles!" she cried. "Where are they?"

"They're coming now!"

On the flat plain toward the water hole, the poaching crew was moving into place, closing in cautiously, determined, the noise of their engines merging with the frightened trumpeting. Sable sat in her father's Land Rover, gripping the seat. She saw Kash driving from the other direction with Mckibber, and the other Land Rovers followed with the armed guards, the Kenya Rifles, led by Mateo.

"Why don't the poachers leave?" she cried. "Even if they kill the herd, they won't have time to take the ivory and get away!"

"You don't know these men, daughter. They outnumber us—and they'll turn their guns on us before they quit now."

"Lord, *please* don't let them kill them all . . . please do something to protect them . . . please. . . ." She watched helplessly.

For a moment her father sat behind the Land Rover wheel just shaking his head as though he couldn't believe it was happening, his gaze fixed on the riverbed. The gray hulks drifted through the green doum palms, and the herd with the last of the calves of various ages were coming out onto the flat arid plain, not trumpeting, not making any sound, but moving rapidly to escape. And in the lead, as they headed away from the poachers, was a large female with a young calf that looked to be a newborn.

"They won't make it," whispered Sable. "Look—its legs are about to go out from under it."

Her father climbed suddenly out of the Land Rover, and Sable, in dismay, recognized the expression on his sweat-stained face. It was a look of pity, of almost irrational determination, and her eyes widened.

"Father! No! No! Don't—"

He was rushing toward the lake to try to turn the elephants back. . . .

"Father!" Sable threw open the door and stumbled out, coming to her feet. She screamed for Kash, then ran after her father, but he was already far ahead with his rifle, like an offering, running to his own massacre. He was shouting, but there was so much noise now from the approaching trucks that she couldn't hear his words. The hunters were driving toward the doum palms and giant euphorbia, where they could come down the embankment onto the arid flat.

Kash and Mckib had seen them, and turning the wheel, Kash accelerated in the direction of Skyler, but he was still running as the matriarch sighted him.

Sable scrambled into the Land Rover and started the engine, driving forward over the rocks and ruts, also trying to reach him.

The elephant was standing, uncertain, her great gray head moving from side to side, one big foot scuffing the ground as she lifted her trunk out toward the Land Rover. The frightened calf moved ahead of her, and she laid her trunk across its small shoulders, edging it into safety behind her as she faced the poachers. The remainder of the herd was bunched up behind her, the older adults making a solid wall of protection with the younger calves behind, all of them alert and roused for the final stand.

As Sable neared, Kash intercepted, the truck's wheels throwing dust and gravel as he accelerated to head her off. Sable saw the truck and quickly swerved, driving off into the bush and slamming the brake in her emotional frenzy. "Father!" she kept shouting.

Skyler stood some fifty yards from the elephants and lifted his rifle to shoot into the air, hoping to turn them back.

But as Browning's and Macklin's two trucks came round the end of the doum palms, there followed an eruption of gunfire from the Kenya Rifles, blowing out the poachers' front tires. Those loyal to Kash, riding with Browning, turned their rifles on the hunters.

In that same moment, as Sable swung around in the seat to look behind her, the great bull Ahmed appeared from the trees. The matriarch saw him and trumpeted. And then something happened that held Sable spellbound. As Ahmed flapped his great ears and curled his trunk, the matriarch charged, not trumpeting, not making any noise, but thundering the dusty plain at great speed, the reddish dust flying from beneath her. And behind her, joining in the final stand, came all the herd except Ahmed. Their trunks were curled underneath their great tusks— their heads held high for the thrust.

"Oh, God—" Sable choked in prayer, watching her father flung aside. Rifle shots split the air, but a cloud of dust from the trucks descended, blurring the vision of the hunters, and now they became the objects of death.

One elephant was struck, another slumped to the earth, but the matriarch kept coming.

Then it was Ahmed! And he was in the lead now, the ground rumbling beneath his feet as though an earthquake were tearing open the ground beneath him. They charged straight for Browning's trucks.

The elephants were now among the poachers, and confusion reigned, with rifle shots ringing out and Browning trying to back out his truck with two shot-out tires. The hunters were shooting and elephants were falling, but the herd came on with Ahmed in the lead, a gray tidal wave that engulfed all in its rage. The matriarch's flailing trunk came smashing down on Browning. Tusks drove into Macklin's Land Rover, sending it rolling over on its side, roof, and finally settling on the other side, with the wheels still spinning and throwing gravel. The hunters were running. Vince emerged from the passenger side of Browning's truck and, stumbling, crawled into a thornbush.

The cows stood their ground, thrusting their tusks into metal objects they deemed the source of their misery, trumpeting their frustration, their fury, then roaring and screaming as more bullets were fired into their hides. Macklin's Land Rover was met by Ahmed. The entire vehicle was lifted and flung into the air like a toy. When it crashed to the earth, Ahmed kneeled on it, reducing it to less than half its height. Then the bull rose, tossing his mammoth tusks toward the sky and scuffing the ground with his foot.

Sable had sunk to the grass, staring—dazed, pale, and in shock.

The elephants were moving on swiftly for the water, and she saw Ahmed disappear into the dark doum palms as the matriarch was gathering her last calf close, her trunk moving over it from head to tail again and again as if to check whether it was hurt. Then apparently satisfied, she edged it off toward the flowing river, where the rest of the elephants were moving down the stream to safety.

The dust had settled, and the Kenyan sun cast a crimson stain on a cloud in the high sky while the earth lay blood-drenched beneath. A wounded elephant opened its mouth in pain, trying to rise from where it had fallen, near the place where Skyler had chosen to make his final stand.

Exhausted and weak, Sable managed to push herself up from the grass, and in a daze, she walked toward the devastation.

Her father lay in a fallen heap, crushed into the ground.

As she slowly drew nearer, Kash moved to steer her away. "No, darling. . . ."

He grasped her in his arms, and she buried her face in the safety of his embrace. She clung to him, heartbroken, too devastated even for tears.

Mckibber came limping toward them, his hard-lined face telling all, his hands clenched about his rifle as his eyes searched for Skyler. He walked over to his body, stooping into the hot, churned dust while the flies found their prey. "There's lots of things that matter, that's worth dyin' for" was all he said, laying a trembling hand on the bloodied shoulder.

Mateo murmured to Kash, "Both dead, Browning and Macklin, and most of the crew. We've arrested the others."

Dr. Vince Adler limped out from behind the bush he had sought for cover and headed toward his Land Rover, still on its side in the dust with the front tire shot out. He leaned there, covered with dust and dripping sweat, a hunted look on his face.

Sable stepped away from Kash and slowly walked toward him. His cheek twitched as he unwillingly met her stare. She remained still in the glaring sunlight, the insects droning, her eyes holding his.

Vince's gaze fell away and he turned his head.

A ripple of dust arose from Kash's boots as he came up beside Sable, his eyes narrowing into heated cobalt, his body looking ready to pounce. But then the tension visibly eased in his muscled body, wet with perspiration.

"Adler, you're under arrest to be handed over to the Kenyan authorities," he breathed.

Vince swallowed and closed his eyes, nodding that he understood.

"You're answering for more than what happened today," continued Kash, his voice dangerously quiet. "There's the death of my brother. There's also the Dunsmoor shipping you used to haul ivory to your Far Eastern contacts." He paused. "Take a good look around you. I want you to remember it in detail . . . for the rest of your life. Decide if it was worth it—for your grand humanistic dream out at Lake Rudolf. Because you're going to live with this memory for a long, long time."

Vince made no reply, his head bent as he crumpled to the ground against the overturned Land Rover, both man and machine a testament to the strength of the matriarch.

Kash took Sable's hand and together they walked away.

The setting sun splashed the vast African sky with ruby fierceness. After darkness settled and the jewels flickered above, a hot wind rippled through the acacia trees. Somewhere a lone lion roared, its rumble sweeping across the vast dried savanna grassland; somewhere a bull elephant stood alone, its ears fanned back and white tusks gleaming; somewhere a matriarch gave comfort, her trunk calming her trembling calf, and hope lived on for another day. Out of the African night, it seemed that the warrior song of the Maasai echoed, dancing on the wind, and all merged into one haunting theme. The song rose higher and higher until it became a plaintive prayer that sighed and moaned for eternal deliverance to break like a joyous flood upon the sin-cursed earth. Then, one day, the Prince of Peace will rule . . . and the lion and lamb will lie down together, and none shall make them afraid.

Kash stood with Sable beside the Land Rover, two dark silhouettes against the pale yellow moon, the wind caressing them. A promised future of their own waited, and they held to each other tightly, two hearts beating as one.

Books by Linda Chaikin

Endangered

HEART OF INDIA SERIES

Silk
Under Eastern Stars
Kingscote

THE GREAT NORTHWEST SERIES

Empire Builders
Winds of Allegiance

ROYAL PAVILION SERIES

Swords and Scimitars
Golden Palaces